TRAITOR

AMANDA McCRINA

TRAITOR

FARRAR STRAUS GIROUX
NEW YORK

Farrar Straus Giroux Books for Young Readers
An imprint of Macmillan Publishing Group, LLC
120 Broadway, New York, NY 10271

10 9 8 7 6 5 4 3 2 1

fiercereads.com

Library of Congress Cataloging-in-Publication Data is available.
ISBN: 978-0-374-31352-4

Our books may be purchased in bulk for promotional, educational, or
business use. Please contact your local bookseller or Macmillan Corporate
and Premium Sales Department at (800) 221-7945 ext. 5442 or by email at
MacmillanSpecialMarkets@macmillan.com.

For Mom

CONTENTS

HISTORICAL NOTE

In September 1939, Nazi Germany and the Soviet Union jointly invade and occupy Poland, dividing the country between them along the so-called Curzon Line. This invasion marks the beginning of what will become World War II.

For nearly two years, the two rival powers maintain an uneasy truce, busy carrying their war elsewhere—to Finland, to France, to Britain. Then, in late June 1941, German forces cross the Curzon Line, setting out to catch the Soviets unawares and crush them.

The invasion is supposed to be over in eight weeks.

Instead, the Soviet Union rallies. The Great Patriotic War against Germany drags on for the next three years. By July 1944, Soviet forces are pouring back into the Polish territories they abandoned to the Germans three years earlier.

One Polish city, Lwów, changes hands for the third time in five years, falling once more to Soviet "liberators."

Lwów is the historic capital and crown jewel of Galicia, a region incorporating parts of both Poland and Ukraine—and, until 1918, part of the Austro-Hungarian Empire. The city was a battleground between Poles, Ukrainians, Germans, and Russians even before Hitler and Stalin laid claim. Its cemeteries house the dead of the First World War, the Russo-Polish War, and the brief, bitter Polish-Ukrainian War of 1918–19—the war that helped establish both the dominance of the city's Polish majority and the national consciousness of its Ukrainian minority.

Both Poles and Ukrainians consider Lwów theirs by right. They've spilled blood to prove it. Invasion and occupation by two different foreign powers have only rubbed those old wounds raw.

July 1944. The Great Patriotic War is all but over. The western Allies have landed at Normandy. Hitler's Germany is on its last legs.

But Lwów's war didn't start in 1939, and it doesn't end here.

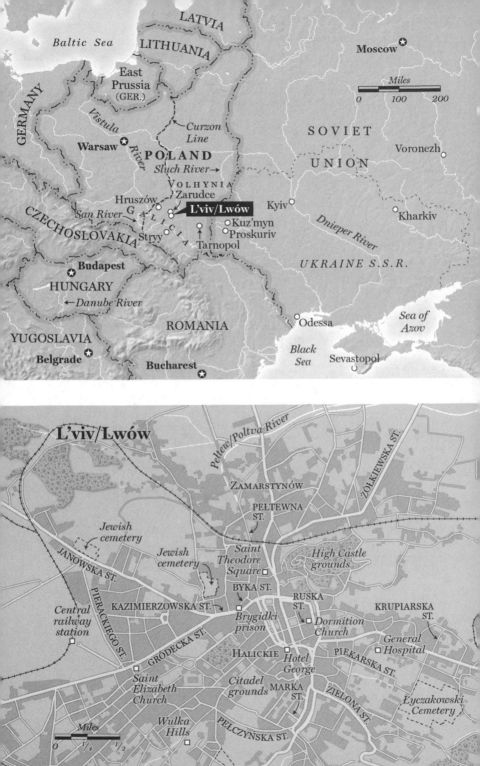

I
TOLYA

Thursday, July 27–Saturday, July 29
1944

1

AT DUSK, TOLYA SHOT HIS POLITICAL OFFICER.

To be fair, he hadn't known at first that it was Zampolit Petrov—official representative of the Communist Party, deputy for political consciousness and troop morale, special commissioner for the liquidation of spies, traitors, and enemies of the Soviet people. It was dusk, and the light was bad. The streetlamps were out because the electricity had been cut in the artillery barrage, and there was a low, gray haze of dust and smoke from the blasted-out buildings. On his way back to the station, he'd come across a soldier assaulting a young civilian woman—or that's what it had looked like anyway. Only after he'd put that first bullet in the small of the *zampolit*'s back did Tolya recognize the olive-drab jacket with the smart red collar tabs.

Then again, he *had* known it was Zampolit Petrov when he set the muzzle of his rifle against the base of the *zampolit*'s skull and put a second bullet in the *zampolit*'s brain.

He knew how he would die for it—piece by piece, in the

dark, in the basement of Brygidki prison—and he knew what his death sentence would say: *Tolya Korolenko, traitor to the motherland.* That was how his father had died (not in the Brygidki, but in a Soviet prison just the same), and that was what his father's sentence had said because his father had been Ukrainian and a Soviet citizen. His Polish mother they'd shot against a wall—no sentence, no interrogation. She hadn't been a traitor to the motherland, only an enemy.

For a second, while the *crack* of that last shot echoed away down the empty street, he and the girl just looked at each other. She'd scrambled out from under Petrov's body when he fell, backing away against the wall. She was sitting very still now, her hands at her sides, her shoulders braced on the wall, one skinny leg splayed out and the other curled up awkwardly under her body. She was small and sunburned and bareheaded, with a scattering of freckles across her nose and cheeks, and a short, stiff chestnut braid sticking out behind each ear. She had a brown wool skirt and a bulky, padded tan soldier's jacket with dark patches where the insignia had been ripped off. Her feet were swallowed in a monstrous pair of soldier's boots.

Tolya crouched on his heels, holding his rifle across his knees. He moved his finger off the trigger and held up his hand, palm out, to show peace.

"Are you all right?" he asked, in Polish. "Are you hurt?"

She shook her head, once, not turning her eyes from him.

"You should go. It's not safe."

She didn't speak. She didn't move. Tolya shifted, glancing back down the street. They weren't far off the main road, Gródecka. The triple spires of Saint Elizabeth Church towered over the rooftops down the row.

"Do you understand? It's not safe here." Somebody had probably heard the shots. "Where do you live? I'll take you there."

When she didn't answer, Tolya slung his rifle over his shoulder and reached for her arm. She slid her hand into her jacket and brought out a pistol. She held it in Tolya's face, finger on the trigger. She stuck out her chin and smiled at him sourly.

"Don't flatter yourself, Comrade. He was mine. And if you were worried about being *safe*, maybe you shouldn't have shot your own officer."

Tolya Korolenko, idiot.

The girl pointed with the pistol. "Rifle and ammunition—quickly."

Tolya slid his rifle off his shoulder and put it on the ground. He took his spare clips from his pocket and laid them beside the rifle.

"Now his pistol," the girl said, nodding at Petrov.

Tolya leaned over Petrov's body and unbuckled Petrov's gun belt. He wrapped up the pistol carefully in the belt. It was a fine, pretty thing—a Mauser HSc. Petrov had gotten it off a dead German officer four months ago, in Tarnopol. The holster and belt were oiled golden leather, as soft as butter. The grip of the pistol was smooth, dark walnut wood burnished to a wet shine. Tolya laid the pistol down.

The girl said, "Open his pockets."

Tolya opened the pockets of Petrov's jacket. There were folded military registration papers and a Communist Party membership card in the breast pocket. These went on the ground with the rest. Tolya felt in the pockets of Petrov's trousers: two cartridge boxes for the Mauser, a wad of paper rubles folded in a clip, a handful of copper-nickel kopecks. Tolya fished them out and turned out the linings so the girl could see the pockets were empty. The girl held the pistol on him with one steady hand while she slipped Petrov's papers and the money into her jacket. She slung the Mauser on its belt over her shoulder. She pocketed Tolya's clips and the pistol rounds and pulled Tolya's Mosin across her knees. She held the rifle on her lap, considering—running her hand along the stock, pausing at the scope, tapping the bent bolt with one finger.

She looked at Tolya as though appraising him.

"Sniper?"

"Yes."

"Do they shoot you if you come back without your rifle?"

"If I'm lucky," Tolya said.

He watched her throw open the bolt and empty the three remaining cartridges into her palm.

"What are you?" he asked. "Resistance?" She must be trying to get out of the city. On Stalin's orders, the death squads of Tolya's front, the First Ukrainian Front, had started rounding up and disarming every Polish Resistance fighter left in Lwów—no matter that the Resistance had been fighting side by side with the Front for months now. They were keeping the officers at the station, which meant they'd be shipping them east to the labor camps when the rail lines reopened. He'd heard that rank-and-file Resistance soldiers were being offered amnesty in exchange for officially joining the Front, but the only rank-and-file soldiers he'd seen were the six Zampolit Petrov had shot in the back of the head that morning in the station square. He supposed they'd refused.

"Alive, that's what, and no thanks to you." The girl shoved the cartridges into her pocket. She held his rifle on her knee and motioned with the pistol. "Up, Comrade. Count ten steps. Then turn."

He counted ten steps down the street toward Gródecka. She was gone when he turned, but his rifle was leaning against the wall.

* * *

What remained, besides the rifle, was that Zampolit Petrov was dead, bleeding into two red puddles on the sidewalk.

That was all right. Tolya had wanted to shoot Zampolit Petrov since Tarnopol—ever since Comrade Lieutenant Spirin, who'd been a friend and a mentor and something very like a father to Tolya these last two years, had crawled wounded all the way back from behind German lines, and Zampolit Petrov had handed him over to a firing squad, saying he must be a double agent or he wouldn't have made it back alive.

The question for reflection later was whether Tolya would still have done it—presented with Zampolit Petrov's back and no witnesses—if not for the girl.

Justice, Father Stepan would say. *Pray for his soul.*

Murder, Father Dmytro would say. *Pray for your own.*

The immediate concern was the *clomp, clomp, clomp* of boots coming toward him down the street—boots and voices, Russian voices.

Tolya slung his rifle and ran, keeping low along the empty shop fronts. They saw him in the half-light and shouted after him. They must have seen Zampolit Petrov's body because there was a split second's silence—weapons being unslung and aimed—then a spray of submachine-gun fire. Plaster shattered above Tolya's head and rained down in a fine, white dust. Bullets kicked up dirt at his feet. He ducked into a side street. Footsteps pounded after him. Shouts echoed along the shop fronts. Tolya cut over on a cross street and turned quickly up another side street—then again, over and up, over and up, north and west through the tangled web of little streets above Gródecka, moving away from the city center. He came out onto a broad, quiet, cobbled street running east-west beneath a low brick wall. There were the railroad tracks ahead of him, open countryside beyond—black-earth grainland billowing gently up to the wooded foothills above the city.

He crossed the tracks and crouched for a little while on the embankment, catching his breath and waiting and watching. It was full dark now. The city center was blazing. The streets were empty and silent. He didn't think they'd seen his face. It was possible they hadn't even seen his uniform in the darkness and smoke and dust. Most likely, they would think he'd been Polish Resistance—that it had been a targeted killing, retaliation for the six prisoners Zampolit Petrov had shot that morning in the station square.

He walked back along the tracks. The moon had set by the time he got back to the station. There was a lone sentry in the ruined train shed, sitting on the edge of the platform, swinging his legs and smoking makhorka.

Tolya said softly, "Vasya."

The muzzle of Vasya's rifle came up smoothly. "Who's there?"

"It's Tolya."

The muzzle dipped. "Where the hell were you? They were looking for you."

"Who?"

"Rudenko. He ordered a search when you weren't back at curfew. He said they'd better find you dead or not at all."

"I got lost."

"Was she pretty?"

"I got lost," Tolya said.

"Sure." Vasya pulled on his cigarette and flicked away the ash with his fingers. "Rudenko's the one you've got to convince. I don't care."

* * *

Comrade Lieutenant Rudenko's office had once been the stationmaster's office. There were old, yellowed timetables on the walls, and a dusty clock, with tall black Roman numerals and thin, scrolled black metal hands, that had run out one morning at 8:17. There was an upright pine desk with a matching letter box and cash drawer, and faded travel posters for Poznań and Kraków, Warsaw and Sopot.

And there was Comrade Lieutenant Maksym Rudenko, disgruntled battalion commander, the newest addition.

He was a meat slab of a man, very nearly two meters tall, bald and red faced and perpetually scowling, with hands the size of dinner plates and fingers like boiled sausages. There was a long, ridged scar across the bridge of his nose—from shrapnel or a bayonet, Tolya didn't know. What he *did* know was that Comrade Lieutenant Rudenko could pick him up, twirl him around, and break him over a knee like a twig.

"I ought to give you to Zampolit Petrov," Comrade Lieutenant Rudenko said. He was holding his pipe in one hand, pouring vodka into a tumbler on the desktop. "Teach you a lesson—all you farm boys, all you unread Cossack shit. Beat it into your thick heads. You all think you're the exception."

He raised the glass. "To hell with that Russian bastard Sokolov," he said, meaning Comrade Colonel Sokolov, commander of their division. "He'd have my head if I sent you to a firing squad." He tipped his head and tossed the vodka back. He set the glass on the desktop, stuck his pipe in his mouth, and scowled at Tolya. "Well? Are you going to say something?"

"No, Comrade Lieutenant."

"Good. Get the hell out of my office."

"Yes, Comrade Lieutenant."

"Korolenko."

Tolya paused at the door. "Yes, Comrade Lieutenant?"

"If you miss curfew again, I'll shoot you myself, and to hell with the *zampolit*. I'll tell Comrade Colonel Sokolov it was an accidental discharge."

"Yes, Comrade Lieutenant," Tolya said.

* * *

He felt his way in the clammy dark over bodies and boots and helmets and packs. He slipped in between Yura and Petya, unslung his rifle, and kicked off his boots. He took off his jacket and rolled it up for a pillow. He lay on his stomach, his hands folded under his chest, so he could pull out the rosary between the buttons of his tunic and hold the crucifix in his fingers while he prayed.

Beside him, Yura lifted an arm from his face. "Where were you?" he asked. He spoke in a low, sleepy whisper, in Ukrainian.

"Around. I don't know. I got lost."

"They were looking for you."

"I know."

"Koval was looking for you."

Tolya didn't say anything. He bent his head, touched the crucifix to his lips, and pushed the rosary back into his tunic.

"What was so important?" Yura asked.

"Nothing. Go back to sleep."

"Because if you're not interested in her anymore—"

"Shut up," Tolya said.

Yura buried his face in his arms again. "Well, you ought to be careful—going *around*. Gives people the wrong idea."

2

KOVAL FOUND HIM IN THE SWITCH TOWER.

He didn't ask how. It was the system they'd worked out between them over the year and a half since they'd first met, back in Kharkiv: He didn't ask how, and she didn't ask why.

There were no trains coming to the terminal now, and there'd been no trains for three months. Polish Resistance saboteurs had cut the main lines back in April, when Lwów was still in German hands, and somebody—Germans, Poles, or Soviets, Tolya didn't know—had since collapsed the train shed and made off with the rails for scrap metal. Sparse, knee-high yellow grass had sprung up between the ties. The gutted ruins of freight cars were piled up under the wall at the end of the yard.

From where he sat—in the signalman's chair, his feet propped up comfortably on the switchboard—he could see clear out of the city, past the empty yard and across Białohorska Street to the low, heather-laced slope where the tanks of the Third Guards were practicing their gunnery. That was westward. Eastward, he could see down the station street all the way to Saint Elizabeth's, and across the smoke-wreathed rooftops all the way to the opera house, at the city center.

He could see the station just below, and he could see Koval coming across the yard from the platform.

He'd cleaned his rifle and was reassembling it now, watching the puffs of white smoke drift over the hillside. She came over from the doorway and sat on the edge of the switchboard, facing him.

"Listen," she said, "we've got to talk."

"All right."

"They're saying somebody shot Petrov."

Tolya held his rifle on his lap and slid the magazine housing into the port. The barrel followed, then the bands, then the nose cap, then the bolt. His fingers moved on their own, from memory.

"So?"

"Last night—in an alley off Gródecka Street. They're saying it was one of us."

Tolya lifted his scope and trained it on the hillside, following the artillery fire across the shoulder of the hill.

Koval reached over and knocked the scope away from his face. "Did you hear me? They think it was one of us. They saw a uniform."

"It could have been Polish Resistance. We've caught them in our uniforms." And it *would* have been, if he'd just let things alone, but how was he supposed to know?

"Where were you, anyway? Yura said you were gone all afternoon."

Tolya wiped the lenses of the scope. He mounted the scope and lifted the rifle, shouldering the butt and resting his cheek on the cool, smooth walnut stock.

"Listen," Koval said, "I'm only asking because the NKVD will be asking too, and they won't be nearly as polite about it."

The NKVD—the Narodnyĭ Komissariat Vnutrennikh Del, the People's Commissariat for Internal Affairs—were the Soviet secret police. If—when?—he ended up in the basement of Brygidki prison, the NKVD would be the ones taking him apart.

"They won't just shoot you," Koval said. "First they'll make you cough up all the other *anti-Soviet elements* in the company."

Tolya shut his left eye and sighted an imaginary target in the poplar trees at the foot of the hill—distance six hundred meters, half wind from two o'clock. He squeezed the trigger and lifted his head, homing the shot in his mind.

"You're short," Koval said dryly.

Tolya lowered the rifle to his lap. He clipped the sling on the stock and butt.

"My grandmother is buried in Łyczakowski Cemetery—my mother's mother. I went to find the grave."

Koval was silent.

Tolya took a clip from his pocket, stripped it into the magazine, and shoved the bolt in.

"I'm sorry," Koval said. "I didn't know."

"That's a first," he said.

He hadn't meant it to sound so sour. She ignored it anyway.

"Are they from L'viv—your mother's people?" She used the Ukrainian name, L'viv, not the Polish Lwów.

"No, they moved to L'viv after the Poles took Galicia. They didn't want to stay on the Ukrainian side of the border."

That was in 1919, after Ukraine went to war with Poland for control of oil-rich eastern Galicia. His mother's family, Poles, had held land in the village of Kuz'myn for more than a century, but Kuz'myn was in Ukrainian territory, and Tolya supposed they'd feared reprisals.

"But your mother stayed," Koval said.

"My mother stayed."

He had wondered, more and more as he'd gotten older, if she'd ever regretted it. She'd been eighteen years old and in love, and even if she'd known her father would disown her for loving a Ukrainian, she couldn't have known the Reds would take Ukraine, seal the borders, and shoot her against a wall for being Polish.

"Are any of her family still here?" Koval asked. "Living, I mean."

"No," Tolya said. That was a lie. More accurately, he didn't know. He knew his mother's father was dead, because he'd found that grave, too, in Łyczakowski Cemetery, and he knew it must have happened in the German invasion because the date on the headstone was July 1, 1941. He'd tried to be sorry, but he wasn't very. He couldn't think of his mother's father as his grandfather. The man had certainly never thought of *him*, the half-breed, as a grandson. His mother's mother had written when she could, in quiet defiance of her husband. His mother's father hadn't broken silence once, even when Aunt Olena had written from Kyiv to tell him his daughter was dead.

He wasn't sure about his mother's brothers and sisters, but they'd never written either, and if they'd ever cared about a mongrel nephew from the wrong side of the border, they wouldn't care now—not when he came wearing the Reds' uniform.

"Listen," Koval said, "I'm sorry, I really am, but the cemetery is on the east side, isn't it?"

"So?"

"Vasya said you came in on the tracks last night."

Tolya didn't say anything.

"Listen to me, Tolya. If I can figure out that you weren't at the cemetery—or not *only* at the cemetery—then the NKVD can too. All they've got to do is ask for names."

"What names?"

"Anybody who had a history with Petrov, cross-checked against anybody who was absent at the time he was shot. You'd fit on both counts—and Vasya will talk. Everybody talks."

Tolya didn't say anything.

"I don't care that you shot him," Koval said. "Somebody should have shot him at Tarnopol. I care about what happens to you."

He looked at her. The breath of wind through the open windows was pulling blond hair from the neat bun under her cap and whipping it around her ears. The sunlight had turned her eyes softly green, the color of moths' wings.

"It's seventy kilometers to Stryy," she said quietly. "You could be in the mountains in two days."

"No."

"I'm serious."

"I'm not running."

"They'll find out. They'll find out, if they don't know already. Everybody talks, sooner or later."

"It's an admission of guilt if I run."

"It wouldn't matter if they couldn't find you."

"They'd come for you. Collective guilt. They'd know you helped me."

"I'd put a pistol in my mouth." Her voice was hard. "I'm not going to be their bait."

"They'd go for your sister," he said.

She was silent. The breeze tugged at her hair. Tolya swung his feet off the switchboard. He leaned over and caught one of the blond strands in his fingers, tucking it behind her ear.

"They can't prove anything," he said.

She shut her eyes. "Don't be stupid, Tolya."

"I'm not being stupid."

"They'll have your name. They'll have whatever *proof* they want once they've got you in an interrogation cell."

"The only way they prove anything is if I try to run."

"Do you trust me?"

He didn't answer. He traced her cheekbone with his fingertips—very lightly because his fingers were cracked and callused. *Peasant fingers*, Koval would say, teasing. She was city born, from Kyiv.

She caught his wrist. "That was not supposed to be a rhetorical question."

He looked away.

"Yes," he said.

"Look at me," she said.

He looked back. He couldn't meet her eyes. He looked at the strands of blond hair slipping loose again from behind her ear.

She said, "You don't have to worry about me, all right?"

"All right."

"So promise me you'll go."

"I'll go."

She held his wrist tightly. "Don't lie to me. Promise me you'll go tonight—as soon as it's dark enough to get past the checkpoints."

"I'll go tonight," he lied.

"You promise," she corrected.

"I promise I'll go tonight."

"Better." She slid off the switchboard, settled lightly on his lap, and leaned into him, lifting his chin with cool fingers so she could lay a row of kisses very slowly and carefully across the base of his throat.

She must have felt his heart lurch, because when she sat back, the corners of her mouth were turned up in a slight, sly grin. She brought his trembling hand to her lips and kissed his callused fingertips, one by one.

"Is that goodbye?" His voice was hoarse. He hadn't quite caught his breath yet.

"It's good luck," she said. "I'll see you again."

He didn't say anything. He had the feeling she knew he was lying. She always knew.

3

IN THE END IT DIDN'T MATTER, THE LIE, BECAUSE
the NKVD came for him at noon mess.

There were three of them, wearing the khaki tunics and the
bloused navy trousers and the blue peaked caps with the bloodred bands. Each carried a sleek sidearm very much like the one
he'd taken off Zampolit Petrov and given to the Polish Resistance girl. They took him from the mess line, and two of them
held him tightly by the arms while the third plucked Tolya's
identification papers from his breast pocket and compared them
carefully to another set of papers that Tolya couldn't see to
read. Then he folded both sets of papers into his own pocket
and jerked his chin over his shoulder.

They took Tolya out to the station square, the two holding
him by the arms, the third walking behind with the mouth of his
pistol pressed in the small of Tolya's back. There was a smooth,
low black car idling by the curb. The driver had a DP-27 machine
gun loose on his lap. They pushed Tolya's head down and shoved
him into the back seat. One of them sat on either side of him.

The third holstered his pistol and went around to sit with the driver, pulling the machine gun across his knees.

The car pulled away from the curb, circled around the square, and went down toward Gródecka. The verdigris spires of Saint Elizabeth's rose up straight ahead. The car turned left onto Pierackiego Street, following the railroad tracks. They weren't taking him to the prison. The car sped along the street, away from the city center—very nearly the same way he'd run, last night.

The one with the machine gun, the one who'd held his pistol on Tolya's back, turned around, cradling the gun in the crook of his arm.

"Don't be afraid, Tolya," he said, in Ukrainian.

Tolya spit at him.

They all laughed—except the driver, who hadn't seen it and who glanced up in the mirror distractedly.

"We're all friends here," the one with the machine gun said. "We're not NKVD."

He took off the blue peaked cap and smoothed his dark hair with his fingers. He was young—five years or so older than Tolya. He had a smooth, tanned face and cold gray eyes that were much older than his face. There was a tiny sliver of a scar, like the mark of a fingernail, on his right cheekbone, below the eye.

"This is Andriy," he said, putting his hand on the driver's shoulder. "That's Taras"—flicking his fingers—"and that's Yakiv. I'm sorry about the uniforms, but I think we pulled it off pretty well."

He slid the gun off his arm and stuck out his hand to Tolya, over the seat.

"Aleksey," he said, "but you can call me Solovey. This is my squad—well, some of it. We're with the L'viv group of the UPA."

Tolya didn't move. It was a trick. He was sure it was a trick. They would speak in Ukrainian, saying L'viv instead of Lwów, and they would tell him they were UPA—Ukrainska Povstanska Armiia, the Insurgent Army, radical Ukrainian nationalists and anti-Communists—and they would try to trick him into talking.

After a moment, Solovey withdrew his hand.

"It's all right, Tolya," he said. "It's all right."

Tolya looked out the window. They were crossing the north fork of the railroad tracks. There was a roadblock with a boom gate at the end of the bridge. Solovey put his cap back on. He slipped a paper from inside his jacket, unfolded it, and leaned across Andriy to show it to the sentry. This time, Tolya saw the heading at the top of the paper and the stamp on the corner.

"Comrade Colonel Volkov's orders," Solovey said to the sentry, in Russian.

Tolya's throat closed. He watched the paper circulate hands outside the car window. Fyodor Volkov was the Front's senior NKVD officer. Tolya had seen him only once, in Kyiv last November, and then only very quickly from a distance: He'd been with General Vatutin, commander of the Front, on an inspection of the ruined city. Five months later General Vatutin was dead, assassinated by UPA partisans, and Volkov had sworn the UPA would pay.

They must think he was UPA. They must think that was why he'd killed Zampolit Petrov. That was the only reason they would take him on Volkov's personal orders. That was the only reason they would be trying to convince him that they, too, were UPA.

The stamped paper came back in through the window. The sentry raised the gate.

"I almost saluted," Solovey said, and laughed. He was speaking Ukrainian again.

"Quiet," Andriy said, glancing up in the mirror.

He didn't know why they were taking him out of the city to work on him. He knew how the NKVD did their business. If they really needed to get somebody talking, they would do it in public, making everybody else watch. They called that the "conference method," and that was how they'd gotten his father. His father hadn't been strong enough—weak enough? hardened enough?—to stand by and watch in silence.

The last of the city was speeding past in a gray, rubbled blur. Now there were bright green poplar trees streaming along the roadside. Tolya's stomach jumped and twisted. He looked away.

Solovey looked back at him over the seat.

"Have you ever been in a car before, Tolya?"

No. He remembered the first time he'd ever seen a car—in Kyiv, at the train station, after Aunt Olena had come to get him and take him away from Kuz'myn. That was three or four days after his mother had been shot. There'd been some high-ranking

Communist Party official getting out of the car, and there'd been NKVD with him, and Tolya had held on tightly to Aunt Olena's hand because they'd looked so very like the men who'd shot his mother against the garden wall. Of course, they couldn't have been the same because it was three hundred kilometers from Kuz'myn to Kyiv and there were different jurisdictions, but that wasn't how a ten-year-old mind worked. You didn't understand distances and jurisdictions. All you really knew was that your mother was dead, and it wasn't the famine that had done it, but the men with the blue caps.

"Our source says you come from Kyiv," Solovey said, as though he'd heard Tolya's thoughts. But that was another trick—to drop names and dates, to pretend you knew things. Tolya didn't say anything. Solovey didn't seem to care. "Turn off here," he said to Andriy. The car eased off the road, the tires spitting up gravel. Andriy put on the hand brake and cut the engine.

Solovey held the machine gun with his left hand and opened his door. He got out, cradling the gun on his arm. They all got out. The road went on ahead between the poplars. It was hot there on the shoulder of the road. The sun was beating down hard and bright in a clear blue sky, the heat curling off the pavement in slick, greasy waves—and Tolya knew suddenly that he was going to die, here and now on the side of the road in the heat and the sunlight.

Solovey kicked the car door shut and said, "Tolya, come here."

He wasn't going to die with a bullet in his back, and he wasn't going to be dragged to it. He went over on his own, holding his head up. His heart was lodged in a cold, tight lump at the base of his throat.

Solovey shouldered the machine gun. He held out the ammunition bag.

"You carry this. We're on foot from here."

Tolya took the bag numbly. He put the strap over his head, looking back over his shoulder. The others weren't paying any attention to him or Solovey. Yakiv was taking a tool kit out of the trunk of the car. Andriy and Taras were lifting the hood, leaning over the engine.

"They'll catch up," Solovey said. "They're wiring the car—a little surprise for our NKVD friends, if they come looking. Know what a tilt fuse is?"

"No," Tolya said.

"I don't really either," Solovey said. "That's why I'm not the one wiring it."

* * *

They walked away from the road. Solovey walked ahead, bent a little under the weight of the machine gun. The ground sloped up and up to the foothills, and they walked in knee-high grass and tall, purple heather. For the first little while, they walked in silence, and Tolya could hear the murmur of the wind in the grass, and the snatches of birdsong in the poplars, and the beat of his heart in his throat.

"All right," Solovey said, "switch—to the trees." He slid the gun off his shoulder and held it out to Tolya. "Give me the bag."

Tolya didn't move. His heart was beating very loudly. "Shoot me if you're going to shoot me. This is stupid."

Solovey planted the butt of the gun on the ground between his feet. He crouched in the grass, leaning on the gun as though it were a walking stick. He looked up into Tolya's face. "I'm not NKVD, Tolya. I'm not going to shoot you. This is a rescue—or an extraction, if you want to be technical."

"On Comrade Colonel Volkov's orders?"

"Not that he knows. That was a forgery."

"That's what you want me to think."

"Well—yes."

"I didn't ask to be *extracted*."

"No. Our source in the Front put in a request through channels, and my commander obliged. Sent his best man." Solovey grinned winningly.

"Who's your source in the Front?"

"Your guess is as good as mine—probably better, actually. I just follow orders and dodge bullets."

"All right," Tolya said. "You followed your orders. Now let me go."

"Go where? There aren't many options for a Red deserter—not in L'viv anyway."

"I'll take my own chances."

"With the Poles? They'll shoot you just for being Ukrainian, never mind what uniform you're wearing. Repayment in kind." Solovey smiled again, without humor.

Tolya's stomach clenched. He knew what the UPA did to Poles. He'd heard it from the small, roving bands of Polish Resistance that had fought together with the Front for a while back in the spring, before Stalin had ordered them disarmed. Then he'd seen it himself, all the way across Galicia from Tarnopol to Lwów—all that stretch of chewed-up, exhausted, godforsaken black-earth country: farmhouses burned, Polish civilians tortured and raped and shot, their mutilated bodies marked *traitor* or *collaborator* or *NKVD rat* and hung up for examples. The UPA claimed Galicia and neighboring Volhynia as rightfully Ukrainian. Poles were a blight on the land, a cancer to be excised.

"The Germans might not shoot you," Solovey said. "They might just take you for slave labor. *Ostarbeit*, they call it. Tidy and efficient—very German. But I doubt you'd make it that far. They're in full retreat across the San. Your chances aren't very good, Tolya."

"You don't understand. I've got to go back."

Solovey's smile disappeared. "You murdered a political officer. They'll hang you on a meat hook."

"You don't know anything about it."

"Sergei Ilyich Petrov," Solovey recited, "thirty-six years old, from Ulyanovsk, just like dear Comrade Lenin. He's been a party member since 1926 and political officer for the Hundredth Rifles since November of last year. You shot him once in the back and once in the head, possibly over differences left unsettled since Tarnopol—"

"You don't know anything about Tarnopol," Tolya said.

"—but definitely with deliberate intent," Solovey finished, "whatever the reason. Anyway, if they don't shoot you for treason, they'll shoot you for desertion. You're absent without leave and consorting with the enemy. Maybe you didn't have a choice, but neither did Lieutenant Spirin, did he? Didn't stop the NKVD from putting a bullet in his head—but I *don't know anything* about that."

"Shut up."

"The point is you don't want to go back. Trust me."

"There are people close to me," Tolya said.

Solovey's chin snapped up.

"Our source said you were alone—no family."

"Not family." Tolya hesitated. He'd never had to explain Koval. She was just Koval—though sometimes, in the safety of his head, she was Nataliya. "A friend."

Solovey scowled. "In the Front?"

"Yes."

"Ukrainian?"

"Yes."

Solovey was silent, leaning on the gun.

"You've got to let me go back," Tolya said.

Solovey looked up. "I'm sorry."

"You've got to let me go back."

"I can't," Solovey said, "not now. I'm sorry. The problem—"

Tolya ran. He stumbled down the bare hillside, fighting through the long grass. There was a little copse of poplars at the foot of the hill, curving away from the road. If he could make it to the trees, he could make it away. Solovey was shouting after him. Tolya didn't stop, and he didn't look back. He was almost to the trees. He heard the *crack* of a pistol shot, and he ducked by instinct. The bullet tore through the trees ahead of him—a warning shot. There was a pause, then another *crack*. The bullet slammed into him, low in his left shoulder, pitching him forward onto his hands.

For a moment, he lay numbly still, breathless with the shock, holding the grass in fistfuls. Then there was pain, spreading out and searching him through with white-hot fingers, and the blood roaring in his ears, and the frantic *thump, thump, thump* of his heart on the grass.

Solovey's footsteps were coming toward him down the hill.

Tolya staggered up and stumbled on, gasping, holding his shoulder.

"Stop, Tolya," Solovey said. He'd broken into a run, his pistol in his hand.

Tolya ducked into the trees—and tripped, stupidly, sprawling over a root, falling on his face on the cool, damp earth.

He fought against Solovey's hands—or he tried anyway, twisting and kicking and swearing. Solovey put a knee into his back and jerked his arms around.

"I'm sorry," Solovey said, sliding the ammunition bag off Tolya's shoulder. He held Tolya's wrists in one hand. He had a scout's knife in his other hand. He cut the strap of the bag. "I didn't want to shoot you," he said, tying Tolya's wrists with the strap. "You've got to understand I can't let you go. They'll torture you if they take you, trying to find us."

His hands lifted Tolya slowly, carefully. He opened the buttons of Tolya's jacket and pulled the jacket down Tolya's arms. He held Tolya's tunic in his hands and ripped it and peeled it away.

His fingers found the rosary around Tolya's neck.

Orthodox didn't pray the rosary. Neither did the Ukrainian Catholics here in Lwów.

A rosary meant Tolya was a Roman Catholic, a Pole—and he knew what the UPA did to Poles.

For a moment, Solovey was frozen, holding the rosary in his fingers and looking at the crucifix on his palm. Very distantly, over the blood in his ears and the wind in the trees, Tolya could hear Andriy and Taras and Yakiv coming up from the roadside.

Solovey yanked the clasp open, tore the rosary from Tolya's neck, and shoved it quickly into a pocket. He tore Tolya's tunic into strips.

"It's all right, Tolya," he said. "It's all right."

4

THEY WOULD TORTURE HIM FIRST, TO SEE WHAT
he knew about numbers and positions and battle orders.

Then they would kill him.

*The Ukrainian nation is against mixed marriage and regards it as
a crime*, the UPA leaflets said. He'd seen them in Tarnopol, in
Zborów, in Złoczów—all the way across Galicia. *The family is the
most important organic unit, the highest cell of the national collective,
and thus we have to keep it purely Ukrainian.*

There were other leaflets listing other crimes: *Death to the
traitors who join the Red Army! Death to the traitors who join the collective farms!* They hadn't stuck with him the same way. Those
other crimes were just things you *did*. Who cared what he'd
done? They would kill him just for what he *was*—or maybe for
what he *wasn't*. He wasn't *purely* Ukrainian. With a Polish mother
and a Ukrainian father, he was an impurity in the blood of the
Ukrainian race.

They would kill him to cleanse the blood.

"You're going to have to walk," Solovey said. He was bandaging Tolya's shoulder with strips of tunic. "There's a reason I didn't aim for your legs. Well, multiple reasons, but that was one of them. However, try to run . . ."

He showed Tolya his pistol, holding it very close to Tolya's face, opening the magazine and letting Tolya see the six remaining rounds.

"I can use every one of them without killing you," he said, "but it would be miserable for both of us, so I'm going to ask you, please, not to run. All right? Be good about it, and I might even untie your hands."

Tolya swore at him in Polish.

Solovey slid a hand over Tolya's mouth. "In Ukrainian, you suicidal idiot."

"*Vyrodok*"—through Solovey's fingers—"*suchyy syn*—"

"I'd conserve the energy," Solovey said. "It's a long walk, and I'm not going to carry you."

* * *

Tolya tried to run.

He knew he wouldn't make it away. There was no question of making it away. But he didn't want to live to go through a UPA interrogation, and he thought, in a sudden rush of panic, that he could make it enough of a possibility that Solovey would shoot to kill.

There wasn't much more thought to it than that. He waited

until they were halfway up the bare-grass slope, very nearly the same place as last time, and he ran.

He'd never tried running with his hands tied behind his back. This time he didn't even make it to the trees. He stumbled ten meters or so, fighting for his balance the whole way, before the soldier called Yakiv—intimidatingly big and surprisingly quick— caught him by an elbow, jerked him around, and shoved him to the ground, planting a heavy, booted foot in Tolya's stomach. Tolya looked up into the gaping metal mouth of Yakiv's rifle.

"Do you know, *zradnyk*," Yakiv said, "you can still walk with a shattered kneecap, given enough motivation."

"Not very quickly," Solovey said lazily, coming down through the grass, "and not for very long, no matter the motivation. Leave him his kneecaps, Yakiv."

"Up, *zradnyk*." Yakiv took his foot off Tolya's stomach and jabbed Tolya's ribs with the muzzle of the rifle.

If he'd been braver, he would have said he wasn't the *zradnyk*, the traitor, not technically, because *he* only shot Germans and Soviet political officers—but he didn't say it. He got up. He rolled over onto his stomach and pushed himself up awkwardly on his knees. Yakiv prodded him with the rifle again, just for good measure, and they walked.

He didn't know how far they walked. He tried to estimate time and distance by the angle of the sun, the way Comrade Lieutenant Spirin had taught him, but Yakiv hurried him roughly along with the muzzle of the rifle whenever he looked up into the trees. Solovey and Andriy were ahead, carrying the machine gun and the ammunition bag between them. Yakiv followed Tolya, and Taras brought up the rear. They were going north and west into the low foothills above the city. He knew that much because when they crested one long, wooded slope he risked a glance back over his shoulder and saw the wood spreading away behind them, the road through the poplars as thin as a thread below them, the city like a smear of ash on the far green floor of the river valley. Then Yakiv nudged him with the rifle, and he stumbled down the slope after Solovey and Andriy.

They rested once. Andriy passed around a canteen of warm, stale water. At first, he was going to refuse because his hands were still tied, which meant Solovey had to hold the canteen for him. But his shoulder was hurting badly, and when he opened his mouth to snarl an oath, he lost his nerve and ended up letting Solovey tip the water onto his tongue—and Solovey must have taken that as his surrender, because afterward he bent over Tolya with his knife and cut the strap from Tolya's wrists.

They walked again. His shoulder was hurting very badly now. The bandage was swollen and soaking. He bit the insides of his cheeks and blinked away blackness from the corners of his eyes, letting Yakiv nose him this way and that with the rifle because that was easier than lifting his head to look.

He tried to think about Comrade Lieutenant Spirin making it all the way back from the German lines at Tarnopol with two broken ribs and a bullet hole in his back, but all he could think about was how Comrade Lieutenant Spirin got a firing squad instead of a Red Star because Zampolit Petrov said he'd been turned in captivity.

Then he tried to think about Koval, calmly picking out shrapnel from her calf after a mortar round collapsed the walls of the slit trench, but all he could think about was that morning in the switch tower, and collective guilt, and how she would put a pistol in her mouth before she'd let them take her.

He must have passed out, because he woke up to find Solovey and Andriy carrying him, Solovey's arms under his arms and Andriy's arms around his knees. Solovey was walking slowly backward, talking over his shoulder to somebody Tolya couldn't see: "Going to have to hurry if you want the light."

"Put him down—here." That was a girl's voice. Somebody put a hand on Tolya's shoulder. He jerked reflexively, hissing.

Solovey's hands tightened under his arms. "Morphine," Solovey said.

"You want to use—"

"Yes."

"Iryna," the girl said.

Tolya jerked again, deliberately this time. He twisted against Andriy's arms, scrabbling for Solovey's hands. He knew what that meant too—morphine. They would give him a little before the questioning, just enough to keep him calm and pliable and to dull the pain so he wouldn't pass out again. That was what the NKVD did. He jerked wildly, kicking.

"Put him down," the girl said. "For the love of heaven, put him down before he hurts himself."

They put him on the ground, spreading his arms. He tried to lunge back up. They pushed him down and held him. Solovey leaned over him.

"Easy, tiger," he said. "We're going to take the bullet out." He had a knee in Tolya's stomach and a hand on either side of Tolya's head, pinning him. "You picked the wrong time to wake up," he said.

"How did it happen?" the girl asked, unwrapping the makeshift bandage from Tolya's shoulder. She had calm, steady hands—warm, red hands, callused from work. There was a Red Cross badge on the sleeve of her coat.

"Stray shot," Solovey said. "The getaway. It was close." He grinned a quick, pained grin down into Tolya's face.

"No one else?" The girl peeled away the bandage and wiped the blood with clean gauze.

"We were lucky," Solovey said.

"*He* was lucky the bullet missed the bone."

"Extremely," Solovey agreed.

Another Red Cross girl swooped in beside Solovey, slipping a bag from her shoulder.

"Fifteen milligrams, Iryna," the first girl said.

"Thirty," Solovey said.

The two girls looked at each other over Tolya.

"Thirty milligrams," Solovey said. "Take it out of mine."

"Fine," the first girl said, "all right. Thirty." She was pinning her hair up. "Give me those forceps," she said to Solovey. "Make yourself useful for a change."

* * *

Afterward, Tolya was under a canvas tarpaulin in the blue half-light, curled up on a blanket on the ground with another blanket over him, blinking up through tangled tree branches to a twilit sky. His head was very thick and very light at the same time. When he moved, it felt as though somebody else were directing his limbs distantly on a puppet string. He lay still, listening to the nightingales. *It's all right*, he thought vaguely, *it's all right*. If they were going to torture him now, they wouldn't have troubled with blankets.

Solovey ducked in under the tarpaulin.

He wasn't wearing the NKVD uniform. He was wearing a green-gray jacket and trousers and a green-gray side cap with the *tryzub*, the Ukrainian trident, in bloodred and black on the badge. He had his pistol at his belt, and the bloodred stripes on his sleeves must mark him as an officer. He was carrying a sausage in waxed paper.

"No hot food," he said. "No fires. I'm sorry."

He sat down cross-legged beside Tolya. He showed Tolya the sausage.

"A present from Anna, to make up for digging around in

your shoulder with sharp metal things. Eating something ought to make you feel a little better. Always works for me, anyway."

He laid the sausage down and spread open the waxed paper. He had his scout's knife in his hand.

"All right," he said, "here's the thing." He held the sausage in his left hand and cut with his right, bracing the spine of the blade on his forefinger and cutting the sausage in thick slices. "Early this morning, our source in the Front contacted command and asked if we could get you out. You'd shot your political officer, and it was only a matter of hours before the NKVD followed it back to you." He picked a strip of sausage skin off the heel of the blade with his thumbnail. "Now, I made it very clear to command—and command, in turn, made it very clear to our source—that I wouldn't even try getting you out unless I knew you could make a clean break of it. That means no living family, no close friends. And I got the unequivocal assurance that you could."

"They lied," Tolya said, through shut teeth. He lay very still under the blanket, watching the knife in Solovey's hand.

"I've thought about it," Solovey said. "Motivation is tricky. Our source is a double agent, maybe, and you're a Red spy. That's as far as that line of thinking takes me."

"I'm not a spy."

"It raises an interesting question. Did you spit in my face because you thought I was NKVD or because you knew I was UPA?"

"I'm not a spy."

"The other possibility, of course, is that *you* lied, in which case motivation becomes a little easier. Our well-meaning but unwitting source delivered you right into the hands of the UPA, and you needed an excuse to get away."

He finished cutting the sausage and wiped his knife carefully on the paper, then on the grass. He glanced up.

"Was that it?"

Tolya didn't say anything. He watched the knife disappear into the lining of Solovey's boot. He was clenching his muscles to keep his empty stomach from muttering, trying not to look at the sausage. He focused on the pistol at Solovey's hip. The pistol was very nearly within his reach, and it would be if Solovey leaned forward just a little.

"Don't even think about it," Solovey said.

Tolya looked away, swallowing. His shoulder hurt, and his empty stomach ached, and Koval would be dead by now because she wouldn't have let them take her, and his throat was tight, and he was very afraid in that moment that he was going to cry with Solovey watching.

Solovey said, "How old are you, Tolya?"

Official UPA policy was to kill every Polish male over the age of sixteen. He supposed it was the conscientious ones who asked first.

"You've got my papers," he said.

"Not at the moment," Solovey said.

"You saw them."

"I was too damn nervous to *read* them."

He knew it was a lie, but he was too tired to keep fighting, and too much a coward. He shut his eyes and swallowed.

"Eighteen in October," he said.

"Conscript?"

He nodded against the blanket. He couldn't speak.

"I guess you'd have to be," Solovey said. "They wouldn't take you at the recruiting stations—not for a frontline rifle company, anyway." Tolya heard the *click* of a lighter. "You're not from Kyiv, are you?" Solovey said. "Not with those fine Galician vowels."

"Kuz'myn," Tolya said.

"Where's that?"

"Outside Proskuriv."

"Andriy would know," Solovey said. "He's from Proskuriv."

His fingers tugged at Tolya's elbow. Tolya opened his eyes. Solovey held out a cigarette. Tolya looked at it, wanted it so badly that his mouth watered, fought with himself, knew that Solovey could see him fighting with himself, and turned his head quickly away because he wasn't going to give Solovey the satisfaction.

Solovey returned the cigarette indifferently to his breast pocket. "How did your parents die?"

He had to get his mind off that cigarette. "My father in the prison at Proskuriv," he said.

"Political."

"They said so."

"Would you not?"

"I mean—he was one of the ones—when the Reds were trying to make us give up our land and go to the *kolhosp*—the collective farm . . ." He risked a glance to see whether Solovey understood.

"Yes," Solovey said.

"He was one of the ones who resisted. But that's not what they killed him for. Lots of people resisted."

"What did they kill him for?"

"He confessed to something he didn't do. So they asked him questions he couldn't answer. He died under torture."

Solovey flicked the ash from the tip of his cigarette and blew a soft, smoky breath. "What about your mother?"

Tolya swallowed quickly. "Against our garden wall, because she was Polish."

He waited. He held the blanket drawn tight in his fists, watching the pistol at Solovey's belt. *The Ukrainian nation is against mixed marriage and regards it as a crime . . .*

But Solovey only pulled on his cigarette and said, "NKVD?"

"Yes."

"How old were you?"

"You mean when they died?"

"Mm."

"Seven when they took my father." The pistol didn't seem to be forthcoming. Solovey was leaning his elbows on his knees, holding his cigarette in two fingers and rolling it absently between his fingertips, not looking up. Tolya shut his eyes again. "Ten when—when it was my mother."

"That was in 1937?"

"Yes."

"And after that—what? One of the state orphanages?"

"My aunt took me to Kyiv—my father's sister. Her husband wrote for the state paper there. *Proletars'ka Pravda*."

"Party members?"

Tolya hesitated. "He was. I think you have to be—to write for the paper."

Solovey was silent for a moment, pulling on his cigarette and breathing out the smoke. Then he said, "Did he make it difficult?"

"You mean . . ."

"For you."

It wasn't the question he'd expected. He swallowed, remembering Ivan's voice through the shut closet door. *Don't you understand? He'll get us shot, the half-breed.*

"Sometimes," Tolya said.

"Abuse?"—quietly.

Tolya opened his eyes. He craned his neck to look up into Solovey's face.

"You don't have to answer," Solovey said. In the glow of the cigarette, the lines of his face were hard and sharp shadowed. "You don't have to tell me anything."

"How did you—"

"You called him your aunt's husband, not your uncle. It was a guess. You don't have to tell me."

"She wanted to leave," Tolya said. "We were going to leave—my aunt and I, together. But she was afraid—because I didn't have the permission to be off the collective—you've got to have a special permission to be off, and I—she had just—"

"She was afraid he'd turn you in if you tried to leave."

"Yes."

Solovey rolled his cigarette between his fingertips. "How long?"

"In Kyiv?"

"Under his roof."

"A year. They took him in one of the party purges—the NKVD." It had occurred to Tolya only much later that it must have been Aunt Olena who'd denounced him.

"And your aunt . . ."

"No, she died at Voronezh, in the retreat. We went to Voronezh when the Germans came."

"Is that where you were conscripted?"

"Yes."

"Sniper," Solovey said.

"Yes."

"I'm told our source spoke very highly of you."

"He didn't know about my mother," Tolya said. There was something bitter on the base of his tongue.

"No," Solovey said, "I imagine not." He was silent, breathing smoke out softly through his nostrils. Then he said, "Were you lying?"

"What?"

"About this friend in the Front."

Tolya was angry suddenly. "Maybe I'm lying about all of it."

Solovey's face was blank. "Because I'm going to look like an idiot trying to make another rescue, if you were."

Tolya blinked at him.

"I owe you that much," Solovey said.

"It's no good."

"What's no good?"

"Rescue."

"We won't be able to pull off the same trick again. That's all right. I know other tricks."

"I mean she can't make a clean break."

"Family?"

"She's got a sister in Kyiv."

Solovey flicked ash from his cigarette. He took a thoughtful drag. "What's her name?"

Tolya didn't say anything.

Solovey let out a low, smoky breath—not quite a laugh, not quite a sigh.

"All right," he said. "Three possibilities. There are more, but let's keep it to three for simplicity's sake." He counted on his fingers, starting with his thumb. "One—I'm NKVD, and it doesn't make a difference whether you tell me her name or not. If they're going to take her, they've taken her already. Two"— holding his forefinger and middle finger together, the cigarette between them—"I'm *not* NKVD, and I figure out her name on my own. She'll probably be dead by then, but at least you know you didn't betray her. Three—"

Tolya shut his eyes.

"Koval. Nataliya Koval. She's a junior sergeant with the Hundredth. Second Battalion."

"Sniper?"

"Yes."

"We'll see," Solovey said.

"I think she's dead already." He made himself open his eyes. He looked up into Solovey's face. "I think she'd have done it herself—before they took her."

Solovey slipped his cigarette back into his mouth. He was silent for a moment, playing with the cigarette between his teeth. Then he took it out again and stubbed it out in the dirt.

"We'll see," he said. "You should eat. I've been politely pretending not to hear your stomach growling."

5

NIGHT CAME DOWN THICK AND BLACK. SOLOVEY was gone, and Tolya was alone under the tarpaulin. For a little while, he tried to keep himself awake, but his stomach was comfortably full of sausage, and his body heavy and numb with morphine, and it was no good. He slept. He woke up once, in darkness, to low voices and the crackle of underbrush in the wood. He lay tensely still under the blanket, listening, but now there was only silence and the far-off hooting of an owl. He slept again, and this time when he woke up there was pale, early sunlight slanting through the trees, and the fresh, damp, clean smell of dirt and tree bark and pine needles.

Somebody leaned over him, blocking the light. He jerked by reflex, thrashing his legs.

"Mind," Solovey said. He was sitting across from Tolya under the tarpaulin, smoking a cigarette. "He's awake."

The Red Cross girl, Iryna, the one who'd brought the morphine, sat back on her heels. She smiled down at Tolya. She was a thin, dark-eyed girl with a long plait of black hair under a kerchief.

"It's all right," she said. "I'm just changing the dressing."

"How is it?" Solovey asked.

"Do you want the technical prognosis?"

"No, please, dear God. I've had a long night."

"Bleeding a little, but it's clean."

"Permanent damage?"

"There shouldn't be. The bullet penetrated below the medial cord."

"You're getting technical," Solovey said.

"There shouldn't be any nerve damage," Iryna said. She was leaning into the sunlight again, holding Tolya's shoulder in cool fingers and wrapping it tightly with a strip of gauze. She glanced down into Tolya's face. "You're awfully quiet. Is that because it doesn't hurt, or because you want me to think it doesn't hurt?"

"It's all right," Tolya said.

"So, yes—it hurts. How badly?"

"It's not bad."

"He remembers you stuck needles in him," Solovey said. "That's the issue. That was his first introduction to you. Now he wakes up with your hands all over him."

"Mind yourself," Iryna said.

Tolya leaned his head back on the blanket, holding the pain behind shut teeth. He looked out into the wood. There was a camouflage net over a pile of ammunition boxes just outside the tarpaulin, and another over the DP-27 and the 120mm mortar, which were mounted a little way up the slope, toward the ridge. There was a stretch of open, grassy ground between. He lay watching the squad share a cold breakfast of black bread and pork drippings. There were five of them. He recognized Andriy and Taras and the other Red Cross girl, Anna. He didn't see the big, bearish one, Yakiv, but the whole squad wouldn't be here in the camp all at once. There would be couriers and scouts. There would be sentries posted at intervals all around the wood.

Iryna tied off the gauze and cut it with a pair of scissors. She rolled up the extra gauze around her fingers and put it in her bag.

"You know what I'm going to say," she said to Solovey.

"Do I?"

"Yes, because it's the same thing Anna will say. It would be better if he came back with us to Toporiv."

Solovey pulled on his cigarette expressionlessly. "I need him here."

"He'll have a better chance at a full recovery in Toporiv."

"You mean there's a risk he won't make a full recovery."

"There's always a risk with this kind of wound. You know that."

Solovey was silent, pulling on his cigarette.

Iryna shouldered her bag and got up. "Even if he does make a full recovery, it'll be a month. He's not going to be doing you much good here."

"I'll keep that in mind," Solovey said.

He came over when Iryna had gone, crouching slowly on his heels by Tolya's blanket. He laid a piece of bread spread with drippings beside Tolya on the blanket.

"Were you lying to her?"

"What?"

"About the pain."

"It's all right," Tolya said automatically.

"There's a Red Cross station in Toporiv. That's what she was talking about." Solovey took his cigarette out of his mouth and spun it in his fingertips absently. "*She* wasn't lying. That's your best option, medically speaking."

Tolya watched him spin the cigarette. His stomach was tight.

"And my other options?"

"Well," Solovey said, "that's what you and I need to talk about."

He put the cigarette back in his mouth.

"I went down to talk to the commander last night," he said, "about your friend—about why I didn't know about your friend."

"What did he say?"

"Not much, as it turns out. I didn't actually end up getting to talk to him. It's hard to work these things out spontaneously, you understand." Solovey shrugged. "I did some poking around on my own, just so it wouldn't be a wasted trip. It's eight hours on foot—there and back. Eight hours total, I mean. Four hours each way."

"And?"

Solovey took out his cigarette. He spun it between his fingers and dropped it on the dirt, grinding it out under the toe of his boot. He looked down into Tolya's face finally.

"You were right," he said.

It took him a second, blinking back up into Solovey's face, to understand.

"Dead?"

"I'm sorry."

Tolya looked away. He looked out into the wood, blinking and swallowing—blinking very quickly so Solovey wouldn't see the tears, then not caring, and letting the tears come, and watching the tree branches blur together, and hearing Solovey say quietly, somewhere very far above him, "She was more than a friend, wasn't she?"—and not having the words to explain, because all he could think about was yesterday morning in the switch tower and the way her eyes turned green, the color of moths' wings, in sunlight.

"You said she's got a sister in Kyiv," Solovey said.

He squeezed his eyes shut. "Nadiya."

"I put a message through to our people in Kyiv. We'll get her out."

He couldn't speak. His throat was closed. *You're lying*, he wanted to say—but he could hear her voice, and he could hear the hardness in it, and he could see the straightness in her shoulders, and he knew it wasn't a lie. *Your fault*, he wanted to say, *your fault, all of it*—but it wasn't, not really. Solovey hadn't shot Zampolit Petrov.

Solovey stood suddenly. He prodded Tolya's ribs with the toe of his boot.

"Get up, Tolya. Eat that bread. Then get your boots. I want to have a look at something."

* * *

He followed Solovey up the slope, away from the little camp. Solovey was carrying a musette bag slung across his body and a pair of binoculars on a strap around his neck. He had his pistol at his hip and a rifle—a scoped Mosin with a bent bolt, very like Tolya's own rifle—propped on his shoulder, the legs of the bipod dangling down his back. He paused every now and then to let Tolya catch up. They crested the ridge. The earth dropped away sharply ahead of them, down into a narrow, shaded ravine, sloping up again across the ravine and rolling on down to the river valley, the way they'd come yesterday. There was the road through the poplars, faint and far below. There was the dark scar of the railroad tracks, and the gray ruin of the city, and there was Gródecka Street, plowing west to the San River, choked with soldiers and trucks and the big *dashka* guns on trolleys.

The Front was moving out of Lwów, pushing west in pursuit of the Germans and new territory to claim for the motherland.

Solovey put down the musette bag and propped up the rifle on its bipod.

"Wait here," he said. "I'll be back."

He went down the slope into the ravine. Tolya watched him through the trees—losing him for a little while in the thick trees at the bottom of the ravine, finding him again on the far slope. Solovey went just about halfway up the slope and took off his cap and hung it on a tree branch.

He came down and crossed the ravine and climbed back up to Tolya.

"What do you think?" he said. "Five hundred meters?"

"Maybe," Tolya said.

Solovey crouched by the rifle, taking the butt on his lap. He took a cartridge box out of his pocket and popped the bolt on the rifle, stripping a clip smoothly into the magazine. He shoved the bolt home with his palm. Then he laid the butt of the rifle carefully on the ground. He sat back, wiping his hands on his trousers. He looked up at Tolya.

"Hit the cap," he said.

Tolya didn't move. He knew this kind of game. He would be playing for his life, but the trick of it was there was nothing he could do to win.

Solovey patted the stock of the rifle. "Try it."

He would die for failing, and he would die for refusing, and very likely he would die when it was done no matter how it went. It was a game he couldn't win unless Solovey decided to let him win.

"I'll allow you a margin of error," Solovey said, "in light of circumstances which are entirely my fault."

Tolya knelt numbly. He went down onto his stomach on the ground, shouldering the butt and leaning his cheek on the smooth wood, balancing the stock gingerly with his fingers. He closed his left eye and sighted through the scope, sliding his fore-finger over the trigger. He lifted his head a little. Closer to six hundred meters—negative elevation twelve meters. There was a strong crosswind cutting through the ravine from nine o'clock, north to south.

He leaned his cheek back on the stock. He squeezed his eye shut and sighted again, willing his hands not to shake. Out of the corner of his eye, he saw Solovey looking through the bin-oculars. He drew a breath, squeezed the trigger, and let out the breath. He lifted his head and slid the bolt back. The empty shell casing spun out. He threw the bolt shut and looked up, tight-throated, at Solovey.

Solovey lowered his binoculars.

"Go get it," he said.

Tolya hesitated, just for a second. There were four rounds still loaded, and they both knew it. He laid the rifle down, wiped his hands, and got up. He walked down the slope, away from

Solovey. There were beech trees all down the slope. He handed himself from one mottled gray trunk to the next, down to the floor of the ravine. He felt the rifle on his back all the way down. He thought he remembered the ravine from yesterday, but there was a wide, shallow stream on the floor of the ravine that he didn't remember, so it must have been right about here that he'd passed out. There were deep, green shadows between the hills and sharp flashes of sunlight when the wind lifted the beech boughs. The air was clear and cool. Thrushes sang back and forth across the hillsides above him. He crossed the stream and went up the slope. He found Solovey's cap on the ground. There was a neat, round hole, the width of his fingertip, through the top of the cap.

He took the cap back across the ravine and went up to Solovey on the ridge.

Solovey was sitting by the rifle, smoking. When Tolya came up, he stubbed out his cigarette against the barrel of the rifle and flicked the butt away.

"You owe me a new hat," he said. He held out his hand and took the cap from Tolya and held it on his lap, putting a finger through the bullet hole. "Why didn't you run?"

"Why didn't you shoot?"

"I wanted you to know I wouldn't. It could have important implications for what comes next. I'm giving you two options, and I want you to make an educated choice."

He moved the cap off his knee and leaned over to open the musette bag.

"I'm not counting Toporiv, by the way," he said, rummaging in the bag. "It might be your best option from a medical standpoint, but you've got a lot more to worry about than that shoulder. Toporiv is our ground—UPA ground. They won't have any reason to think you've got Polish in your blood unless you give them reason to think you've got Polish in your blood, but it won't take too many innocuous questions before somebody figures out you came in with the Front, which is just as bad. Anna and Iryna won't betray you, but they won't be able to protect you either—and at that point neither will I. The commander could, but he wouldn't."

"I thought you said he ordered the extraction."

"The commander," Solovey said, still rummaging, "is what you might call a utilitarian. Do you know what that means?"

"No."

"Means his interest in your well-being is directly proportional to his estimation of your usefulness. And his estimation of your usefulness is inversely proportional to the number of people who know you fought with a Soviet rifle division. In other words—"

"I live only as long as I'm useful."

"And you're useful only as long as you're safely anonymous. They find you out in Toporiv, he throws you to the wolves. Otherwise the wolves turn on him." Solovey held up a little plastic vial between thumb and forefinger. "So. American morphine syrettes, thirty milligrams apiece. The Red Cross gets them through to us sometimes. Like gold, these—you could bribe your way across a border with them. Also some iodine, courtesy of Iryna; another sausage, courtesy of Anna; and these. Very important." He held up a thin red-leather wallet. "New identification papers, and a Young Communist League membership card. We had to tear up your military registration for the photograph. I'm sorry. You're now a party-appointed schoolteacher on your way to Stryy. Do you know where Stryy is?"

Tolya looked away, swallowing quickly. His throat was very tight.

"In the mountains," he said.

"Due south. On foot, it will take you three days—two, if you push yourself. I wouldn't. I'd take it easy, with that shoulder. And, because party-appointed schoolteachers don't carry sniper rifles . . ."

Solovey unbuckled his gun belt and handed the pistol in its holster to Tolya.

"Easier to keep hidden. There are rounds in the bag. Not many, so you'll have to be judicious."

He sat back on his heels. "That's your first option. It's not as simple as it sounds. Do you believe in God, Tolya?"

The question hung on the air between them. Tolya's tongue was tied by reflex, weighed down with years of careful silence.

"You're either a believer or an idiot," Solovey said. "Those are the only people carrying prayer beads in Stalin's army."

The anger was by reflex too. "Why do you care?"

"You've thought about your contingency plans?"

"What?"

"Your contingency plans—for instance, if the NKVD take you. It's a very good chance they will, if we're being realistic. There's seventy kilometers between you and the mountains. Open farmland, most of it."

Solovey covered Tolya's hand with his hand and lifted the pistol, pressing the mouth of the pistol gently to Tolya's temple.

"What do you think?" he said. "Would God forgive you this?"

The pistol was holstered and safety locked, but even so Tolya's stomach jumped. He didn't move.

"I don't know," he said.

"Think about it. Do you trust him enough to pull the trigger? Do you trust him enough *not* to pull the trigger? You're wagering body and soul on a decision you make in a second—the hardest and loneliest decision of your life. Could you do it?"

Thump, thump, thump went Tolya's heart against his ribs.

"Could you?" he said.

Solovey smiled. His fingers were cold.

"I've got more faith in God's mercy than in the NKVD's," he said.

He let go of Tolya's hand.

"Second option," he said. "Fyodor Volkov. What do you know about him?"

"He commands the NKVD rifle division with the Front." Tolya hesitated. "He says he's going to make you pay for killing General Vatutin."

"He's the highest-ranking NKVD officer in all of western Ukraine, and he's going to hang us publicly in our own village squares, to be exact—yes. He's more worried about us than about the Germans, so he and his rifles are staying behind in L'viv while the rest of the Front pushes across the Vistula." Solovey patted the stock of the rifle again. He looked up into Tolya's face. "So—second option. You stay with me, and I get you within five hundred meters or so of Volkov."

"And then?"

"You put a hole in his head."

"I mean after that."

"I can promise you the NKVD won't give a damn about one runaway Galician conscript after that—even if you did murder a political officer."

"What about the UPA? Will I still be *useful?*"

Solovey was silent for a moment. He looked away into the wood. The muscles in his cheek tightened, fluttering.

"This is between you and me," he said, "not the UPA." He looked back, smiling just a little. "Yours won't be the first secret I've kept. I can promise you that too."

Tolya didn't say anything.

"Think about it," Solovey said. He stuck a hand in his pocket. He brought out Tolya's rosary and spilled it into Tolya's hand. "I'll be down the hill."

* * *

Tolya sat on the ridge, running the rosary between his fingers.

He didn't know how to pray the beads as his mother had prayed, in Latin, but he knew the first three beads after the crucifix were the prayer to the Theotokos, and he didn't think the Theotokos really minded that he did it in Ukrainian instead.

Rejoice, O Virgin Theotokos, Mary, full of grace, the Lord is with thee. Blessed art thou amongst women, and blessed is the fruit of thy womb, for thou hast borne the Savior of our souls.

He made the prayers in turn: to the Theotokos; to his patron and the patrons of his family, holding the icons in his head one by one; and last of all to Christ, holding the crucifix tightly in his hand, *for Thou art the Resurrection and the Life and the Repose of Thy departed handmaiden* . . .

Then he faltered, because he couldn't bring himself to say her name.

It was very quiet in the wood. The wind had died. The midmorning sun was pouring through the trees there on the hilltop. With his eyes closed, he could hear the murmur of voices up from the camp and—distantly—the low hum of engines. The Front was still crawling along the floor of the river valley, westward, away from Lwów—away from *him*.

It was a strange, empty feeling—being left.

He had imagined running. He'd lain awake in the darkness between Yura and Petya, thinking about what it would be like to run. Of course, the only way you could do it, really, was to do it the cowards' way, slipping away quietly in the night or in the ragged confusion of battle. But he'd still liked to think they would *know*, somehow—that he was Tolya Anatoliyovych Korolenko, his father a murdered Ukrainian peasant farmer and his mother a murdered Catholic Pole, and he wasn't going to fight the murderer Stalin's war any longer—as clearly as if he'd stood up and shouted it.

Anyway, it had only been imagination. Koval couldn't run, and he wouldn't run without her.

He'd killed her just the same.

He'd killed her by killing Zampolit Petrov, and he'd killed her sister, Nadiya, too.

We'll get her out, Solovey said, the same way he said *I'm sorry, Tolya* and *It's all right, Tolya* and all the other things he didn't really mean—not lies, exactly, but the kinds of things you said only because you didn't know what else to say, the kinds of things you believed only because it would hurt too much if you didn't.

The truth was they were dead, and he'd killed them.

He could follow the trail of ifs. *If* he hadn't shot Zampolit Petrov, *if* Zampolit Petrov hadn't killed Comrade Lieutenant Spirin, *if* Comrade Lieutenant Spirin hadn't seen him drop that German *Oberleutnant* from seven hundred meters across the river in Voronezh two years ago—*if* and *if* and *if*, all the way back to Kuz'myn.

But he couldn't change the truth, and he couldn't outrun it—not if he kept running for the rest of his life.

All he could do was choose not to try.

* * *

He put the holstered pistol down on the grass by Solovey's knee, slipping the musette bag from his shoulder.

Solovey looked at the pistol. Then he looked up into Tolya's face.

Tolya expected a question. He had an answer ready. But Solovey only leaned over the field book spread open on his lap, picked up the pistol, and held it out again.

"Keep it," he said. "You need something you can use one-handed, for a while."

II
ALEKSEY

Friday, June 27–Saturday, June 28
1941

6

DOWN IN THE STREET, A GAGGLE OF SCHOOL-
boys was throwing rocks at the shuttered, barred windows of
Lwów's Brygidki prison.

"Hey, *moskali!*" A cobblestone bounced off one of the
bricked-up doors—*clatter-rattle-clatter*. "Better run, *moskali!* The
Germans are coming for you!"

They clomped down the empty sidewalk in the shadow of the
long, white wall, alternating rocks and taunts.

"Hey, *moskali!* Better run while you can!"

Ukrainians, these—*moskali* was their slur for the hated Russian interlopers. Poles said *ruski*.

They were braver than I was.

No, stupider. Very important distinction. Never mistake stupidity for bravery. Both can kill you, but only one can kill you
for a purpose.

I'd been there all afternoon, watching, waiting for darkness. It
was nearly eight o'clock now. The sun was touching the tops of
the northwestern hills. The streetlamps were coming on below

me. In the silence—when the boys had vanished around the corner onto Kazimierzowska Street—you could hear the long German eighty-eights thundering from across the San River, ninety kilometers west.

They're coming for you, moskali.

The Germans would be here by Monday. We all knew it. The Reds knew it. They'd abandoned the city's westernmost districts three days ago, when the bombs started dropping. But they were still holding on to the radio towers and the NKVD offices on Pełczyńska Street and the prisons at Zamarstynów and the Citadel, and they were still holding on to the Brygidki.

They wouldn't move all their prisoners. That was simple mathematics. For two years, they'd been stuffing every dissident, every subversive into the cells of Lwów's prisons—Ukrainian, Polish, and Jewish, indiscriminately. There were four thousand prisoners in the Brygidki alone, by my count, maybe more.

Not all of them were political prisoners, of course—and not all the political prisoners were the Reds'.

Anyway, they wouldn't try to move all of them. They wouldn't waste the manpower. Realistically, they had no choice but to leave most of their prisoners behind.

Most. Not all.

They would take the high-profile prisoners, the really important ones—the ones they could break for intelligence or barter for concessions.

They would take my father if they knew who he was: Yevhen

Kobryn, hero of the Ukrainian nationalist movement, jailed as a terrorist by the Poles for his part in the assassination of an interior minister seven years ago.

I wasn't sure they knew, but I wasn't taking chances.

I didn't have much of a plan. I had a couple of stick grenades—last resorts—and a battered rifle, all lifted from a vodka-drunk sentry down at the station. If I'd had the nerve, I'd have cut his throat with his own bayonet when I took his weapons. The best he could hope for from his own people was a bullet in the back of the head.

His own people. For all I knew, he'd been Ukrainian—a conscript from the steppe, maybe. He'd had high Cossack cheekbones in a gaunt peasant's face. That didn't matter. He'd put on the Reds' uniform. He was the enemy. Anything else was unnecessary complication.

It was beside the point, in the end. I hadn't had the nerve.

What I *did* have, in addition to the weapons, was an NKVD officer's jacket, a pair of bloused uniform trousers, and a fine pair of golden-leather cavalry boots. The officers came down to the Hotel George sometimes to have their uniforms laundered and pressed, and I'd filched this one right off the line and smuggled it home in a potato sack. Repayment in kind—these weren't NKVD-issue boots. Some Polish officer had been shipped off bootless to the camps when the Reds took the city two years ago.

I had neither the NKVD's red-banded peaked cap nor the

sidearm—officers didn't carry rifles—but it was enough to fool at first glance. I hoped.

Most importantly, I had a pretty good map of the interior of the Brygidki. Father Yosyp had made it for me this morning on the back of a Psalter page. Before the Reds came, Father Yosyp had gone once a week into the Brygidki to hear the confessions of the faithful among the prisoners and to administer the Eucharist, and his memory was good—better than mine. I'd been into the Brygidki too, twice. The first time, I was twelve, and we'd just put Mama into the ground. The second time was two years ago, just before the city fell. I was seventeen, and that was the last time I'd seen my father.

I wasn't sure he was still alive, but I wasn't taking chances.

Father Yosyp hadn't asked why I wanted the map. He knew— and I think he knew I was going to do what I meant to do anyway, map or no.

He would look after my brother, Mykola, if I failed. I knew that of him.

The sun was slipping behind the hills. The Brygidki stretched long and silent and ghostly pale below me. It stretched a full block along Kazimierzowska Street—a squat, square complex of blocky sandstone buildings around a broad central courtyard. At one point in its long history, it had been a convent of the Bridgettine order of nuns. It had been a prison and a killing place since the time of the Hapsburgs, but the name had stuck—Brygidki— clean and innocent as the whitewashed walls.

A whitened sepulchre, this place, full of Ukrainian blood and Ukrainian bones.

Below me, down in the shop, the door from the alley creaked open and swung shut again. Footsteps echoed over the shop floor—two pairs of heavy, booted footsteps, clomping toward me up the stairs.

I dove behind the long bar counter, slipping the rifle from my shoulder. I curled up against the cabinet with the rifle across my knees, holding my breath and listening. They came up to the landing. They paused in the doorway. I could smell cigarettes on them—the bitter, burnt grass smell of rough makhorka tobacco. Their shadows ran over the ceiling in the light from the streetlamps.

I could see the silhouettes of rifles.

"I thought you said you could see into the yard," one of them said.

"The back yard. You can see the garages."

One of the shadows dipped. The first man ducked through the doorway. He stopped short just inside, hissing a low, sharp breath.

My momentary relief—they'd been speaking Ukrainian, not Russian—shifted back into fear. He'd seen my fresh footprints on the dusty floor.

"You," he said. "You, behind the bar. Show me your hands."

I didn't move.

"I know you're there." He unslung his rifle, unlocking the bolt. "Come on, hands up. Come out of there."

I said, with my heart in my throat, "What happens if I don't?"

"Stop wasting time. Show me your hands."

"I'm genuinely curious. What are you going to do with the gun?"

A pause.

"I've got a gun too," I said. "It does me just about as much good as it does you." The Reds might be willing to ignore a few rocks chucked by bored schoolboys, but they weren't going to ignore a firefight on their doorstep.

Another pause while he came to the same conclusion. "All right," he said grudgingly. "All right. Get up, and we'll talk it over. You're Ukrainian?"

"*Tak*," I affirmed, and remembered only as I stood that I was wearing an NKVD officer's jacket.

The first man, the one whose rifle swung back up toward me as though by instinct, was obviously the senior of the two. He had maybe ten years on me. He had coppery red-blond hair cut close under his cap and a scattering of bristly red-blond stubble on his chin. His blue eyes were hard and unblinking. Besides the rifle in his hands, he had a pistol holstered neatly under his arm.

The other, hanging back silently in the doorway, was my age, or close, with a sharp, serious, pale face. He met my eyes, blinked, and looked away. He was holding his rifle very tightly.

"Hold your hands up," the blond man said to me, "above the bar, where I can see them. Come around here."

"Or what?" It was stupid to keep pushing him, but I was very afraid just then. I had no identification on me. I hadn't been *that* stupid. I had an NKVD uniform—most of it—and a Red's weapons. This could go very badly.

"All right," the blond man said. "We'll play it like this."

He lowered his rifle and slung it back over his shoulder. He brushed open his jacket and slipped a long knife from somewhere inside. He showed it to me, holding the blade between his thumb and two fingers.

"That's not a throwing knife," I said.

"Come around here," the blond man said.

I went. My feet started moving on their own, and I went, holding my hands up. The blond man watched me come around the bar.

"Stand there," he said, pointing with the knife. Then to the young one: "Search him."

The young one slung his rifle and approached me cautiously. He crouched at my feet and patted down my legs, straightening slowly as he worked his way up. He took the grenades from my pockets very carefully and laid them on the bar. He took out the spare clips for the rifle. He unfolded Father Yosyp's map with stumbling fingers.

"What does it say?" the blond man asked. He hadn't turned his eyes from my face.

"It's a map," the young one said softly.

"Of what, half-wit?"

"Of the Brygidki."

"Give it to me," the blond man said. "Let me see. What about papers? Any identification?"

The young one felt along my arms and slipped his hands shyly into my jacket pockets. He shook his head, not looking in my face. "No, nothing."

"All right." The blond man folded up my map and put it in his pocket. "Tie his hands. Use that twine."

At this point, I didn't have much to lose by being frank.

"Look," I said, "I'm not NKVD."

"So?" the blond man said. "Then you don't have anything to worry about, eh?"

They tied my hands with a scrap of fuzzy packing twine snaking through the dusty debris on the floor. They pushed me down against the bar, and the young one stood over me watchfully while the blond one went around to pick up my rifle from behind the bar. More footsteps on the stairs, and another man came in from the landing. He was short and burly and bearded, with the rolling gait of a sea captain—ship's commander Golikov fresh off the battleship *Potemkin*. He was cupping a pipe in one hand. He had a sidearm holstered at his belt, under his coat.

"Problems?" he said, and then he saw me under the bar.

The blond man came back around the bar, carrying my rifle. "He's NKVD."

"I'm not NKVD, you son of a one-eyed Russian goat," I said.

The bearded man went down on one knee and looked at me in the half-light. From his lonely sidearm I knew he must be the commanding officer here, and from his silence I knew—at once but with certainty—that he was a man to be afraid of.

"He had these," the blond man said, showing the bearded man my rifle and grenades, "and this." He took my map from his pocket and gave it to the bearded man. "No identification."

The bearded man spread my map on the floor, flattening the creases carefully with his fingertips. He turned it over to look at the psalm on the other side, then over again wordlessly. He looked at it for a long time, puffing on his pipe.

Without raising his head, he said, "Bring up the gun."

We waited, Commander Golikov and I, while the other two went out. Their footsteps went away down the stairs. There was a stiff silence in which I could hear my heart beating in my throat.

Commander Golikov sat back on his heels and looked at me.

"The Germans will be here in three days," he said. "Do you know how I know?"

"Used your eyes?" I asked.

He reached into a pocket and brought out something small and flat and silvery. He held out his hand. On his callused palm lay an eagle, wings outstretched, stitched in bright silver wire on a black cloth patch the size of my thumb. I recognized it from the Reds' latest propaganda posters, though I'd never seen one in real life.

It was a Wehrmacht officer's breast eagle.

"Did you kill him?" I asked. If he meant to scare me, he'd have done better to keep his mouth shut. It was his silence that scared me.

He returned the eagle to his pocket. His face was blank.

"No," he said. "It's mine."

I'd seen that, too, in the Reds' propaganda. There were certain Ukrainians, traitor Ukrainians, *enemies of the motherland*, who'd taken commissions in the German army.

I wondered whether this man knew my father. I wasn't fool enough to ask.

"It's very nice," I said. "Shiny. Better not let the Reds catch you with it."

He ignored that. "Do you know who we are?"

"Deserters?" I guessed wickedly.

"Nachtigallen," he said.

I could tell he expected me to be impressed. The Nachtigallen were the elite—an all-Ukrainian special-forces unit spearheading the German advance.

"I've heard of them," I allowed.

"You can believe me when I say the Germans will be here in three days."

"Nobody's arguing that."

"My point," he said, "is that it might be better if you just waited."

I didn't say anything.

"Who is he?" the bearded man asked. His voice was quiet. He was watching my face. "Father? Brother?"—not unkindly— "What's your name, son?"

"None of your business," I said. The *son* galled me.

"They'll leave their prisoners when they pull out."

"Not all of them." *Not the ones that matter.*

The other two were coming back up the stairs. They came in from the landing, wheeling a machine gun between them. A third man, whom I hadn't seen before, followed with the ammunition pans. I watched them take the gun over to the window and lock the wheels of the mount.

"Was it political?" the bearded man said to me.

"What isn't?" I was bitter now, nursing the gall.

"Who was it? Reds or *lyakhy*?" He used the derogatory word for Poles.

"Does it matter?"

"Maybe," he said. "Maybe not." He let out a long, exaggerated sigh. He folded up my map and put it in his breast pocket. "Andriy," he said, "come over here."

The young, pale one came over from the window. "Yes, sir?"

"Take him downstairs. Put him in the cellar for now."

"Yes, sir." Just a hint of a wince.

"Look," I said, as Andriy pulled me up gingerly by my elbow. I wasn't going to make too much of a fuss. I was pretty sure I could take Andriy once we were alone, even with my hands tied. But it was the principle of the thing. "Look—you know I'm not NKVD. You might as well let me go."

"I know you're not NKVD," the bearded man said, "just like I know the NKVD would pay very, very handsomely to know we're mounting a machine gun across from the Brygidki gate—yes?"

He had to tilt up his chin to look me in the face now. It would have been satisfying in a way, if I weren't so very sure that this man could kill me in a second, effortlessly and without remorse. "Give me your name, and I might reconsider," he said.

"Liar," I said.

Gunfire hammered distantly somewhere out in the darkness—a long, spattering burst of submachine-gun fire, rolling away slowly into silence.

"What the hell was that?" said the blond man.

"It's coming from the prison," said the other man, the one who'd carried the ammunition pans. He was looking out the window.

"Get away from the window," the bearded man said.

The submachine gun picked up again. There was another long, unbroken burst of gunfire, then silence, then another long burst, and with it a popping fusillade of pistol shots. This time it seemed to stretch on forever. We stood there nervously in the half-light, all of us, looking at each other and listening.

"Using up their ammunition before they let the Germans get their hands on it?" the blond man guessed doubtfully when the gunshots had finally died away again.

But I knew what they were doing—with sudden certainty, as I knew to fear the bearded man's silence.

"They're shooting the prisoners," I said.

And I knew he knew it, too, because he didn't say anything.

I jerked my elbow from Andriy's unresisting hand. The

bearded man must have been anticipating that. He'd closed the distance between us and hooked a foot neatly around my ankle before I'd taken one full step toward the doorway. I sprawled facedown on the floor, just catching myself on my bound hands.

He put a foot between my shoulder blades.

"Andriy," he said, over my head, "Marko. Take him downstairs and keep him there."

"Cowards," I snapped, jerking and twisting against their hands, stupid with panic. "Don't you *understand*? They're shooting them—they're *killing* them, you bastards—you cowards—let me *go*—"

"Keep him quiet," said the bearded man from somewhere above me.

One of them—Marko, the blond one—slipped his arm around my neck, crooking his elbow and clamping his hand over my mouth. They got me up to my feet, holding me by the arms between them. They half carried, half dragged me out to the landing. I wrenched against their hands furiously, trying to jerk my head away from Marko's hand—achieving a short-lived victory when I got two of his meaty fingers between my teeth and bit down hard. He snatched his hand away with a curse.

Andriy slammed his rifle butt into my stomach.

I think it surprised both of us. For a second, as my breath spilled out and the world spun, we gaped at each other openmouthed, like fishes. His face had gone green, the color of lichen.

Belatedly, I realized that was probably because most of what had been in my stomach was spilling out too.

After that, I let them drag me. They took me down through the shop and into the cool darkness of the cellar.

Faintly in the distance, the gunfire had picked up again.

7

THE CELLAR WAS A WINE CELLAR AND STORE-
room—or it had been at one point, presumably when the bar
upstairs was still a bar. There were smashed crates and empty
bottles all over the floor, and a row of fat barrels with spigots
lining the long, brick-faced western wall. They put me down
on the floor below the barrels, and Marko untied my hands and
retied them behind my back, tightly. He tied my ankles too, for
good measure, with something that looked like curtain cord. I
think he was still sore about his wounded fingers. Then he went
back upstairs. Andriy sat on the stairs in the low light of an oil
lamp, his rifle across his knees.

We both jumped when the machine gun opened up—or he
jumped. I twitched like a trussed pig.

"So," I said. They'd put me down on my stomach, and with
my hands tied behind my back I had to crane my neck awkwardly
to look him in the face. "Why *are* you mounting a machine gun
across from the Brygidki gate?"

He wasn't really looking at me. He was studying the ground

between us, his eyes half closed, as though he were trying very hard to bring something into focus. The machine gun pounded away above us. Brick dust drifted down lazily from the vaulted ceiling.

"I can't tell you that," he said piously.

"You're a real saint, aren't you?"

He didn't say anything.

"I'll bet you're his favorite," I said.

He shifted uncomfortably, swallowing.

"Who is he, anyway?"

He looked up now—eagerly, like a dog. "Not your enemy."

"Just a German whore, like you?"

I wanted to hurt him. I was bitter and aching, inside and out, and I wanted to hurt him. I wanted him to hurt like I was hurting, and I wanted to see it in his face.

He blinked and looked away.

"I'm sorry," he said.

"Save it." I hated him for that apology because he genuinely seemed to mean it. I wanted a rise out of him. "If you were really sorry, you'd get me out of here."

He turned blank, dark eyes on me. "I can't."

"Why? Would he shoot you?"

"Yes."

"*That* kind of friend, is he?"

"He isn't my friend. He's my commanding officer, and he gave me an order. It would be necessary discipline."

"My mistake," I said viciously. "You're a zealot, not a saint."

He didn't say anything.

"Look, at least untie me," I said. "I think I'm losing circulation."

He hesitated. I'd played him well. By comparison, it was a perfectly reasonable request.

"What are you afraid of?" I said. "You've got a gun, and you know how to use at least *one* end of it."

I knew I'd got him. Guilt is a powerful motivator. He flinched ashamedly and slid over to me across the floor, slinging the rifle on his shoulder. He slipped a knife from his boot and leaned over me. He loosed my ankles first, his thin, cold fingers fumbling uncertainly at the cord in the half-light. Then he cut the twine from my wrists, careful not to nick my skin—one loop at a time, until my hands swung free.

I threw myself into him, dropping my shoulder and bowling him over to the ground.

He fought with surprising ferocity even with my knee in his stomach—squirming and twisting and kicking under me, like a pinned beetle. He got his knife hand free from my fingers and slashed wildly at my throat. I reeled back by instinct, and he slid away from me, rolling onto his stomach with the knife in his hand.

I jerked him back by his rifle sling and slammed his face into the floor.

Even then he tried to fight, gathering his limbs together

slowly and dazedly, trying to push himself up on his hands and knees. He hadn't made any noise this whole time—shock or stupidity, I thought, but then it occurred to me that calling for help would require an unpleasant explanation of how and why, exactly, my hands had come free.

I prised the knife from his limp fingers and dug a knee into the small of his back. I tore the rifle off him, slinging it on my own shoulder. Then I slipped the knife under his chin, bracing his head with my free hand.

"Do you have guards at the alley door?"

He didn't say anything. His hands were clenched in fists on the floor. He was holding his head up bravely, defiantly, stupidly, but I could feel him shivering under my knee.

"Answer me." I opened the skin across his windpipe with the edge of the blade, just enough to draw blood. "Don't think I won't do it," I said, through clenched teeth. "I've done it before. How do you think I got this uniform? How do you think I got those weapons?"

By this point, I was really hoping he would open his mouth because I knew, from past experience, I couldn't do it. But he just shivered silently beneath me, holding his head up like an idiot, waiting. Martyr, not zealot.

"Look." I was desperate now. "Look, idiot. You're already dead, as far as he's concerned. You might as well—"

The cold mouth of a pistol pressed against my skull, behind my right ear.

"Drop the knife," the bearded man said.

So that was that. I hadn't heard the machine gun stop firing, and I hadn't heard their footsteps.

I tossed the knife away and let go of Andriy's head. They pulled me off him. Somebody slipped the rifle off my shoulder and slung it away somewhere, and the bearded man motioned me down against the wall with his pistol. Two of them had gotten Andriy up to his feet, holding him by the arms—he unresisting between them, his face as white as a sheet. There was a thin, beaded line of blood across his neck where I'd nicked him.

They shoved him against the wall beside me and stepped away from him.

The bearded man stooped to pick up Andriy's knife without taking the pistol off me. "Your own knife, Andriy?"

Andriy said nothing.

"Andriy, Andriy." The bearded man shook his head. He stuck the knife in his belt. "'He who is faithful in the least is faithful also in much'"—as though he were reciting it for the Sunday liturgy— "'and he who is unfaithful in the least is unfaithful also in much.'"

"I'm sorry, sir," Andriy whispered.

"You understand why this has to happen?"

"Yes, sir."

"I'm sorry too," the bearded man said.

He lifted the pistol away from me and put the muzzle to Andriy's forehead.

Necessary discipline.

My fault.

"Wait," I said. "Stop—don't. My name is Aleksey Kobryn, all right?"

He looked at me. They all looked at me—except Andriy, who was leaning his head back against the wall, eyes shut. The muscles in his throat moved as he swallowed.

"My father is Yevhen Kobryn," I said.

They looked at me. They didn't speak. I floundered.

"We—we were in school together. Andriy and I. Old friends. He recognized me."

"Is that so?" the bearded man said.

"Not at first, I mean. It's been a while. I wouldn't have recognized him if he hadn't said something."

"Is that so, Andriy?" the bearded man said. He seemed amused.

Just say yes, idiot. Just say yes.

Andriy shifted his head slightly. He didn't open his eyes, and he didn't speak.

"It was in primary school," I said, hating Andriy very fiercely. "It's been a long time."

The bearded man wiped the blood from Andriy's throat with his thumb. Andriy flinched.

"Friendly little argument, is that it?" the bearded man said.

"Something like that," I said.

He knew I was lying, of course. His lips twitched, as though he weren't sure whether to laugh in my face. But he took the pistol away from Andriy's forehead.

"Get him out of here," he said, in a voice of long suffering.

He crouched on his heels, holding the pistol on his thigh, while they took Andriy upstairs. Then he looked up into my face.

"A soft heart is a liability. If you're going to last this war, you'd better learn."

"Save it," I said.

He sighed. He holstered the pistol at his hip.

"Why didn't you tell me?"

"That Andriy and I were in school together?"

"Andriy," he said, "is from Proskuriv. Orphaned in the Reds' famine. God knows how he made it across the border. He won't tell me. I found him barefoot and begging in the streets seven years ago." He was lighting his pipe. "I meant about your father," he said. "I didn't know Yevhen Kobryn had a son."

"Neither do the *lyakhy*," I said. "Neither do the NKVD."

"I see." He studied my face closely, as though trying to find my father there. He dropped his eyes and looked me over, head to toe. Unexpectedly, he reached and caught my hand and held it up, circling his fingers tightly around my wrist—all the way around.

"When's the last time you ate?" he asked.

8

MARKO, THE SECOND-IN-COMMAND, SAT SMOK-
ing and watching while I ate. The bearded man—Marko had
called him Strilka—was gone, and evidently Marko was under
orders to make sure I didn't slip away in his absence. He had his
pistol out.

I hadn't eaten so well in a long time. There was black bread
and cold sausage and fat boiled dumplings stuffed with potatoes
and onions, spread over the floor on pieces of oil-splotched
newspaper. I ate slowly, in measured mouthfuls, letting Marko
think only that I was savoring it, but each time an underling
came down the stairs to say something into Marko's ear, I folded
another sausage or dumpling in newspaper and slipped it quickly
into my pocket.

I took a long time eating. Strilka came back before I was
done. I didn't know where he'd been, but there was the smell
of smoke on him—the smoke of a fire, not pipe smoke. He sat
down across the newspapers and started asking me questions—

casually and at easy intervals, but I wasn't an idiot. I knew what he was doing.

"How old are you, Aleksey?"

I answered him around mouthfuls. Why not? I'd already spilled the biggest thing I was going to spill.

"Nineteen this August," I said.

"In school?"

"Lwów Polytechnic. Just finished my first year."

"Studying . . ."

"Mathematics."

He seemed to consider this. "Why mathematics?"

I shrugged. "Only thing I didn't fail in grade school."

A stretch of silence. "Where did you learn weapons?"

I finished the last of the sausages, sucking the savory grease off my fingers. "Rifles from my grandfather. Taught myself the rest."

He looked dubious. "Your grandfather."

"My mother's father. Used to take me hunting up in the hills outside Brzuchowice. He had a cabin on the lake."

"Rifles, you said."

"Mosins, Mausers, Winchesters—"

"Ever used automatics?"

"Sure."

"Ever actually hit anything?"

"Sure," I said, "I've hit things."

"Show me," he said. He unholstered his pistol and laid it on the papers between us.

I picked it up, testing the weight. Out of the corner of my eye, I saw Marko's finger curl around the trigger of his pistol. Knowing I came of Ukrainian nationalist royalty apparently wasn't enough to put *his* mind at ease.

"What am I hitting? Him?"

"Preferably not," Strilka said. "Hit the bulb."

"Which one?" I asked, turning to look and seeing the line of electric bulbs strung down the length of the cellar—unlit, of course, but gleaming dimly in the lamplight.

"The farthest," Strilka said.

It winked at me in the darkness—twenty meters, maybe. The light was what made it tricky. I opened the magazine and checked the rounds. Then I shoved the housing back in and adjusted my grip, cupping my hands and willing them not to shake. I shut my left eye, sighted, and pulled the trigger.

Or I tried anyway. The trigger was stuck. I tried again impatiently, mashing my finger down. Nothing. I lowered the pistol. My face was burning.

"Safety," Strilka said softly, trailing pipe smoke from his lips.

I flicked it off without looking at him and lifted the pistol again. This time the trigger yielded smoothly under my finger, the pistol recoiling quickly and sharply in my hand. The spent cartridge clattered at my feet. The echo of the shot rolled away over the brick-faced walls.

"Your technique isn't bad," Strilka said, taking out his pipe. "Accuracy takes time and effort. You're a mathematician—you know that. One miscalculation, one sloppy mistake, and the whole equation goes to hell." He stuck the pipe back in his mouth and held out his hand for the pistol. "How about a job?" he asked.

I handed him the pistol. "At the Hotel George. Night porter."

"No," he said. He brought out a cartridge box from his pocket. "I mean that I'm offering you a job."

"What kind of job? Hired gun?"

"Let's call it a chance to continue your father's work. You've met Commander Shukhevych, I'd imagine."

"Ah," I said.

I'd met him. He would probably even remember me. Roman Shukhevych had been head of the UPA, the militant arm of the Ukrainian nationalist movement, and mastermind behind the assassination for which my father had been jailed. He'd been in and out of our flat all that spring, 1934. I'd been eleven years old—old enough to know he wasn't just one of Papa's army friends, no matter what Mama might say. I had no idea he was working with the Germans now. The last I knew, he'd been with Papa in the Brygidki.

I couldn't help the bitterness needling at me. How come he was free, and not Papa?

Strilka was still going on about his Nachtigallen.

"You'll take your oath to Hitler and the Third Reich. You'll take your orders from me."

"And you'll shoot me if I refuse?"

He avoided the question neatly. "Why refuse?"

"My war is right across the street," I said. "Not with the Wehrmacht."

He was reloading the pistol, not looking up. "Your father is dead, Aleksey."

"What—you've seen him?"

"I saw enough."

"What's that supposed to mean?"

He pushed the cartridges into the magazine with his thumb, one by one. "The Reds pulled out about an hour ago—tried anyway. We finished them in the street. Went in to see if we could find survivors. Found a few in the upper prison—the rats and collaborators, the ones they left for us to deal with. The lower prison . . ."

He let that hang in the air between us.

"I want to see," I said.

"No, you don't."

"I want to see."

"These weren't the first shootings. These were the last. They'd already finished with the cellars. Must have been at it for days. Nobody's alive down there. Too far gone to identify, most of them. Maybe you could do it if you knew clothes and personal effects, but you'd need a respirator."

I think that was when I knew he wasn't lying. His hands were shaking as he refitted the magazine, though his voice was steady.

"They left the upper prison burning. Clumsy attempt to cover—"

"All right," I said, "all right."

The strange thing was I didn't feel anything now, not really. I was vaguely angry at Strilka, and I wasn't exactly sure why. Maybe because he'd so very obviously orchestrated all of this— not the shootings, I mean, but *this*, the food, the job offer, the trump card at the end: *Your father is dead, Aleksey.* He hadn't been counting on that, but he sure as hell didn't mind using it. But I didn't feel anything for my father. Shock, I guess. Staggered by the irony. I'd have broken into the Brygidki to find him already dead after all.

I fought a sudden, wild urge to laugh.

Strilka holstered his pistol. He looked up.

"Commander Shukhevych is the better speechmaker. If he were here, he could tell you all about the glory of the fight. 'Ukrainian blood on Ukrainian black earth.' Very pretty. But instead I'm here telling you that you can have your revenge." His eyes were sharp and cool on my face. "You tell me. How did it feel bowing and scraping to them—the people who took your father from you?"

"I don't know," I said. "I've never tried it."

"No?"

"I don't bow to Poles. Or to Reds. Or to Germans. Or to you."

"They made you speak Polish, didn't they? They wouldn't want your dirty Ukrainian tongue in a high-class place like the

Hotel George. Believe me, they knew exactly what they were doing." Strilka blew a low, smoky breath. "I know you want revenge, Aleksey."

"On my own terms. Not on the Germans'." *Not on yours.*

He dropped his eyes to my bulging pockets pointedly.

"Not even for thirty Reichsmarks a month?"

"Thirty Reichsmarks?" I said, like an idiot. My face was burning again.

"A month," he repeated. "That's base pay. You'd have opportunity for promotion, of course. They want college-educated men for officers."

Thirty marks—more than sixty rubles. More money at once than I'd seen since Mama died.

"Think about it," Strilka said. "Revenge against the Poles, freedom, food on the table—all that to gain and nothing to lose."

"All that and thirty pieces of silver," I said, but oh, what I could do with sixty rubles. The first thing, of course, would be to pay Father Yosyp back the rent he'd covered these last three months. But after that—

"Think about Mykola," Strilka said.

I was up so quickly that I think I startled him a little. He leaned back, one hand swinging down to his pistol. Quick as I was, Marko was quicker. He'd been watching and waiting for this moment. He closed the distance between us in one long step, slipping one arm around my chest, the other across my throat, hugging me close and tight, pinning my arms.

Strilka let go of his pistol. He puffed on his pipe—calmly, as though I hadn't just caught him off his guard. *Bastard.*

"Where did you get his name?" I snarled, as menacingly as I could with Marko's arm crushing my throat.

He took my map out of his breast pocket. "This is from an Orthodox Psalter."

"So?" But I knew where he was going.

"So I went to the church. I wanted to know if you were who you said you were. The priest gave me your name. Father Yosyp."

"He wouldn't."

"He would if he thought you were dead."

"He wouldn't give you Mykola's."

"Name—no. I'm capable of reading baptismal records. Address and flat number—yes, unintentionally. The good father didn't realize he was being followed."

I jerked against Marko's grip, kicking at his shins, trying to snap my head back into his face. He hooked a foot around my ankles and sent me neatly to my knees.

"I'm trying to get you to think about consequences," Strilka said. He worked at his pipe unhurriedly, watching my face. "If you want to know your father's one weakness, I think that was it. He accepted consequences for himself. I don't think he ever understood what it meant for you."

"If only he'd had *you* to explain it to him," I said by reflex. I didn't want to give him the satisfaction of knowing how right he was—how much that stung.

"And you, Aleksey Yevhenovych, ready to die in the Brygidki tonight, and never once stopping to think it through."

"What can I say? I'm my father's son."

"For instance," he said, ignoring me, "you didn't think about what would have happened if they'd taken you alive—and they would have, almost certainly. You didn't think about how much you'd spill under torture. You didn't think about how much your father would spill when they brought him in to watch. Otherwise you'd have made a priority of getting Mykola out of the city first. Yes?"

I didn't say anything.

"You were careless," Strilka said quietly. "You can't afford to be careless—not if you're going to last this war."

"All right," I said, "all right. What do you want me to do? Kiss your feet?"

"Get up," he said. "I want you to see something."

9

THEY BROUGHT DOWN THE PRISONER FIRST, dragging him by the arms. His broken legs trailed limply and uselessly behind. Polish Resistance, Strilka said, one of the ones they'd found alive in the upper cells—one of the very few, which meant most likely he'd collaborated, which meant he was no good for ransom. Evidently, he hadn't proven much good for information either.

By then I knew why they were here, Strilka and his Nachtigallen. They'd come to pick over the Reds' leavings and take prisoners—and vengeance—of their own.

He didn't really look like my idea of Polish Resistance. Stupidly but inevitably, my idea of Polish Resistance was something like the grim, hard-faced men in long navy coats and peaked caps who'd burst into our flat, torn the place apart, and taken Papa away into the night in a terrifying blur of efficiency. Their efficiency had struck me very clearly. The plainclothes officer who'd been in charge of the whole thing hadn't really even needed to give any orders—just stood watching from the doorway, pulling lazily on a cigarette. Most of my memory of that night was a vague shambles, but that had stayed with me.

But he was about my age, this prisoner, tall and bony and barefoot, wearing the thin, fluttering gray tatters of what had once been a fine, store-bought suit. Maybe he'd been a student. Who knows? Maybe I'd even seen him on campus. He slumped silently against the wall when they let him go, folding up over his ruined knees, looking at nothing—but when Strilka said "collaborator," his chin jerked up.

"I'm not a collaborator." He said it in Ukrainian, sounding it out very slowly and stiffly, as though his tongue were out of practice. "*Ya . . . ne . . . ye . . . kolaboratsionist*"—then again, more confidently. "*Ya ne ye kolaboratsionist.*"

Marko came down the stairs with Andriy. At that moment, I understood what they were going to do. I don't think Andriy did. He cast one darting, shamed glance over the Pole, another over me. When Strilka held out the pistol, he just looked at it for a second, blankly.

Then his face went white.

"*Ya ne ye kolaboratsionist,*" the Pole said.

"Andriy," Strilka said.

"*Ya na ye kolaboratsionist,*" the Pole said. Then he switched suddenly to rapid Polish, shutting his eyes. "*Ojcze nasz, którys jest w niebie, swiec sie imie twoje . . .*"

Our Father, who art in heaven . . .

Andriy looked at the pistol in Strilka's hand. The lump in his throat was going up and down, up and down. He was blinking very quickly. He shook his head once, just perceptibly.

Out of the corner of my eye, I saw Marko, leaning against the wall, slip his own pistol quietly from its holster.

"Andriy," Strilka said, "take the gun."

". . . *odpusc nam nasze winy*," the Pole said, "*jako i my odpuszczamy naszym winowajcom . . .*"

Andriy took the pistol. He cradled it against his stomach, fumbling blindly at the magazine housing. His hands were shaking.

"It's loaded," Strilka said blandly.

Andriy snapped the action and cupped his trembling hands around the grip. He lifted the pistol and trained it. Then he lowered it again. He looked back pleadingly at Strilka.

". . . *ale nas zbaw ode zlego*," the Pole finished.

Deliver us from evil.

"Go on," Strilka said. "Deliver him."

I looked away at the moment of the shot. I heard the bullet casing clatter and the body slump to the floor. When I looked back, Strilka had pulled Andriy in close, slipping his arms around Andriy's thin, shaking shoulders. He pressed Andriy's face to his shoulder and stroked Andriy's close-cropped hair gently with his fingers, murmuring into Andriy's ear: "You did well . . . you did well."

But he was looking at me over Andriy's head.

10

I HAD TWO HOURS, STRILKA SAID.

A bullet-riddled NKVD car straddled the sidewalk below the Brygidki wall. It had smashed nose first into the wall and hung now at a gentle tilt across the curb, three wheels on the sidewalk and one in the street. A couple of Nachtigallen with blue-and-yellow armbands and submachine guns were standing guard at the Brygidki gate. The upper prison was still burning. The gate doors stood open, and I could see into the yard—just a glimpse in the smoke and firelight, just enough to see the row of limp, lumpy bodies piled waist-high against the far wall.

That was enough. I didn't try to go in.

I ditched the NKVD uniform down a drain—everything except the boots, which were far better than my own shoes and could be sold later for a good price if need be. I could probably have sold the rest of the uniform too, but I didn't want to be shot by some trigger-happy patriot before I got the chance.

The clock atop City Hall was tolling six when I went up the street stairs to our flat. I'd already used up a precious thirty minutes. The sun was up over the rooftops. The stairwell was dark even in daylight, stinking of grease and fried onions and cat piss. I fumbled for a second in the half-light, trying to fit my key into the lock. There was a trick to the door that involved pulling the door slightly toward you as you turned the key, then nudging it in very quickly with your foot as you slipped the key out. It would be less effort just to kick the door down if anybody really wanted to break in, so I guess the joke of it was that any place with a door like that wasn't likely to be a place worth breaking in to. Anyway, nobody had ever tried.

And really it wasn't much of a place. It was a single bare, square room, with a cracked linoleum floor and peeling, yellow-papered walls thin enough that you could hear the cockroaches scuttling in them at night. There was a woodstove and a washbasin with a tap on the western wall—left, as you came in the door. There was a corner cabinet with four chipped china plates and three mismatched glasses. There was a sagging wooden shelf on the far wall, the northern wall, that held our books, the ones we couldn't bring ourselves to sell or burn: Papa's carefully slipcased literary journals; Mama's beloved natural histories; yellowed paperbacks of all the traditional nationalist writers; Mykola's well-worn copy of *Solovey the Robber*, his favorite adventure story. There was one narrow, single-paned window on the eastern wall, looking down on the street five floors below, and there were our icons: Christ and the interceding Theotokos, above, then each of our name saints—Yevhen of Trebizond and Larysa of Crimea, Aleksey the Man of God, Mykola the Wonder-Worker.

Most everything else had gone for fuel.

I kicked the door shut. Mykola was asleep in his corner, curled up knees to chest in his bed of tattered blankets—fully dressed, to his shoes. He'd pulled one blanket over his head, as always. I could just see the tip of his nose between the folds. He didn't stir when the door swung to, and I didn't wake him.

I went to the icons and made my prayers in silence—to Christ first, with the sign of the cross, then to the Theotokos, then to the saints in turn, Saint Yevhen last of all.

Only then, bending to kiss his icon in that holy silence, did I let the tears come—and only for a moment because I'd promised myself six years ago, on the day we buried Mama, that Mykola would never see me cry.

He must have felt me block the sunlight when I crouched to tug the blanket from his head. He woke up with a jerk before I'd even touched him. He thrashed his legs, flinging out an arm.

An empty vodka bottle rolled out from somewhere among the blankets, rattling away across the floor.

I snatched it back. "Where the hell did you get this?"

He fell back against the blankets with a groan, digging the heels of his hands into his eyes. I could smell it on him now—straight alcohol and the stink of vomit. I stripped the soiled blankets away roughly, jerking them from under him.

"What—the—*hell*"—punctuating each word with a jerk of a blanket—"were—you—*thinking?*"

He didn't speak. He curled against the wall, drawing up his knees. He looped his arms around his shins and buried his face between his kneecaps. I kicked the bottle away and went to fill a glass with water from the tap. I brought it over, knocking it sharply against his bowed head.

"Drink."

His voice came up muffled from between his knees. "Leave me alone."

"Drink it or you get it in the face."

He muttered something into his knees, but he lifted his head. He let me pry his arms apart and uncurl his clenched fingers and put the glass in his hand. He sat holding the cool glass against his temple, kneading his forehead with his fingertips and looking across the room at nothing, while I mopped his sick off the floor with one of the blankets.

"So?" I said. "I'm waiting."

"Thought you were dead," he said, not looking at me. "He said you were dead."

"Who? Father Yosyp?"

He made a noise in his throat. He was swallowing a long mouthful of water—tossing back the whole glass in one gulp.

"He was misinformed, obviously."

"He said you'd gone to the Brygidki."

Bitterness in his voice now. It was an accusation. I kicked the blankets over to the dustbin. Our saints watched expectantly— Saint Aleksey, who deceived his own family out of love for God, Saint Mykola, who smacked people in the face for the sake of truth.

"Do you think I'm an idiot?" I said.

He didn't take the bait.

"Where were you?"

"I didn't get off till two. They'd stopped the trams. I had to walk all the way back from downtown."

"It's past six."

"I got lost."

"You're lying," he said. "You always lie."

"I was seeing a girl."

"You went to the Brygidki."

"The point is you don't know, do you, because you were too busy spewing your guts all over the floor."

He was silent. Out of the corner of my eye, I saw him swallow twice, blinking, and I realized he was trying very hard not to cry.

I relented.

"Hey, I'm not dead, all right?" I crouched beside him and started emptying my pockets of sausages and dumplings. "Here—look at all this."

He watched hollowly, unmoving, while I unwrapped the sausages one by one, then the dumplings, only slightly squashed.

"Is Papa dead?"

I spread the newspapers on the floor between us. I didn't look up. I didn't want to look into his face just then, and I didn't want him to look into mine. I wiped my fingers on the papers.

"Eat."

"Is he dead?"

"Eat, Mykola."

"He's dead or you'd look me in the face."

"He was dead two years ago," I said. It wasn't really a lie. Maybe they hadn't put the bullet in his head until last night, but he was dead two years ago.

"I wish he'd been," Mykola said.

"Eat," I said.

But he was crying now—silently but without trying to stop it, leaning his elbows on his knees and resting his face in his hands, shaking with trapped sobs.

"Mykola, you're fun when you're drunk." I clambered carefully over the newspapers to sit down beside him against the wall. I slipped my arm around his shoulders. "It's all right," I said. "We'll be all right. Take a look at this." I took out the wad of crisp marks Strilka had given me—my first month's pay, in advance. I pushed the wad between Mykola's fingers. "We're getting out of here."

He lifted his head to look at the money in his hand. He unfolded the bills and smoothed them carefully against his knees, turning them over one by one, as though to make sure they were real.

"It's German," he said with a sniff.

"Very good. You didn't drink yourself blind."

"Where did you get it?"

"That's where things get tricky."

"You stole it?"

"Trickier." I took the money from his hand and put it back in my pocket.

"You joined," he said.

I lifted my arm from his shoulders. "Wrap that stuff back up if you're not going to eat it. Put it in your pack."

"You joined one of the volunteer battalions."

"They think I did."

"What does that mean?"

"It means we need to get the hell out of here. I wasn't kidding about that." I got up, nudging his ankles. "Wrap that stuff up. Thirty marks doesn't mean we can start throwing away food."

11

THE UKRAINIAN CHURCH OF OUR LADY'S DORMI-
tion on Ruska Street was the only church in Lwów to survive the
Reds' invasion. All the Catholic churches, Roman and Greek,
had been closed up and carted off piece by piece to the Historical Museum. The idea was that the Orthodox faithful could be
shepherded into Moscow's fold, given enough time. It wasn't a
bad idea in theory, but it wasn't going to work—not here anyway, not in Lwów, where our church had been our one freedom
under Polish rule. We couldn't speak Ukrainian in our schools or
our offices, but we could speak it in our liturgies. We couldn't
publicly keep our holy days, but we could keep them quietly to
ourselves in the shelter of our church walls.

The Reds couldn't win. Either they had to treat our priests
like the Catholics—ship them to the camps or shoot them, in
which case they could damn well forget about herding us back
to Moscow like meek, compliant sheep—or they had to tolerate
them, which meant tolerating the memory of freedom.

The Brygidki was still burning—black smoke roiling up over

the rooftops westward, past the opera house. Too close. My two hours was nearly up, and Strilka would know I'd cheated him. He wouldn't care about the thirty marks as much as he'd care that I'd taken him for a fool, even after his little lesson on *consequences*. Would he care enough to hunt me? Part of me didn't think he'd waste the time. Part of me was pretty sure he wouldn't consider it a waste.

If he did hunt me, this would be the first place he'd look.

He was right. I'd been careless.

There was no answer to my knock at the door of Father Yosyp's flat, adjoining the belfry. It was a little past seven now. The church doors were still locked. The deacon, Father Kliment, wouldn't be along for another hour. I kicked gravel down the empty sidewalk.

"He didn't say anything about going anywhere?" I asked Mykola. "Last night—when you talked to him."

Mykola had sat down on the church steps, leaning his head against the wall, eyes squeezed shut against the bright morning sunlight. "Probably went to get your body. Thinks you're dead in the Brygidki."

I wasn't careless. I was an *idiot*.

Because he would. He wouldn't take no for an answer. He never took no for an answer—not from the Poles, not from the Reds.

Not from Strilka.

I kicked Mykola's ankles. "Up."

"We can just wait for him."

"You need to burn off that alcohol. Come on."

* * *

There was some kind of riot going on at the Brygidki gate.

I couldn't see anything but people—hundreds of people, pressed elbow to elbow along the sidewalk below the gate wall—but somewhere up ahead, in the lingering smoke and the tangle of bodies, there were shouts and screams and the intermittent *cracks* of pistol shots. *NKVD*, I thought. They were trying to retake the prison, and the Nachtigallen were fighting back. But the crowd was pushing and shoving *toward* the gate, not away—eager, not afraid. Whatever this was, it wasn't a firefight. I'd seen enough of those two years ago, when the city fell. Crowds didn't run toward a firefight.

A couple of nurses in the uniforms of the State Medical Institute broke away from the crowd just ahead, hauling a bloody-faced, stumbling girl between them. The girl's netted hat was askew, her dress torn. They hurried her past us, moving her along so quickly that her feet never really touched the sidewalk.

At the edge of the crowd, a thin, graying woman in ratty furs picked up a cobblestone and flung it after them.

"Hey!" I caught her wrist. "What the hell?"

She wasn't paying any attention to me. She was shouting after them: "Bolshevik whore! You did this!"

I shoved her away. "Shut up."

"You did this!"

I shoved her again, sharply. She staggered back, caught a heel on the curb, and sat straight down, her mouth open—*oh*.

Somebody's fist connected soundly with my jaw.

The sidewalk and the crowd and the Brygidki wall slid away and back again, like a yo-yo. I reeled, head spinning. Something small and dark shot past me—Mykola, dropping his pack and lunging, head down. He caught the punch thrower neatly around the middle and carried him down to the sidewalk.

It was like a schoolyard fight—and nowhere close to my first or Mykola's first—except I had no idea who we were fighting or what we were fighting about. In the schoolyard, it was always because some Polish snot had been stupid enough to call me *chachoł* or *savage* or *salo-eater*, or to try to get me to spit on the blue-and-yellow bicolor or admit that Shukhevych and Kobryn were traitors who deserved the gallows. They didn't know Yevhen Kobryn was my father, of course, but sometimes I fantasized about telling them—preferably *after* we'd taken Lwów back, and *they* were the ones having to bow and scrape. Anyway, there'd never been any question about who or what or why. But these were Ukrainians—at least, the fur lady had been screaming in Ukrainian, and that tall fellow in workman's clothes who was trying to kick Mykola off the punch thrower swore in Ukrainian when I socked him.

Marko broke it up. He popped up from somewhere with a pistol in his hand and cleared the sidewalk by squeezing off a few shots into the air. He holstered the gun and yanked Mykola off the punch thrower. He nudged the prone man with his boot.

"Get out of here."

He stood holding Mykola by the arms while the crowd shuffled resentfully along. Then he spun him around to face me, keeping his hands on Mykola's shoulders.

"Yours?"

There wasn't any denying it, really. Mykola would always be smaller, but we had the same long, straight nose and square jaw, Mama's, and the same dark hair and gray eyes, Papa's. Mykola's eyes were on me now. He didn't say anything — he was much too sharp to say anything, even hung over—but he was watching me, reading my face, trying to figure out what he was supposed to do.

The problem was I didn't know.

My mouth was full of blood. No teeth out—I must have bit the inside of my cheek. I spit blood onto the sidewalk and picked up Mykola's pack.

"Mykola," I said, "Marko. Marko, Mykola."

Marko didn't let go of Mykola's shoulders. I noted, with satisfaction, the tooth marks on his fingers.

"The commander said two hours. You're late."

"Going to be later the longer we stand here jawing. Where is he?"

Marko was silent for a long moment, looking at me. Finally, he jerked his chin over his shoulder, toward the shop. He shoved Mykola at me sharply.

"Watch that tongue, Kobryn," he said.

I very nearly promised him I would watch my teeth too, but thought better of it. He had a pistol. I did not.

Mykola was silent as we walked. I could see him putting things together. His lip was split, bleeding a little. There was a set of knuckles imprinted in perfect duplicate across his left cheekbone, red turning purple.

"She was a Jew," he said suddenly.

"What?"

"That girl. She was a Jew." He was nursing his lip carefully with the tip of his tongue. He must have been expecting a question because he said after a moment, "She works at Altenberg's. I see her there sometimes."

He meant the bookseller's in the shop front below the Hotel George.

I glanced back down the sidewalk. Marko was standing in the street, watching us go, his hand resting on the butt of his holstered pistol. There was still a crowd pressed close at the Brygidki gate, shouting indistinctly, though the shooting had stopped.

Bolshevik whore! You did this!

My stomach tightened. It was an old idea—that this was all just some Jewish conspiracy, that the Reds were nothing more than Jewish thugs—and it was a stupid one. Jews died with NKVD bullets in their heads just like the rest of us. But it was the kind of idea somebody like Strilka wouldn't mind using if he thought he could get something out of it, and it was the kind of idea angry, hurting people latched on to, when they couldn't touch the real culprits but still wanted to feel they could do *something*.

Andriy was standing guard at the alley door—sitting guard, at least. He was huddled against the jamb, leaning on his rifle, shivering the way he'd shivered in the cellar when I'd had the knife at his throat. He jumped up as though he'd been kicked when he saw us through the smoke.

"Glory to Ukraine," I said.

He was supposed to respond with "Glory to her heroes." It was stupidly obvious, both password and countersign, because that had been the nationalists' standard greeting for years, and everybody in Lwów knew it. But he didn't say it. He didn't say anything. He was scrubbing hastily at his face with the back of his free hand. He'd been crying.

Opportunity presented itself.

I took the rifle away from him. I didn't trust him holding it toward me when he was shaking like a leaf. He didn't protest— didn't resist at all. I gave the rifle to Mykola and sat Andriy back down on the step, crouching in front of him with my hands on his trembling shoulders. Holy hell, he was thin. His collarbones poked up sharply under his loose coat. His teeth were chatter-ing, though it was hot enough in the breathless, smoky stuffiness of the alley that I was sweating.

"It's all right," I said. "It's all right. I need your help."

He looked warily into my face, but he didn't speak. I took that as a good sign. He was willing to listen.

"I'm looking for somebody. A priest—Father Yosyp, from the Dormition Church." He wouldn't wear his cassock out in the open, but still. "Commander Strilka went to talk to him last night. You know who I'm talking about?"

Andriy darted a glance down the alley, then to Mykola, then back to me.

"It's all right," I said again.

He swallowed. He nodded once—a quick, shamed dip of his head. *Yes.*

"Have you seen him?"

"Here?"

"We think he might have come looking for me."

He didn't say anything. He shut his eyes. I couldn't tell whether he was trying to remember or just trying to shut me out.

I prompted him. "Some time last night or this morning."

"No," he said finally, in a choked kind of voice. "No, I don't think so."

"Nobody's tried to get in to talk to Strilka?"

A shake of the head, this time—*no.* "He just got back."

"Strilka? Back from where?"

He didn't answer. I thought I'd finally got him to stop shivering, but he started again now, violently.

"Andriy," I said.

He flinched as though I'd hit him.

"It's all right," I said. "Look at me."

He opened his eyes and looked. His lips quivered.

"I'll get you out of here," I said.

It wasn't an outright lie—I'd do it if I could, and I'd try my best even if I couldn't—but it was overly optimistic. I felt guilty for saying it and even more guilty that it actually seemed to calm him.

I was as good at this as Strilka.

Andriy sucked a long, steadying breath.

"They've got another prisoner—down there," he said. "They brought him in from the Brygidki." He looked into my face quickly, almost desperately, as though to make sure I understood.

I did. I held on to his shoulders tightly. "Polish?"

"I don't know."

"What did he look like?"

Another shake of the head. "They had a hood on him."

They hadn't hooded the Pole. They wouldn't hood a prisoner for the thirty-meter stretch between here and the Brygidki gate unless they didn't want that mob seeing who they'd got.

The local parish priest, for instance.

I squeezed Andriy's shoulders and looked at Mykola.

"I'm going to go take a look. You've got the rifle. If I'm not back in twenty minutes—"

"Run for the hills?"

"I was going to say come rescue me."

"I'll think about it," he said.

"I love you too," I said.

12

IT WASN'T FATHER YOSYP.

His hood was off by the time I got down there. They'd made me wait at the top of the cellar stairs while they'd sent down to ask whether Strilka wanted me just then. The prisoner was my age or Andriy's—not much older anyway—prison pale and shaven-headed. He was tied to a chair in the middle of the floor, ankles lashed to the chair legs, arms wrenched behind the chair back and tied at the wrists. Blood dribbled from his nose, running in two red lines around the corners of his bruised, battered mouth, then in a single wide streak down his chin. He'd tilted his head back against the chair, trying to stanch the flow. He saw me come in.

"Got a new pet?" the prisoner asked Strilka, in Ukrainian.

Strilka was leaning against a wine barrel, dabbing absently at his split knuckles with a handkerchief. It was just the two of them—and me, gulping like a dying fish there in the shadows at the foot of the stairs.

"Aleksey," Strilka said, not looking up from his knuckles, "come here."

I went. I slunk around the edge of the lamplight, trying not to look at the prisoner. But I could feel his eyes on me, unblinking and contemptuous.

Strilka folded his handkerchief unhurriedly and put it in a pocket. He took me by the elbow and pulled me over, putting his hands on my shoulders, holding me easily in front of him, the way Marko had held Mykola.

"One more chance, Vitalik," he said to the prisoner. "Make it good."

"If I'd talked," Vitalik said, in a measured voice, dead calm, "why wouldn't I have told them about *this*?"

"What about this?"

"I could have had them waiting for you here last night."

"How would you have known?"

"Put it together. Two and two. Bringing in the gun. Asking Andriy to case the sightlines from the window—making sure you could get a shot at the gate."

"And he told you I'd asked," Strilka said lightly. His hands were very still on my shoulders.

Vitalik hesitated.

"Look," he said, "the point—"

"The point is I've got a rash of loose tongues, apparently. An epidemic."

"I didn't talk. I didn't tell them anything."

"You shared a cell with Yaroslav and Borys. Yaroslav and Borys are dead. You are not."

"I told you. The Reds came in shooting. I hit the floor and played dead. They were in too much of a hurry to make sure."

"Hit the floor with a body on top of you. Don't neglect your details, Vitalik." Strilka's voice was bland. "Is there anything else you'd like to say?"

"Not to you. To your pet, there. Aleksey." Vitalik smiled at me savagely, baring bloodied teeth. "Six months, maybe a year. You do everything he asks. Then he gets a new pet, and this is you."

Strilka put his pistol in my hand.

I'd been expecting it, but I still flinched a little at the touch of the cold steel. I curled my fingers around the grip—loosely, so my hand wouldn't shake. Strilka's left hand was still resting on my shoulder, his thumb braced gently on the back of my neck. I went through the motions unhurriedly. I checked the magazine, just to be sure. I checked the safety—I remembered this time—and snapped the action.

Vitalik leaned his head against the chair back. He licked the blood from his lips and smiled at me. His face was white.

I turned under Strilka's arm, sidestepping him. I put the mouth of the pistol to Strilka's breastbone and pulled the trigger.

Just like that—*pop, thump*, silence—and I'd killed a man.

I waited for the pangs of conscience. It was never as easy as you thought it was going to be. I knew that because I'd failed every time before. I hadn't even been able to kill that Red sentry, down at the station. I hadn't been able to kill Andriy, and I hadn't been able to watch Andriy kill that Pole.

It wasn't supposed to be this easy.

"They'll have heard the shot," Vitalik reminded me in a low voice, after a moment.

"They'll think it was for you," I said.

I tucked the pistol in my waistband. It was because I didn't have time to think about it, I decided. It would be harder later.

I crouched to untie Vitalik's ankles. Marko's handiwork—the curtain cord was pulled so tight that Vitalik's bare feet were purple, the color of borscht. His toenails were gone. *That* must have happened in the Brygidki. The nail beds had had time to scab over.

I spent a couple of minutes picking ineffectively at the cord.

"There's a knife in his boot lining," Vitalik said finally.

His fingernails were gone, too, and the ends of his little fingers, below the knuckle. I stared a little too long, and he twisted to look at me reprovingly over his shoulder.

"Having trouble?"

"No—sorry."

The cuts weren't clean. I knew they were hurting him, because he stiffened when I touched his hands. The stumps were weeping pus. His fingers were streaked purple and puffy even after I'd rubbed the circulation back into his wrists. His skin was fever hot under my fingers.

"Can you stand?" I asked.

He didn't bother to reply to that. He spit blood and wiped his mouth with the back of his hand. He got up, leaning lightly on the chair.

"Guards?" he said.

"Two at the top of the stairs."

"What about the street?"

"The alley door's open."

"That's suspicious." He limped over to Strilka and crouched to tug off Strilka's boots. He sat there lacing the boots on his own mangled feet slowly and carefully.

"Andriy's there," I admitted.

"Thinks you're a friend of his, doesn't he?"

When I didn't answer, Vitalik looked up, smiling that sharp, cold smile.

"Don't worry about it. He thinks everybody's his friend. Thinks it's his fault when he realizes they're not."

He got up, sucking a breath.

"Ever killed a man with a knife?" he asked.

"No."

"Better give it to me, then," he said.

I handed him the knife. He caught my wrist and jerked me expertly around, pulling me tight against him, sliding an arm across my throat. He twisted my wrist until the knife slipped from my numb fingers. Then he liberated the pistol from my waistband and pressed the muzzle to my temple.

"What are you—NKVD?"

"I thought that was *you*," I said.

The muscles in his forearm contracted, and I gagged.

"I'm expendable," he said, low and tight into my ear. "Strilka wasn't. You should have known better, you Red bastard."

I pried frantically at his arm. Hot blood hummed in my ears.

"Wouldn't have—blown cover—"

"What?"—without loosening his grip.

I got two fingers under his arm finally and gulped a long, sobbing breath.

"If I were NKVD. Wouldn't have blown cover for you."

He was silent, considering this.

"I'm not Nachtigall either," I added after a moment. At this point, it couldn't hurt to be honest.

His voice was cool. "What are you?"

That was a damn good question. I wasn't my father, as much as Strilka might have been hoping. In over my head, that's what I was. Pulled in too many directions by too many obligations. Angry. Desperate. Scared.

An idiot, in sum. P → Q, where P is *Aleksey is angry and desperate and scared* and Q is *Aleksey acts like an idiot.*

"Look," I said, because it couldn't hurt to be honest, "I don't care about the glory of Ukraine. I've got a sixteen-year-old kid brother, and I'm going to get him out of Lwów or die trying."

He was silent. I didn't think he was going to shoot me. The guards at the top of the stairs might have been expecting one gunshot, but they'd be suspicious about two. But his arm was still clamped convincingly tight across my throat. I waited.

Finally, abruptly, he slid his arm from my neck and took the gun away from my head.

"We've all got our own little wars," he said.

He stooped to pick up the knife.

"They don't know anything's wrong," he said, jerking his chin to the stairs, "so you walk out of here like there's nothing wrong. Send them down. Tell them he wants them to come down and take care of the body. Casual, got it?"

"Casual," I agreed.

"I'm doing you a favor, so you're going to do one for me. You're going to take Andriy with you."

I looked at him. He didn't look at me. He was digging through Strilka's pockets, looking for spare clips.

"Your own little war?" I asked.

"One of them."

I hesitated. I didn't like the idea of leaving him.

"You could come," I offered.

"I've got business here."

"They'll kill you."

He opened the magazine of the pistol and pushed a new cartridge in. Then he shoved the magazine home against his palm. He looked up, smiling coolly.

"Why? You're the one who shot four men."

"Four?"

"Three killed, one wounded."

"You want me to shoot you?"

He rolled his eyes. "I want you to get the hell out of here. I'm buying you time."

"You're going to shoot yourself?"

"You heard the commander." He shrugged. "It looks suspicious if I come out unscathed."

* * *

Andriy was alone on the alley doorstep. He jumped up when I came out. He was holding his rifle.

"I'm sorry, I'm sorry—"

"Relax," I said, "it's me. Where's Mykola?"

"I'm sorry," he whispered.

My stomach lurched as though I'd stepped off a ledge.

I hauled him up by his collar and backed him against the wall. I towered over him.

"Where is he?"

His eyes were shut, his teeth chattering. "They're bringing the b-bodies out. He s-said he'd be ba—"

I was halfway down the alley before I remembered what I'd promised him, what Vitalik had asked of me.

I went back.

"Come on," I said. "We'll find him."

He'd crumpled against the wall like an empty paper bag when I'd let him go, curling up into a miserable, tight ball, clutching his rifle.

"He'll kill me," he said to his kneecaps. "He'll kill me . . ."

I pulled him up by the elbow, slipping the rifle from his hands. With two fingers, I tugged the blue-and-yellow band from his upper arm and shoved it into my pocket.

"Strilka? He's got other things to worry about now," I said.

13

IT DIDN'T TAKE US LONG TO FIND MYKOLA. THEY
were bringing out the bodies from the prison courtyard and laying them out for identification on the wide sidewalk along Kaz
imierzowska Street. He was sitting by one of the bodies—just
sitting there, cross-legged, looking at nothing, not hearing when
I shouted at him through the crowd.

Oh God, no. He'd found Papa's body.

But it wasn't Papa's body. It was Father Yosyp's.

He hadn't been dead very long. There was a single bullet hole
between his eyes, and the blood was still wet. Execution style,
with a pistol. I thought of the shots I'd heard earlier. I thought
of the pistol in Marko's hand.

It was stupid, but I bent to check his pulse. I don't know why
I did it. I wouldn't have felt it anyway. My fingers were numb.

He *was* wearing his cassock, I noticed. Why not? The Reds
were gone. There was nothing to fear.

I tugged at Mykola's sleeve. He shoved my hand away.

"Mykola," I said.

"No."

"Come on."

"No."

I tugged harder, and he jerked away, folding limply across Father Yosyp's body, burying his face in the black folds of the cassock.

"Why did they do it?" he said, his voice muffled in the heavy fabric. "Why did they do it?"

I slung the rifle. I sat on my knees and pulled him up and slipped my arms around him, tight.

"Listen," I said into his ear, "we've got to go."

He shook his head against my shoulder. He didn't speak. He was crying the way he'd cried for Papa—shaking but silent. I rubbed his back in slow circles, feeling his rib cage rise and fall in long, racking sobs under my palm.

"It'll be all right," I said. "It's going to be all right."

Andriy was standing on the edge of the sidewalk, watching and saying nothing. His eyes fell on mine, just for a second. Then he blinked and looked away. I wondered if he thought I was lying. I wondered if he thought I'd lied to him.

Somebody touched my elbow gently.

"Let me take a look."

It was a Polish voice.

One of the institute nurses knelt beside me in a faint gust of lavender perfume. She was tall: Our faces were level when I looked up. She was about the age my mother would have been. She looked like a film star even in the drab nurse's uniform: slim but broad-shouldered, cool blond hair done up in an elegant chignon, tiny pearls in her earlobes. She was the kind of woman who'd make you look up from your newspaper on the tram, the kind of woman whose eight hatboxes I'd have to juggle in one go from her chauffeured Daimler sedan to her suite—the kind of woman to whom I'd have to be very careful to say only *Yes, madam* or *No, madam*, so she wouldn't hear the Ukrainian under my Polish.

Her manicured fingers slid over my forearm.

"Let me take a look," she said again.

"He's all right, ma'am."

"Mm." She pried at my arms as if she hadn't heard.

"He doesn't need your help," I said, through my teeth. My accent was unmistakable when I was angry, but I didn't care. I wanted her to go away.

She ignored me. She pulled Mykola's hands across her lap and uncurled his battered fingers one by one, pressing gauze across his bloody knuckles. He let her do it, lifting his head a little to watch. He was still crying—I could feel him trembling—but his shoulders had stopped heaving.

She was trying to calm him down.

I was too ashamed to protest when another nurse pulled me away. I sat beside Andriy on the curb, craning my neck to look for Nachtigallen in the crowd, while the second nurse tried to hold my chin in two fingers and wipe the blood off my face. I'd forgotten about taking that slug to the jaw.

"I'm sorry," the nurse said.

I didn't know what she was apologizing for—the slug or the sting of the iodine or the way she was holding my chin or the bullet in Father Yosyp's head or all of it or none of it. I shrugged indifferently, teeth clenched, before I realized she'd said it in Ukrainian.

I looked up at her, caught off guard.

"I saw the fight," she said. "Fascist bastards. You did the right thing—standing up to them."

She was younger than the Polish nurse. She was my age, with dark hair plaited neatly in a bun at the nape of her neck and laughing eyes the color of linden honey.

I shut my eyes and opened them, trying to clear my head.

"Why are you here? Little late, aren't you?"

It was a sour, shitty thing to say, and stupid anyway. There'd be wounded among the survivors. There'd be others like Vitalik. What did I know? Maybe her father was rotting with mine down there in the lower prison.

My turn. "I'm sorry," I said.

She pretended not to hear. She wadded the bloody gauze and stuffed it into her ragbag.

"You were close?"

"What?"

"To the priest."

He'd been more a father than Papa had ever been. I couldn't explain that because I couldn't explain about Papa, who was—had been—one of her *fascist bastards*.

"I owe him my life," I said, which was vague but true enough.

I skirted back to safer ground. I waved a hand toward his body. "Did you see it?"

Her mouth was tight. "I saw it."

"What did they say? He was a collaborator?"

She shook her head. "They ordered the Jews out—those nationalist goons. One girl wouldn't go. The officer shot her. The priest tried to go for the gun, so he shot him too."

The Polish nurse came over. She'd left Mykola sitting with a cold compress beside Father Yosyp's body. She murmured something to the dark-haired nurse and knelt beside me on the sidewalk.

"May I talk to you for a minute, Aleksey?"

I was so startled by her effortless Ukrainian that for a second I didn't even notice that she'd somehow managed to pull my name out of Mykola.

"I'm Renata Kijek," she said, ignoring my gaping. "I'm the director of the Department of Pediatrics at the Medical Institute." She paused, as though to make sure I appreciated that. "I'd like to take Mykola in for some testing."

"He's not hurt," I said automatically—not hurt that she could help with anyway.

"He's malnourished to the point of starvation. He has all the signs of rickets. We'll do the testing to be sure, but I can tell you right now that both of you could use vitamin supplements." She glanced at Andriy, who was sitting very still beside me, studying his boots. "All of you," she said.

"What kind of vitamin supplements?"

"Calcium. Vitamin D. I'll be able to tell you more once I've done the blood work."

"And they'll cure it? The vitamins?"

"In combination with a good diet—a much better diet than he's been getting." She was looking at me in a way that made me think she could see right through me. "The longer it goes untreated, the more likely the damage will be permanent."

"Damage," I repeated, like an idiot.

"To his bones." She explained it patiently, as if to a child. "He's still growing. His bones are still developing. In order for them to develop properly . . ."

I looked away. There was bewildered panic fluttering in the pit of my stomach, and underneath it a sick, tight ball of despair. I couldn't think—couldn't focus. I didn't know what to do. All I knew was that I'd failed.

She laid a hand on my arm.

"Aleksey, he'll be all right. He needs good food and time, that's it."

I had neither of those things to give him. I had thirty German marks with which to get us out of Lwów and keep us alive for the foreseeable future—three of us, which had not been the plan—and I had a target on my back, or I would have any minute now, as soon as Marko and the Nachtigallen sorted out who'd killed Strilka.

"Let me help you," Director Kijek said, her hand still on my arm.

There'd be a target on her back, too, if she helped me.

I weighed the lies in my head. She would believe me if I told her I couldn't pay for the medicine. She thought we were starving. The problem would be if she were the kind of saintly person who didn't care that I couldn't pay.

Alternatively, I could show her the blue-and-yellow Nachtigall armband in my trouser pocket and the Reichsmarks under my coat and tell her I'd go to hell before I accepted help from a Pole.

I didn't even have to lie. I could tell her who I was, who my father had been, and she would spit in my face and tell me she'd go to hell before she helped me.

Damn it, I didn't want her hatred. I couldn't take her help, but I didn't want her hatred.

"We're going to Kraków," I told her.

She looked skeptical. "Do you have family there?"

"An uncle."

She was silent.

I waited. I resisted the urge to embellish the lie. The trick to lying was to say the least possible at any given point. You played details like pieces on a chess board—never without careful consideration.

She let go of my arm. She slipped her hand into the pocket of her apron, then laid it over mine, squeezing my fingers gently, pushing something into my palm.

"If you change your mind," she said.

14

"WHAT DID SHE GIVE YOU?" MYKOLA ASKED.

I gave him the calling card wordlessly. He spent a moment puzzling it over, sounding out each gilded character softly to himself. He could read Polish, but not well.

"*M-a-r-k-o*——"

"Marka," I said. "Marka Street, number twenty." It was in the Halickie District, not far from the Citadel—the moneyed part of town. I could have told him it was in Halickie before I'd opened my fingers to read it, just from those pearls she was wearing.

Mykola handed the card back. "She gave me chocolate," he said, sounding pleased that he'd gotten the better deal.

Andriy trailed behind, his head down, walking carefully, as though he were stepping a waltz—left, right, drag—so that he never trod on the grooves between the paving stones. He was hugging himself tightly around the ribs, but he'd stopped shivering.

"You don't have an uncle in Kraków," he said.

It was the first time he'd spoken since the alley doorstep.

"Not as such," I said.

He scuffled his feet over the paving stones.

"Are we going to Kraków?"

"No," I said.

Away from the Brygidki, the streets were quiet enough that you could hear the low rumble of German artillery fire rolling down from the western hills—low, but louder than yesterday. Fifteen kilometers, maybe. Infantry would be closer.

There were shutters over the windows at Altshuler's pharmacy. There was a cardboard sign on the door, so new the paint still looked wet: CLOSED FOR SABBATH.

The Reds were gone. There was nothing to fear.

I left Mykola and Andriy down an alley with the gun while I went across the street to the Polish-owned pharmacy, Nowak's. I practiced the Polish under my breath all the way up to the counter. *Witamina D* was nearly the same as the Ukrainian. Calcium was *wapń*. I remembered that from the Deming table of elements on the wall in the lecture hall at the polytechnic.

The words were easy enough.

There was a lone clerk, a reedy student type, reading a newspaper behind the counter—one of the smeary Polish underground papers, the *Information Bulletin*. He folded it away just as I caught the headline: *Inna Twarz, Ta Sama Walka*.

Different Face, Same Fight.

"Help you?" he asked.

I had the advantage of being taller. There's something confidence inspiring about being able to look down at people.

"I need vitamin supplements," I announced. "Calcium and vitamin D."

He didn't show any sign of noticing my accent—no blinking, no recoiling, no curling of the lip—but neither did he show any sign of caring that I was every bit of 1.9 meters and needed vitamin supplements.

"Have the prescription?"

I opened my mouth and closed it.

"A doctor's order," he prompted.

I parried weakly. "For vitamin supplements?"

"For anything. Store policy." He moved his newspaper so I could see the notice taped on the countertop.

"Give him the vitamins, Janek," the dark-haired nurse said in Polish, shutting the street door. "I'll write him a prescription. He's Renata's patient."

"And I'm the one who's going to get chewed out for it," Janek said, but he disappeared into the back.

The dark-haired nurse slid in beside me at the counter, taking a prescription pad from her pocket. She reached across me for the pen by the cash register.

"That was quick," she said.

She said it in Ukrainian. Janek was still within earshot. I could hear him rummaging around in the back.

She must have seen the look on my face. "You don't have to be afraid," she said. "Not here."

I leaned casually on my elbows on the countertop, to show her how not afraid I was. "What was quick?"

"Changing your mind about Kraków."

"I haven't changed my mind."

"Because you were never really going to Kraków." She didn't look up from her writing. "You're not as clever as you think you are."

"Who says I think I'm clever?"

"Full name," she said.

"What?"

"I need your full name."

"It's not for me."

"I'm writing one for each of you. Full name."

"Aleksey Yevhenovych Shevchuk," I said. That was the name on my fake Soviet passport. There were enough Shevchuks in Lwów that it was safely anonymous.

"And Mykola Yevhenovych Shevchuk." She wrote in Latin letters, in a pretty, swooping hand. "And the other boy?"

"Andriy Andriyovych Proskurivskyi." *Andriy, Andriy's son, of Proskuriv*. Easy enough.

She tore off the forms and handed them to me. "Take these with you. You can fill in the dates as you need."

"That was just your ploy to get my name, wasn't it?"

"Not as clever as you think you are," she said, starting on another form.

"It got me *your* name, Anna Kostyshyn," I said.

"Good to know you can read," she said.

I tucked the forms into my coat pocket. I took out my wad of Reichsmarks and slid it under her hand.

She paused midstroke, lifting her wrist to look. Then, deliberately, she moved her hand away and laid the pen down.

"We seem to have misjudged each other," she said coldly.

"It's all I've got. I'm sorry."

"Where did you get it? Your friends up there at the Brygidki?"

"They're not my friends."

"Strictly business?"

"Strictly nothing. I'm not with them."

"Not since you realized you needed our help?"

"We're good capitalists. Money is money," I said.

Her shoulders were straight, her chin up. "Not to me."

"Never been on the street, have you?"

"That's not an excuse."

"Because you've never been on the street."

"Because I have principles."

"All right," I said, "so how long is the waiting period for principled people? How long did you wait before you started touching rubles? Or maybe you're interested in other methods of payment, if you know what I mean. I'm willing if you are."

She slapped me.

She put some muscle into it too. I'm pretty sure I would have gone flying if I hadn't had the counter to catch me.

Her face was flushed—little blossoms of red on each cheek. She smoothed her apron with stiff, careful dignity.

"Get out," she said.

I shoved the money back into my coat and tossed her prescription forms onto the countertop. My jaw was smarting. My left ear was ringing like a church bell.

"I don't need your help," I said, "yours or your Polish friends'"—loudly, just in case Janek could understand Ukrainian.

"Get out," she snapped.

My pride lasted me out the door and across the street. Once I was safe in the half-light of the alley, I kicked the wall and swore until I'd exhausted my supply of invectives in Ukrainian, Polish, and Russian. Andriy and Mykola watched from a safe distance—Andriy owlishly, his mouth open, Mykola through half-lidded eyes, with the beatific expression of a saint.

"No medicine for you, *chachoł*," he said when I limped over.

"Not for Nazi money, that's for sure."

"Now we start selling our bodies," he said.

"Surprisingly ineffective." In hindsight, I'd deserved that slap. Honestly, I was lucky she hadn't decked me. She *could* have—no doubt about it. "Just let me think."

The obvious thing would be to take advantage of the fact that Altshuler's was closed. I'd stolen before, of course, when I'd needed to. It was easy to justify stealing from Poles and Reds. They were the ones who'd created the need in the first place. Repayment in kind—God would understand and forgive. But this was different. I had nothing against Altshuler. If anything, I owed him. He'd given us Mama's medicine on credit all that winter before she died.

I could leave money and a note. It still meant breaking in, and there was no guarantee the money would be there when the old man opened up again. But my conscience would be clearer.

"I can get the medicine," Andriy said.

I looked at him too sharply. He shrank back, hugging his knees.

"I mean I know how to get it," he said in a smaller voice.

"For Nazi money?"

"They won't care," he said.

"Good capitalists," I said sourly. "Very reassuring."

15

EVIDENTLY, GOOD CAPITALISTS WERE TO BE found in an apartment block across the train tracks on Żółkiewska Street, not all that far from our own place in Zamarstynów. We waited in the lobby, Mykola and I, while Andriy conducted business up in one of the flats—not ideal, but necessary. They knew Andriy. They didn't know us.

"These aren't Strilka's people?" I ventured casually, just to make sure.

"I'm not an idiot," Andriy said.

He looked so hurt that I felt guilty for asking. I gave him the money. He counted out ten marks with careful fingers and handed the rest back to me.

"They'll search me," he said. "Never let them know everything you've got." He smiled at me shyly.

No, he wasn't an idiot.

He gave me the knife from his boot lining. He wouldn't take the gun. I wished he would. Good capitalists might see a chance to make ten marks at no loss.

He was gone for a long time. There weren't any chairs in the lobby. Mykola stood gravely studying the buzzer panel, hands clasped behind his back. I wasn't going to bother trying to look inconspicuous. What was the point? I didn't have any way to hide the gun. Anybody who saw us would know we weren't just a couple of innocent loiterers. I sat against the wall and took the opportunity to close my eyes. I hadn't done that in a while.

"Aleks," Mykola said.

"Mm?"

"You don't have to lie to me."

"Mm."

"Or pretend to be stupid about it."

"I never have to pretend to be stupid." I was only half listening. "What are we talking about?"

He was silent for so long that I opened an eye to make sure he was still there. He was scowling at the buzzer panel, obviously fighting some battle with himself. His hands were clasped very tightly.

"Am I going to die?" he said.

Oh.

"We're all going to die," I said. "God's truth."

"I mean she told you I'm going to die."

He'd been holding this in since the Brygidki. I should have realized.

"She told me you don't eat enough. No surprises there."

"She wanted me to go to the hospital."

"You don't need to go to the hospital."

"She said—"

"She said you need vitamin supplements. We're getting you vitamin supplements. You're not going to die, Mykola."

"She said I should go."

"You know why you can't go," I said.

"Because she was Polish?"

"Because you don't have identification, idiot."

He shrugged. "Maybe I burned all my Red papers."

"It's too risky. You'd let something slip, or I'd let something slip."

"It's not like I sing the 'March of Ukrainian Nationalists' in my sleep."

"Think about it. Why can't you read Polish? Somebody would start putting things together."

"So?"

"So they give you to the Poles. The Poles put a gun to your head and tell the UPA they want the names and whereabouts of every cell leader in Lwów, or else."

"I don't care," he said. "I don't care about the UPA."

"The problem is the UPA don't care about you. They'd let the Poles blow your brains out."

He didn't say anything. He scowled at the buzzer panel.

"Mykola," I said.

He flung me a sullen glance.

"If you needed the hospital, I'd take you to the hospital. All right? I'm not going to let you die."

He shrugged again.

"Papa let Mama die," he said.

I knew better than to try debating that just then.

"Well, I'm not Papa," I said.

Andriy came back down the stairs. He was empty-handed. I pretended not to notice.

"Any luck?" I asked. Mykola watched hollowly from the buzzer panel.

"Tomorrow," Andriy said.

I gave him his knife. My stomach was tight. "We come back tomorrow?" I didn't want to spend another night in Lwów. At this rate, there could be German infantry in the city streets by morning.

Andriy knelt to stick the knife back in his boot. His hands, I noticed, were trembling again, fumbling nervously at his boot laces. He'd seemed almost confident on his way up the stairs—in his element. Something up there had shaken him.

"Andriy," I said.

He didn't look up. "They want ten more marks."

Did he think I'd be angry about the money? I knew how black-market bartering worked. Honestly, I was surprised they weren't asking for more. I'd fully anticipated having to use all thirty marks and throw in my boots and possibly Andriy's wristwatch on the side.

"We can do ten more marks," I said. "We're just going to have to find some place where we can lie low until tomorrow."

He was still fidgeting blindly with his boot laces.

"Andriy," I said, "it's all right."

"There's an order out for you." He looked up finally. "It's all over the city. Two thousand marks for your capture. Commander Shukhevych signed it himself."

16

THERE WERE PLENTY OF PLACES TO HIDE IN Lwów. The trick was finding someplace that I knew and the Nachtigallen didn't. Andriy didn't seem to think Commander Shukhevych was in the city yet—he would come in with the Germans, he and the main body of the Nachtigallen—but we still had the immediate problem of Marko and his advance party and the fact that their communiqués seemed to be covering a lot more ground a lot faster than we were.

"Is he from Lwów?" I asked Andriy. "Marko?"

He seemed puzzled by the question. "No, from Radziechów."

"What about the others? Anybody besides you?"

He shook his head. "Most of them are from the General Government."

He meant the part of Poland under German occupation, not Soviet.

"Would Marko know the sewer tunnels?" I asked.

A century ago—back when Poland was still under Hapsburg rule—they walled in Lwów's river, the Pełtew, and built right over it. The main channel ran for several kilometers, south to north beneath the city center, on an exact line with the grand boulevard. The sewer system fed into the channel. You could move all around Lwów through those tunnels, provided you had a good head for direction and could stand the mud and the stink and the faintly disconcerting sensation that you'd been buried alive. None of the tunnels were much wider than a good armspan.

Andriy was scowling, still puzzled. "Commander Shukhevych might know about them."

"But Marko wouldn't necessarily, unless somebody had specifically told him."

Another slow shake of the head. "No. I don't think so."

The tunnels were as good a place as any—or as good a place as I was going to think of until I'd had some sleep anyway. But I made Mykola and Andriy wait above while I went down the Pełtewna Street drain with the rifle and the box of matches from Mykola's pack and had a look around. I wasn't worried so much about the Nachtigallen and the price on my head right then as I was worried about the ordinary scum—thieves, smugglers.

We were pretty far from the city center here, and it wasn't bad in the tunnel, just dark and damp. The quiet was welcome. We sat on the narrow concrete shelf above the water and shared around the last of the dumplings and sausages in the thin light of our grease lamp, the battered tin one we used to take with us when we went camping with Grandfather in the hills above

Brzuchowice. Afterward, Mykola carefully divided up his chocolate bar into three exactly equal pieces and handed one piece to Andriy, one to me.

"So what's the plan?" he said calmly.

He didn't have to say a word about the lobby. I knew this was his apology.

"Istanbul," I said.

He looked up. "Istanbul?"

"Istanbul."

He broke his chocolate into even smaller pieces and laid each piece on his tongue one at a time, making it last.

"Overland?" he said finally.

"Or you give me to the Nachtigallen and buy your passage on a ship with your two thousand marks."

"If we gave you to the Nachtigallen," he said, placing his last piece of chocolate on his tongue and shutting his eyes in an exaggerated show of savoring it, "we wouldn't need to go to Istanbul in the first place."

He was joking the same as I was, but it was uncomfortable being reminded that this was all my fault. Andriy didn't think it was funny anyway. He picked at his chocolate in silence, not looking at either of us.

It wasn't going to be easy. If we made good time, it would take us two months. We would be living off the land the whole way—and by *living off the land* I meant scavenging, because we wouldn't have much chance to get more ammunition for the rifle. We'd have good weather—even moving on the slower side of my estimations, we'd be out of the mountains by August and across the Turkish border by September—and we'd have the advantage of being far behind the front. Romania and Bulgaria were both staunch German allies, therefore unoccupied. But two months in the Carpathian wilderness was still two months in the Carpathian wilderness, never mind weather and the war.

Anyway, the front didn't matter to the UPA. If they wanted me dead badly enough, they could reach me anywhere. There were UPA cells as far away as America.

I didn't say that aloud. No need—Mykola and Andriy knew it as well as I did.

We agreed to take a watch in shifts of three hours. Andriy took the first shift. I went to sleep in the happy anticipation of six uninterrupted hours before my shift, and I was groggy and a little peevish when I woke up to Mykola shaking my shoulder insistently after what seemed like only a couple of minutes.

"All right," I said, "all right. You're not mixing a martini."

"Andriy's gone," he said.

He shifted on his heels so I could sit up and see. He'd relit the grease lamp. The tiny flame sputtered and bobbed in the draft down the tunnel. The empty shelf stretched away into yawning darkness. Wherever Andriy had gone, he'd taken the gun.

"How long?" I asked.

It was a stupid question. He'd been asleep as I had, and anyway, neither of us had a wristwatch. My head felt thick and heavy. That little bit of sleep was just long enough to remind me how bone-tired I was, not long enough to do anything for it.

Mykola avoided the question graciously. "He was gone when I woke up just now."

"You probably woke up because you heard him leave. He's gone off to piss."

"Without saying anything?"

"He didn't want to wake us up."

"The point of being on watch is so he can wake us up if he has to," Mykola said.

"Rats carried him off," I said. "He's skinny enough. Almost as skinny as you are. The question we have to ask is—was it many small rats or one big rat?"

"That's not funny," Mykola said. He was afraid of rats.

"The possibility we don't even want to consider is that it was many big rats."

"Shut up," Mykola said.

"Which would you rather fight—a hundred one-kilogram rats or one hundred-kilogram rat?"

"Shut up."

I yawned and rubbed my face, digging the heels of my hands into my eyes.

"We'll give him a couple minutes. Then we'll panic. Put that light out."

We sat in darkness, listening to our breaths and the distant *plop* of dripping water. There was a faint splash that I hoped for

Mykola's sake was a fish, not a rat. I was almost asleep again when I heard the soft patter of footsteps coming down the shelf from the direction of the drain—quiet enough that I could tell they were trying to move stealthily, whoever they were, loud enough that I could tell there was more than one of them. Electric torchlight jumped over the walls.

I snatched at Mykola's arm. We retreated down the shelf, staying just ahead of the torchlight. They were making more noise than we were—they wouldn't be able to hear us as long as they were moving—but they had the advantage of being able to see where they were going, which meant they were moving a lot faster. Sooner or later, the shelf would start splitting off into smaller side passages and we'd be able to lose them, but we'd have to keep pace with them until then.

They stumbled across our pack. Somebody flashed a torch up and down the shelf. They knew we couldn't be far. We pressed flat against the wall, holding our breaths. I hadn't had the presence of mind to grab the pack, and I consoled myself with the thought that something in it would have clinked or rattled if I had—the lamp or the tins or the vodka bottle filled with drinking water. At least I still had the money, tucked safely in my coat pocket. At least I still had my boots. But I ached at the loss of our icons.

They were conferring over the pack. I nudged Mykola's elbow and jerked my chin. He slid quietly along the shelf. I followed him, careful to keep my weight on my toes. We moved stiffly down the shelf, huddled against the wall like rheumatic old peasants.

Mykola tripped over something in the darkness. I heard the thump and his soft, hissed breath, then the wet smack as he caught himself on his hands.

There was a moment of absolute silence—nobody moving, nobody talking, nobody breathing.

Then there was gunfire.

I hauled Mykola up and shoved him. We ran. Bullets drilled after us, chewing across the shelf and up the walls, spitting clumps of concrete dust. Muzzle flashes lit the tunnel in short, skittering bursts—enough that I could see the gaping black hole in the wall where a side passage veered off, just ahead. We ducked into the passage. My relief at the way it banked and twisted lasted a good ten seconds. Then the passage turned one last corner and slapped up solidly against a brick wall.

Dead end.

I spent a frenzied moment groping blindly across the wall and came across a set of iron rungs bolted into the brick—a manhole ladder. We weren't out of options just yet. I followed Mykola up the rungs. Footsteps pounded after us, echoing down the passage. Torchlight raced across the floor and up the walls.

Mykola fumbled at the manhole cover.

"It's stuck—it's stuck—Aleks—"

"Punch it! Pretend it's a rat."

I heard the dull clatter of metal on cobblestone just as the gunmen rounded the corner. Mykola pulled himself up through the opening. He swung his legs up and vanished into sunlight. I scrambled after him. I had one hand on the last rung, one hand on the ledge, when the guns opened up.

I lost my footing first. A wave of nausea hit me before the bullets did. The anticipation of pain is as bad as the pain itself—as incapacitating anyway. I was already sliding off the rung when the bullets tore across the backs of my legs. No taking it in noble silence—I had no more control over the scream that came out of my mouth than I had over my buckling knees. Holy hell, it *hurt*. I lost my handholds under the sheer force of the pain, every muscle in my body overwhelmed by my urgent need to curl up into a ball and sob.

I didn't fall. That confused me. Even as a quivering mass of pain, I knew I should have fallen when my hands slipped. Instead, I was moving steadily upward, thumping painfully over the rungs. I yelled. Mykola yelled back into my face. He was hauling me bodily up the ladder, yelling and crying and pulling all at once. He dragged me over the ledge and dumped me onto the street. I lay writhing and gasping on the cobblestones while he heaved the cover back over the manhole.

There were people all around us. It was late afternoon, and we'd come out right in the middle of Saint Theodore Square, just off the boulevard. Somebody who wasn't me or Mykola was screaming incoherently. I don't know whether that was because of the blood and shooting or because you just don't expect people to come popping up out of manholes like that. Nobody stepped up to help—I couldn't blame them, really—but nobody tried to stop us either. Mykola pulled my arm across his shoulders and half carried, half dragged me away from the manhole and into an alley.

He zigzagged through alleys and side streets for ten minutes before he put me down against a low brick wall, under the cover of some scraggly trees. We were at the western edge of the old High Castle grounds, and we were alone. He shook my arm off and dropped to his knees beside me, panting with the effort. He wiped the sweat and tears from his face with his sleeve, sniffed, shook his head, and reached for my legs. I hissed when he stretched them straight. I was past the point of being able to scream. He flinched, though he didn't let go.

"I've got to wrap them," he said. "Aleks, I've got to wrap them. It's too much blood."

I watched him tug my boots off. His hands were shaking.

I tried to help. "Can't be the artery," I croaked. "I'd be d-dead already."

He didn't respond. It was a lot of blood. I hadn't really had a good look at the damage until now. There was blood bubbling through the holes in my trousers—two holes on the inside of my left thigh, just above the knee, where the bullet had punched in and out again; one hole at the back of my right calf, where the bullet must have gone straight to the bone. Mykola took off my coat and shirt and tore the shirt up into long strips.

"Twenty m-marks in the pocket," I reminded him.

"Lot of good it's done us," he said, but he stuffed the bills into his own coat.

The nausea hit me again when he peeled off my trousers. I focused on my boots. My boots—my fine, twice-stolen Polish cavalry boots. I wouldn't be able to sell them now, except for scrap. The bullet had gone through the boot on its way to my shinbone. Maybe a museum would want them. The bullet hole and bloodstains would make them an object of interest in a couple of centuries or so, assuming the war was over by then. Maybe we could eat them, if things got bad enough.

I didn't realize I'd closed my eyes until Mykola shook me. There was blood slicked all over his hands, and he must have rubbed his face at some point, because there was a long, red smear across his cheek. I knew he was saying something because I could see his mouth moving. I couldn't hear him. I wasn't really concerned. I was comfortable—a little cold, but blessedly numb. I'd be asleep if he'd stop shaking me.

I closed my eyes again. Whatever it was, I could safely assume it would still be a problem when I woke up. It could wait.

III
TOLYA

Saturday, July 29–Sunday, August 6
1944

17

FOR THE FIRST TIME, TOLYA WISHED HE'D PAID attention when Comrade Lieutenant Spirin tried teaching him to read a map.

He hadn't really seen the point then. He'd already learned how to use the sun and the stars, and anyway, the only other map he'd ever seen was the big framed one of Kyiv that had hung in Ivan's apartment. He'd made the mistake of assuming Comrade Lieutenant Spirin could just read the map for him if they needed to read a map. He'd made the mistake of assuming Comrade Lieutenant Spirin would *be there* to read the map for him.

They'd been going over maps of Lwów all afternoon—street maps, building maps, sewer maps, more kinds of maps than Tolya even knew existed—so he was about three hours too late to admit he didn't really have any idea what he was looking at.

Most of the squad was here, gathered in a tight circle on the open ground below the gun mounts: Andriy, and Yakiv, back from wherever he'd been that morning, and a Crimean Tatar called Ruslan, and Valentyn, who'd been one of the German auxiliary police in Lwów. He still wore his German uniform jacket, though he'd ripped off the insignia. The Red Cross girls would be going back to Toporiv as soon as it was dark. They would be walking all night and tomorrow, so they were resting now under the tarpaulin.

"Windows," Solovey said, marking right angles with the side of his hand, "here, here, and here."

They all leaned in to look—except Ruslan, who'd made the map in the first place. He sat smoking his cigarette, patiently waiting. He wasn't much older than Tolya, and he hadn't been here much longer. Two months ago, Stalin had ordered all the Crimean Tatars deported east, deep into the steppe, but Ruslan had escaped by making his way to the port at Sevastopol and stowing away on a ship for Odessa. He didn't speak much, but that could be just because he didn't speak much Ukrainian— Tolya wasn't sure. When he did speak, it was only to Solovey.

"As many windows as you could want," Solovey said, "all with clear lines of sight into the headquarters building. We don't know precisely which office is Volkov's, but we know he uses the staircase, here"—scribbling with his pencil—"which can be seen from *these* windows across Pełczyńska Street. How far, Ruslan?"

Ruslan took out his cigarette and rubbed his lean jaw with his thumb. "Fifty meters."

"So. Distance isn't our problem. Tolya made that distance ten times over, this morning." Solovey tossed his pencil down. "Our problem—*one* problem—is that this whole stretch of Pełczyńska south of the Citadel is crawling with reconstruction crews. We go in with one of the crews and smuggle the rifle in by pieces—not impossible by any stretch—but here's the other thing: It's heavy security anyway, but they know they've got this problem with windows, and they're anticipating some idiot will try what we're trying. Nobody makes a move on Pełczyńska Street without Volkov knowing."

"That was all one problem?" Andriy said.

"The first problem. The second problem is that they've put in new window glass since the barrage—both buildings. Stationary panes. How does glass affect the shot?"

There was a long stretch of silence before Tolya realized Solovey was directing the question to him. He was still staring at the map, trying to figure out how the floors of the office building fit together.

He peeled his tongue off the roof of his mouth. "I'd have to take out the near pane."

"What about the staircase window?"

"Won't deflect it much—not a straight shot."

"That's no good," Valentyn said. "The game's up as soon as the pane comes out. They'll spot an open window a kilometer away. You might be able to get the shot off, but you sure as hell won't be making it out."

"An eventuality to be considered," Solovey said blandly.

There was another stretch of silence.

"Look," Andriy said, "this doesn't have to be a suicide mission. What if we blow the windows first?"

"No good," Valentyn said. "Every Red in the city will be watching the building after that."

"Do it a couple of days before—time enough for things to quiet down, but not time enough to replace the windows."

"Or we forget Pełczyńska," Valentyn said. "We get Volkov in his car between headquarters and the hotel. Take the shot from the empty apartment block on the corner of Byka and Kazimierzowska."

"It's too tight," Andriy said. "You couldn't make the shot eastward. There's trees lining the street all along the facade. And you wouldn't have enough time westward. Look at the angle of the street. You'd only have from here—where the car clears the southeast corner of the Brygidki—to here, at which point it passes out of the line of sight—"

"Twenty-five meters," Ruslan murmured to Solovey.

"—and you've got the car moving at, say, thirty-five kilometers an hour, which means—"

"About two and a half seconds," Solovey said.

Andriy shook his head. "Too tight."

"Could you do it?" Solovey asked Tolya.

Four more faces turned to Tolya expectantly.

He swallowed. "One shot, maybe."

"No insurance shot, you mean."

"Not in two and a half seconds—not a moving target. First shot would have to be the kill shot."

"First shot is the driver, then," Valentyn said. "Solves the moving-target problem."

"And gives Volkov time to duck," Solovey pointed out, "and we're stuck in a firefight with every gun in the Brygidki. So really it's one shot only, moving target or no."

"All right," Valentyn said, "but think about this. We miss the shot from Byka, we make it away and try again. We miss from Pełczyńska, we don't get another chance—whether we blow the windows or not. Nobody gets out of that building."

Solovey and Andriy exchanged a glance.

"It's Tolya's call," Solovey said.

"When did we start taking tactical advice from collaborators?"

That was Yakiv. He was looking at Tolya across the map. His eyes bored into Tolya's face, and Tolya looked away. He didn't dare look in any of their faces. He looked at the pile of ammunition boxes, which was safely outside the circle.

"We were shooting collaborators, last I knew," Yakiv said.

There was silence, like a held breath.

Tolya studied the ammunition boxes. He could see some of the stamps through the camouflage net. He knew the Soviet ones, and he knew the German ones by the Reich eagle, though he couldn't read the lettering. There were others he didn't recognize, but they had Latin lettering like the German boxes, so he knew they were Polish.

Solovey leaned back on his heels. He took his cigarette out of his mouth and flicked away the ash with his fingers—slowly, deliberately. His face was blank.

"Only one of us here has bagged a *zampolit*," he said, "and it wasn't you."

"Only one of us here put on a Red uniform. We all had the choice."

"Most of us were wearing Wehrmacht uniforms three years ago," Andriy said quietly.

"In good faith. The Reich stabbed us in the back. The Reds have had knives at our throats for twenty years."

"German knives, Russian knives. What difference does it make?"

"I'm not trusting the judgment of a collaborator."

"You're taking orders from me," Solovey said, "or I'm shooting you."

Yakiv was silent.

"Tolya's shot," Solovey said. "Tolya's call." He put his cigarette back in his mouth.

"When were you thinking?" Andriy asked him. "The longer we wait, the trickier it's going to be, no matter where we do it."

"It can't be tonight," Yakiv said.

"Got other plans?" Solovey said. His voice was cool. Andriy tensed.

"Volkov isn't in the office today," Yakiv said.

"Where is he?"

"Up in Zhovkva."

"Why wasn't I told?"

"I didn't know until this morning, all right? The girl at the hotel said they went up to Zhovkva. If I'd known you were planning an assassination, I'd have asked him politely to stay."

"Did she say how long—the girl at the hotel?"

"No, and they didn't leave a forwarding address for me either. Look—all I know is they cleared out of their rooms, and the girl said they went to Zhovkva."

Solovey was playing with his cigarette with two fingers, breathing smoke softly—thinking.

"Well," he said finally, "good news for Tolya's shoulder." He stubbed out the cigarette in the dirt. "All right. Watch headquarters and the hotel—four-hour shifts, no breaks. I want to know when he's back."

* * *

Tolya tried to approach Solovey alone, later. He wasn't even sure why, except the shame pushed him—to explain? To make excuses? To apologize? It hadn't seemed like collaboration two years ago, only hunger. He wasn't sure how to explain that. He didn't think Solovey would understand, even if he could find the words to explain. Yakiv wouldn't. *We all had the choice.* He wasn't sure how to explain that hunger made the choices for you. He wasn't sure he believed it himself anymore.

Level-headed Andriy would understand, if any of them would. He was from Proskuriv, Solovey had said. He would understand hunger. He would understand you were still learning to think in hard, unbending terms like *resistance* and *collaboration*, not in soft, shifting ones like *survival*. But it was Andriy's shift on the watch, or something. He'd left right after the meeting.

The Red Cross girls were leaving too, and Solovey was kissing Anna under the tarpaulin. Tolya didn't see them behind the ammunition boxes until he'd nearly walked into them. He spun around quickly on his heel before either of them noticed. He fled to the other side of the piled boxes and sat pretending to clean the pistol Solovey had given him—fumbling at it one-handed because Iryna had put his arm in a sling after she found out Solovey had made him shoot. ("Idiots, both of you," she said. "He made the shot," Solovey said, half defensive and half smug.)

Afterward, Solovey walked the two girls to the edge of the camp. He was holding Anna's hand, fingers threaded through hers. They kissed again at the trees. Then Solovey stood leaning on the mortar, watching the girls go up into the darkening wood.

That was Tolya's chance, but somebody caught his good arm when he started for the gun—Yakiv, pulling him back and spinning him around and holding him tightly by the elbow with thick, strong fingers.

"Where do you think you're going, *zradnyk?*"

It was just the two of them there in the long, blue shadows of the ammunition boxes. Tolya tried to pull his arm away. Yakiv's fingers were tight as a vise.

"I want you where I can keep an eye on you," Yakiv said.

"I n-need to talk to Solovey." It stumbled out in a whisper. His throat was closed.

"Listen, *zradnyk*—this is the only thing you should be worrying about." Yakiv made a pistol with two fingers and pressed his fingertips to Tolya's forehead. He pursed his lips and let out a soft breath, *bang*, pushing hard with his fingers and then jerking his hand tautly back, as with recoil. "Understand? There's only one reason you're here and not spattered against a wall in L'viv."

Only as long as you're useful, Tolya Korolenko.

And then?

He realized, in that moment, that Solovey had never really answered the question.

18

HE DIDN'T SPEAK TO SOLOVEY FOR THE REST OF the afternoon. He pretended to sleep through the meal, and he pretended to sleep while Solovey sat across from him under the tarpaulin afterward, making notes in his field book in the last of the sunlight.

Then he must really have been asleep because he woke up to machine-gun fire.

Tracer rounds flashed in the darkness, pouring down in long, white streams through the trees. He was back at Tarnopol, face-down against the earth, waiting with his hands over his ears for the shrieks of the Stuka bombers.

But it was wrong, all wrong. There hadn't been any trees at Tarnopol—not by the time it came to a close fight. Maybe never again. There'd been a month of shelling and dive-bombing, raid-ing and retreating, blow for blow, before the final push. It was gravel and gray mud and a German garrison dead nearly to the last man, Tarnopol.

He raised his head.

He was under the tarpaulin on the hillside, and the wood was alive with tracers and muzzle flashes and shouts and pounding footsteps and the hammering of the machine gun.

Somebody slid in heavily beside him from somewhere in the darkness—Solovey, with a pistol in his hand.

"Keep your head down," he said. He was on his stomach, his cheek against the dirt. He pushed a clip into the magazine of his pistol. "We're blown," he said. His hands moved carefully, steadily. "Do you have your pistol?"

"Yes."

"Loaded?"

"Yes."

"They're trying to cordon us off. I think they've only got the one machine gun—on the ridge." Solovey refitted the magazine against his palm. "You're going to run when I say—west, as fast as you can. Keep low. I'll be behind you. If I drop, you keep running. Believe me—I'll do the same if it's you, and I won't lose any sleep over it. Do you understand?"

"Yes."

Solovey snapped the slide of his pistol. "Do you remember what we said about contingency plans?"

"Yes."

"Wait until he reloads," Solovey said. He grinned against the dirt. "Should have gone to Stryy." Then, after a pause: "Go."

Tolya stumbled out into the darkness. Bodies dotted the open ground—black lumps in the afterglow of muzzle flashes. A dark shape loomed up in front of him. The long shadow of a rifle bent toward him. There was no time to duck, no time to think—just the pistol in his hand, and the trigger under his finger, and the quick, sharp jerk of his wrist. Then he was running, weaving through the trees down the slope—running and running, head down, heart in his throat, the machine gun hammering after him, the tracers arcing past in white streaks, Solovey's footsteps pounding behind.

He didn't know how long he ran, or how far. The wood was close and black. His legs gave out on the far, mossy bank of a thin stream. He caught himself awkwardly on one hand, keeping his weight off his left arm. He untied Iryna's sling with numb, fumbling fingers and wadded it into his trouser pocket. Then he eased himself down and lay still, feeling the cool, wet moss on his cheek. There was no sound but his own gasped breaths, and Solovey's footsteps coming up behind him, and the soft calls of the nightingales in the trees above.

Solovey crouched beside him. "Are you hurt?" His voice was very quiet.

"No. I don't think so."

"We'll listen just for a bit," Solovey said.

They sat on the bank, listening. The trees shivered and groaned in the wind off the hillsides. There was a sudden fluttering of wings somewhere out in the darkness. Beside him, Solovey bent down, pressing his ear to the earth, lying so still for so long that Tolya wondered whether he'd fallen asleep. But then he sat back up slowly, holstering his pistol. He let out a long, low breath.

"Andriy's dead," he said. He leaned his elbows on his knees, resting his face in his hands. After a moment, he kneaded his temples with his fingertips and lifted his head. "Presumably Yakiv and Valentyn. They had the watch on the ridge, and there was no alarm. I think Taras might have made it away." He took out his pistol again and opened the magazine, counting the rounds. "Didn't they teach you to sleep with your boots on in the army? You're going to have a hell of a time running."

"I'll be all right."

"I'll leave you behind if I have to. I'm not joking."

"Were they NKVD?"

Solovey was reloading the magazine, cupping the loose cartridges in his palm. "Yes," he said. "Bad news for us."

"Did they track us? Yesterday?"

"No," Solovey said. "If I had to guess, I'd say they took Anna and Iryna." He refitted the magazine, slamming the pistol butt against the heel of his hand. "Come on," he said. "They'll be tracking us now."

* * *

This time Solovey led. They alternated running and walking, weaving a jagged line through the trees. They didn't speak, and they didn't stop. At first they paused, every now and then, just for a little while, to catch their breaths and to listen—Solovey going down on the ground as he'd done back at the stream, leaning on his shoulder and pressing his ear to the earth. Then he seemed to have satisfied himself about whatever he'd heard, and wherever he'd heard it, because they didn't pause again.

They were deep in the hills now. The wind had died, and it was dark and late and very still. The madness back in the camp on the hillside seemed long ago and far away and uncertain, like the edges of a dream. It was a heavy, humid night, the stars overcast and the air thick, and there was sweat crawling down Tolya's face and neck, trickling between his shoulder blades, soaking his shirt and the waistband of his trousers.

He'd stopped trying to keep track of direction. There was only Solovey, ahead in the darkness, and the endless black earth under his bare feet. He moved mechanically, one leg after the other—up and down, up and down, like pistons. His feet were scratched and bloody. He'd found the sharp edge of a stone in the dark and opened a long, thin gash along the instep of his right foot. There was a stitch in his side, a jabbing pain in his shoulder, an ache at the back of his throat. There was salt on his lips and the metallic taste of blood on his tongue. His fingers had seized up stiffly and uselessly on the pistol grip. But they didn't stop.

The air cooled and cleared toward morning. The wind picked up again, pushing against them gently. They were near water. He could hear the soft, shivering, mournful whistles of lake divers coming up on the wind through the trees.

In the gray half-light before dawn, Solovey finally stopped. He put a hand on a tree trunk and crouched on his heels.

"Tolya," he said, in a low voice, "come here."

They were on the shoulder of a low, pine-clad hill. The water shimmered through the trees down the slope, silvery in the half-light. Tolya crouched beside Solovey. He opened his curled fingers one at a time and wiped his palm on his trousers.

"How are your feet?" Solovey asked.

"They're all right."

"They look like hell."

"They're not bad," Tolya said. There was a cold fist of fear in the pit of his stomach. *Only as long as you're useful, Tolya Korolenko.* He was useless now, and he was too slow, and he knew too much.

This was where Solovey put a bullet in his head.

But Solovey turned a little and sat against the trunk, easing himself carefully down with his hands, sucking a soft breath through his teeth.

"I need you to do something for me," he said. He braced himself against the tree and stretched out his legs stiffly. "Take off my boot—my right boot. My knife's in the lining."

Tolya hesitated, just for a second. Then he laid his pistol on the grass and unlaced Solovey's boot. The trouser leg beneath was dark and wet with blood. He looked up into Solovey's face. Solovey grinned.

"It's all right," he said. His face was slick with sweat. "Machine-gun slug."

"Where?"

"Below the knee, just on the—yes. There." Another grin, fainter this time. "You found it."

Tolya felt the bone under his fingers. "Is it broken?"

"I think so," Solovey said calmly. "Do you think you can make a splint?"

"All right."

"You'll need a stick—a good, stout one. Take the knife."

The pines were no good for sticks, but he found beech trees toward the water. He cut a beech bough about the width of his thumb and took it back up the slope to Solovey. He rolled up Solovey's blood-soaked trouser leg and unwound the footcloth, wiping the blood with his fingers. The bullet had gone straight to the bone through the back of Solovey's calf. There were old white scars peppering the fleshy part of the calf. This wasn't the first bullet he'd taken—or, Tolya suspected, the first time that bone had broken.

"Wrap it up," Solovey said. His voice was low and tight, his teeth clenched. "Use the cloth."

Tolya wrapped the wound with Solovey's footcloth. He measured the stick to Solovey's shin and cut it down and tied it against the bone with long strips cut from Iryna's sling. Then he wiped Solovey's knife on his thigh and put the knife back in the boot.

"Lace it up tight, Tolya," Solovey said. He had his shoulders braced stiffly against the tree. He was holding his pistol in white-knuckled hands. "Is that what I should call you—Tolya? Or do you want me to be formal and say Anatoliy? I should have asked before."

"Tolya."

"I'm sorry for presuming."

"It's all right," Tolya said.

* * *

He went down to the lake shore to wash. Solovey was up on the ridge, "having a look," he said. Tolya washed Solovey's blood from his hands. He cupped water in his palms and drank and doused his face and neck, rinsing off the sweat. Then he rolled up his trousers and stuck his blistered, battered feet into the pebbly shallows, holding his tongue in his teeth and hissing softly at the sting.

The first pink glow of dawn was coming over the pine wood. There was a wispy, pale mist rising off the lake. There were little concentric rings here and there on the surface of the water where the fish were feeding. He watched, sitting very still, holding his breath and listening to his heart beat, while a young elk came down from the edge of the wood to drink.

An engine broke the silence. An olive-drab biplane rattled up over the ridge—one of the ones they called *kukuruzniki*, corn cutters, flying low-level reconnaissance out of Lwów.

Tolya dove up the bank, sliding on his stomach under the

cover of the trees. The elk started at his movement, head flying up, knobby legs stiffening. It broke into a lumbering run up out of the water. Tolya lay on his stomach on a thick carpet of pine needles and watched the plane come over. It cleared the ridge and went away westward over the lake—too high and too fast to be hunting here. Bigger prey was retreating west across the San.

Tolya pushed up on his hands. The elk was gone. Solovey was coming down from the ridge through the trees. In daylight now Tolya could see his limp and also the way he was trying to hide it. His trouser leg was crusted to the knee with dried blood, the color of rust.

"I don't think that was for us," he said.

"No."

Solovey holstered his pistol and went down to the water. He knelt at the edge, splashed his face, and tipped water down his collar. He bent stiffly to drink. Then he sat back on his heels, wiping his mouth with his sleeve.

"Do you fish, Tolya?"

"What?"

"Have you ever fished?"

"Oh—no." Tolya hesitated. "We used to fish the Sluch River—people in Kuz'myn, I mean, before the famine. Then the Reds said we couldn't fish."

"We fished this lake before the war," Solovey said, "my grandfather and I—my mother's father. There are marvelous pike in this lake." He was sitting with his hands cupped on his knees, looking out over the water. "First thing I'm going to do when the war is over," he said. "Come up here, drink Polish beer, fish all day. That's when I'm going to know the war is over."

He was somewhere very far away, and Tolya didn't say anything. There was the wind in the trees, and the lap of the little waves at the shoreline, and the low, sad whistles of the divers carrying across the water. Just for a second, he thought about trying to say what he'd wanted to say yesterday—to apologize, at least, if he couldn't explain. But the words wouldn't come, and he didn't think Solovey would really hear him right then anyway.

Solovey came back slowly. He looked up at Tolya and smiled. "Soon," he said. "Not yet."

19

THEY WENT AROUND THE LAKE. THE SUN CAME
up, and it was hazy and humid in a way that meant it would be hot
later. They weren't running now. Solovey was walking ahead, trying not to show his limp. They were going north by west. They'd
been going roughly north by west all night. Tolya could see the
smoke above Lwów when he looked back over his shoulder.

He didn't dare ask Solovey where they were going—hadn't
cared last night, didn't dare now. They weren't going to the Red
Cross station in Toporiv—his first guess—or they would have
turned east by now. He didn't have any other guesses. He didn't
know what Solovey had heard last night in the darkness with his
ear to the ground, and he didn't know what Solovey had seen
that morning from the ridge.

What he *did* know was that they weren't going to Toporiv.

They hadn't spoken since the lake shore at dawn. It was full daylight now. The lake was away below them. The sun was hot through
the trees. He could feel the silence like an arm across his throat.

"Solovey," he said.

Solovey looked back. "All right?"

"I'm sorry," Tolya said. He fumbled, stammering a little. "I-if it was Anna," he said. He couldn't finish it.

"She knew what she was doing," Solovey said. "She knew the risks. We all did."

"I know," Tolya said, "but I'm sorry."

Solovey had stopped now. He was leaning on one hand against a tree, his weight off his right leg. He wiped sweat from his face with the back of his gun hand and swore once, softly but soundly.

He looked up at Tolya. "Take the boots."

"What?"

"I'm slowing you down, and you know it, so don't act like an idiot. Take the boots. I've got three full clips for my pistol. That's twenty-four rounds. You can have twenty-three of them. I'll need the pistol."

"No."

"You keep going along the shoulder of this hill," Solovey said, ignoring him. "Follow the lake around. There's a cabin—six kilometers or so. Right up from the water. My grandfather's. We've been using it as an ammunition dump—also a rendez-vous point in case things went to hell, which they've done." He smiled. "Haven't been up in a while, but it ought to be stocked pretty well. Everything you need. Let this cool down a bit, then get the hell out. Can you remember an address?"

"Listen—"

"Ruska Street, number five. The Dormition Church. You can

see the bell tower from the boulevard. Ask for Father Kliment. Tell him I sent you."

"No."

"I mean it."

"Not without you."

Solovey let out a soft breath between his teeth. "I said don't be an idiot."

"I'm not being an idiot. I can't go without you. They don't know me. They won't believe me. If I show up saying I'm the only one who made it away, they'll shoot me as a spy—even if they don't find out I've got Polish in my blood."

Solovey didn't say anything.

"Anyway, I can't let you shoot yourself," Tolya said.

"Worried for my soul?" Solovey said.

"If they're anywhere close, they'll hear the shot."

Solovey was silent, holding on to the tree.

"All right," he said finally, "all right—but you take these, to save time later." He dug the spare clips out of his pocket. "Look at me, Tolya. You leave me if you have to, do you understand? Because I swear I'd leave you."

"Shut up," Tolya said.

* * *

The *kukuruznik* came back just after noon.

They heard the engine muttering over the water before they

saw the plane. They dropped flat on their stomachs under the trees, waiting for the flyover. Ahead of them, the pine wood marched away down a long, low slope. There was a reed marsh at the foot of the slope and a swath of bare grassland sweeping back up to the eaves of the wood on the far side of the marsh. The *kukuruznik* passed over south by east, on a line for the city. Tolya picked himself up on his hands and knees, sitting back on his heels.

Solovey's fingers snaked around his wrist, jerking him back down.

"What is—" Tolya started, but Solovey crooked an arm around his neck, slipping a hand over his mouth. He motioned with his pistol. Through the reeds across the marsh, Tolya could see two NKVD riflemen going up the grassy slope, away from the water. They'd been filling their canteens.

There were more riflemen at the edge of the wood.

Tolya's throat closed. He watched the squad split and spread out across the shore. Their voices carried over the water—a murmur, a snatch of laughter, a sharp command in Russian: "Quiet!" They came closer, working through the reeds on the mud bank, looking for footprints in the wet black earth at the water's edge. He could see the red-enameled order star above the right breast pocket of the nearest man's jacket.

Then they were past, moving slowly away down the shore. The *crunch* of boots on underbrush faded away. There was no sound but the rustle of the marsh grass and the whine of the mosquitoes and the *thump, thump, thump* of his heart against the pine needles.

Solovey let go of Tolya's mouth. He lifted his arm from Tolya's neck. He lay still for a moment, his eyes shut, his forehead pressed to the earth, as though he were praying. Then he raised his head and smiled. His face was pale.

"Well," he said very softly. "That's that."

"You think they found the cabin?"

"I think we've got to assume they did." Solovey rolled away from him and sat up. "Anna didn't know this place," he said. "Neither did Iryna. The others did." He was silent, holding a hand absently on his splinted calf. "Do you know what's funny about it?" he said suddenly.

"What?"

"They went right past us in the night, and neither you nor I saw or heard them, and they didn't see or hear us. What do you think? What's the most obvious explanation?"

"They didn't go past us in the night."

"They were already here, waiting for us. We were betrayed." Solovey got up, kicking the ground with his good foot. Then he put his hand on a tree trunk and stood for a moment, head tipped back, eyes shut.

"How are your feet, Tolya?" he asked. His voice was calm.

"They're all right."

"Your shoulder?"

"All right."

"Liar," Solovey said. "But I guess the best of us are."

He opened his eyes. He pushed himself away from the tree.

"Come on," he said. "It's two days due west to Hruszów."

20

THEY RESTED IN THE HEAT OF THE DAY. THAT WAS
Tolya's decision. Solovey didn't want to stop.

"Five minutes," he said.

He was still sleeping an hour later, bowed over his knees
against a tree trunk, and Tolya didn't wake him.

The shadows crawled slowly across the pine-needle floor of
the wood. Tolya sat with the midafternoon sun warm and hard
on his back, his pistol braced on his updrawn knees. He threaded
his rosary carefully out through the neck of his shirt and slipped
the cool glass beads between his fingers.

*Rejoice, O Virgin Theotokos, Mary, full of grace, the Lord is with
thee . . .*

He spoke their names into the silence of the wood—Andriy
and Yakiv and Valentyn. Those probably weren't even their real
names, just their war names, but God would know he spoke
in sincerity—or Christ and the saints could intercede with sincerity, at least, where Tolya couldn't manage. He wasn't sorry
about Yakiv.

He didn't know about the rest—Taras and Ruslan, Anna and Iryna on their way to Toporiv. Anyway, he wasn't sure what to pray for Ruslan, who was Muslim. In the end, Tolya made a prayer to Saint Mykola for guidance and protection and a prayer to Saint Yuriy, the helper of soldiers, pressing the crucifix to his lips in amen.

Solovey was awake, watching him.

Tolya pushed the beads back into his shirt quickly, sliding the crucifix off his palm.

Solovey straightened against the trunk, bracing himself on his hands and shifting his legs very carefully.

"Was it your mother's?" he said.

"What?" Tolya said stupidly.

"That rosary." Solovey's voice was neutral. "Was it your mother's?"

Tolya swallowed. "Yes."

"Is that how they knew—the NKVD?"

"No, by her name—her maiden name, I mean."

"Marriage records?"

Tolya took the time to put his words together. Koval had asked him once. That was the only time he'd ever talked to anybody about Kuz'myn. Aunt Olena had never asked. At first, he'd thought that was just because she was afraid of Ivan, but she'd never asked even after Ivan was gone—and Comrade Lieutenant Spirin had never asked either, and Comrade Lieutenant Spirin wasn't afraid of anything.

Then he'd realized it was because they knew how much it hurt.

"They wanted names," he said, "the NKVD. Somebody had been putting out leaflets, telling people not to deliver their grain quotas, telling people that it was better to slaughter their stock than to let the Reds take it. They wanted names. So they made us come down to the churchyard—all of us, the whole village—and they made us watch. Took people at random and whipped them to pulp. Said they'd do it until they got a confession. My father confessed. Couldn't stomach it." He shrugged. His shoulders were tight. "They didn't know who he was when they took him. Just a face in a crowd. I mean—probably didn't take them long to find out, but the point is they didn't know to take us with him—my mother and me. They'd have sent us to one of the camps if they'd known—for being kin of a traitor."

That, too, had taken him a long time to understand. All you knew at seven was that the men with the blue caps were taking Papa away, and you couldn't go with him. Mama and Mrs. Tkachuk had held you back when you tried.

"My mother started using her maiden name after that. We were registered on the collective under her maiden name." He shrugged again, suddenly conscious of how much he'd let spill. "So. That was how."

Solovey was studying him. "Nobody betrayed you—not in the village, not on the collective?"

"No." And then, angry by reflex: "It doesn't make a difference when you're starving—Pole, Ukrainian. They were our people. We understood that in Kuz'myn."

"Somebody could have turned you in for an extra grain ration," Solovey said.

He had a knack for pricking the vulnerable spots. Tolya didn't say anything.

Solovey checked his wristwatch. "Wake me up next time, all right? The NKVD might if you don't, and I'd rather it was you."

"I betrayed them," Tolya said.

"What?"

"My mother. My father."

Solovey paused, halfway to his feet, leaning one-handed on the tree, looking at him.

"The Reds killed them," Tolya said. He swallowed against the knot in his throat. His heart was beating loudly in the silence—*thump, thump, thump* against his ribs. He wasn't going to make excuses. What was he going to say—*I was hungry in Voronezh?* "I collaborated," he said. "I fought for their murderers. I'm the one who betrayed them."

Solovey straightened very slowly, keeping his weight off his right leg. His face was blank.

"Is that what you think?" he said. "Or is that what you think I want to hear?"

Thump, thump, thump went Tolya's heart against his ribs.

"I don't know," he said, because he didn't.

"It's an easy word to throw around," Solovey said, "*collaborator.*"

"I put on the uniform," Tolya said.

"The uniform isn't what matters," Solovey said.

But he was looking away into the wood now, and Tolya knew he didn't really mean it.

* * *

They walked in the cuts between the hills, where the pine wood was deep and silent—Tolya ahead now and Solovey behind, handing himself carefully along by the pine trunks as though they were crutches, keeping his weight off the leg. He was sweating with the effort, though the air was cool.

"Tell me when to stop," Tolya said.

Solovey looked up blankly. "What?"

"Tell me when you need to stop. We'll stop."

He expected a hasty objection—the hissed breath and the half smile and *Don't be an idiot, Tolya.* He hadn't said as much, but Tolya knew he was embarrassed about sleeping so long earlier.

But Solovey didn't object. "All right," he said.

A little while later he said, "Mykola."

He'd dropped his pistol. He was holding himself up between two trees, his arms spread. Sweat ran on his face in dirty streaks. His skin was the color of ashes.

"Just for a second," he said. He grinned apologetically.

"Sit down," Tolya said.

"I'm all right. Just need to——"

"Sit down."

"You go," Solovey said. He was holding on to the trees very tightly. "I'll catch up."

"That's not going to work."

"I'll catch up, Mykola."

"I'm not Mykola." He picked up Solovey's pistol and tucked it in the waistband of his trousers. "Give me your knife," he said—and then, because Solovey had gone too far away to hear, he knelt and unlaced Solovey's boot and took the knife himself. "I'll be back, all right? I'm going to get you some water."

He left Solovey sitting there on the pine-needle floor. He pushed through bracken and birch brush, slipping over the moss beds, ducking the low branches. As he'd guessed, there was water farther down the cut—a thin, pebbly spring stream not yet run dry. He cut a strip of birch bark, curled it in a cone, and took water in the cone back up the cut.

Solovey was sitting with his back against a pine trunk, his legs stretched out. His face had cleared, though his skin was still pale.

"Tolya."

"Here—drink."

"I'm sorry. Didn't mean to scare you like that."

"It's all right. Drink."

Solovey took the cone. He cupped it in his hands, covering the seam to keep it from dripping.

"You should go," he said.

"I don't go unless you go. We already decided."

Solovey tipped the cone, drank a little, and dashed the remainder on his face. He smiled wearily.

"*You* decided—but you've got both guns, and the knife, so I'm not really in a position to argue."

"Who's Mykola?"

Solovey flung the bark away. "So you're asking the questions now too, is that it?"

"You know enough about me. I don't know anything about you—except that you had a grandfather and you like fishing and Polish beer."

"What else is there to know?"

"I don't even know your full name."

"Neither do the NKVD, and I'd like to keep it that way. Give me the gun." Solovey was holding out his hand. "Give me the gun, Tolya."

"Give me your name," Tolya said.

It was stupid and pointless, but they were both going to be dead soon, and he was tired of secrets, and he was tired of lies.

Solovey dropped his hand to his lap. He leaned his head back against the trunk. His face was blank.

"You've got to trust me," he said.

"All I've done is trust you. Why can't you trust me?"

"You're holding both guns, and the knife. It wouldn't exactly be *trust*, at this point."

Tolya didn't say anything.

"Give me the gun," Solovey said very quietly.

Tolya hesitated. Solovey's hand was outstretched again, waiting. Tolya took Solovey's pistol from his waistband and handed it over, grip first. Solovey took it and opened the magazine to count the rounds. Then he shoved the magazine back in. He looked up.

"Aleksey Yevhenovych Kobryn, from L'viv. I was studying mathematics at the polytechnic before all this. First year. I worked nights as a porter at the Hotel George to pay for my books, and the most daring thing I'd ever done was hop the tram between the city center and Zamarstynów. I'd used the last of my fare money to see Czarni play for the ice-hockey championship at the Citadel." He smiled again, wryly. "I wanted to play. Not for Czarni—they were Poles only. You understand. There was an all-Ukrainian team—Ukraina. But Czarni was the best."

Tolya digested this piece by piece—Solovey the mathematics student, Solovey the night porter, Solovey who spent his tram fares on ice-hockey matches. "And Mykola?"

Solovey holstered his pistol. He bent to lace his boot.

"My brother," he said. "About your age. He was."

Tolya's throat tightened with sudden shame. "He's dead?"

"Three years, three days."

July 27, 1941. It hadn't been the Reds who'd killed him. They'd abandoned Lwów a month earlier in the face of the German advance.

"The Germans? Why?"

Solovey's hands moved very slowly and carefully, threading the laces over the tongue of his boot.

"The Nazis made kill lists when they came," he said. "Jews they just killed indiscriminately, but for the rest of us there were lists. Political dissidents, academics, clergy, prominent citizens—the intelligentsia, the core of a potential resistance movement. You understand. The Reds had done the same thing two years before." He pulled the laces tight, breathing softly through his nose. "They had the names of some of the Polish faculty at the polytechnic, at the university, at the Medical Institute. The SS murdered them—twenty-five professors, with their families. Afterward, people started asking questions—why those names? Why only Poles? And then they started saying it was Ukrainian students, collaborators, supplying names and addresses for the lists. And then there were reprisals." He knotted the laces, looped them around, and knotted them again, not looking up. "They had my name," he said, "the Polish Resistance. They came looking for me. They found Mykola instead."

He finished with the laces. He brushed his nose with the backs of his fingers. He sat up, cupping his knees in his hands. His knuckles were white.

"We were going to get out," he said. "We were going to make for Turkey. We'd been planning it for weeks—us and Andriy. But we'd had a run-in with some Nazis, and I was laid up in a friend's place with a bum leg, and she and Andriy and I all had bounties on our heads and our photographs plastered on the

Nazis' wanted posters all over the city. Mykola was the only one who could risk going out for supplies."

He rubbed his knees absently, flexing his fingers.

"Andriy went out looking for him when he wasn't back by dark that night. Found him in our old flat. I don't know if he'd gone there on his own or if they'd just dumped him knowing we'd look for him there. Don't know how they'd have gotten the address. But they left a note for me on his body—stuck on a bayonet in his spine. Made sure I knew everything they'd done to him. Made sure I knew how long it took."

Tolya didn't say anything. Solovey took his pistol back out, snapping the slide. Tolya looked away. He swallowed the knot in his throat and waited. There was the murmur of the stream coming up faintly through the trees, and the whisper of the wind, and the beat of his heart, and there was the pistol in Solovey's hand.

But Solovey only pulled himself up against the tree, sucking his breath through his teeth.

"I could use that beer," he said.

Tolya shut his eyes. He couldn't look in Solovey's face.

"Solovey," he said.

"It's all right," Solovey said. "It's all right."

* * *

The cut gaped open onto a sunken streambed running north-south at the foot of a low ridge. They crossed the stream and went north for a while, walking in the streambed until the bank ran down. The sun had dipped behind the ridge. Moonlight shimmered across the water. Solovey was coming slowly behind, his head bowed, his shoulders hunched, one hand stretched to the bank. He caught the toe of his boot on a lip of rock and fell forward on his hands. His pistol clattered away over the rocks. He pushed himself up quickly. He was smiling, but his face was white.

"I'm all right," he said, brushing away Tolya's hand. "Just a bad step. Go get the gun."

Tolya picked his way back across the streambed. Machine-gun fire flashed out of the darkness on the east ridge. Bullets spat up sand on the far bank, splashing toward him across the water. He reeled and staggered back, feet slipping on the slick rocks, arms flailing. He fell, sprawling. He scrambled frantically backward, kicking over the rocks, scrabbling blindly with his hands.

Solovey was there, hauling him up and shoving him away.

Tolya caught Solovey's arms. "No," he said, "no, I'm not going to—"

"Yes, you are." Solovey tore his arms free. He put his hands on Tolya's chest and shoved, hard. "Run, Tolya."

Solovey stumbled around to face the hillside. "*Khay zhyve vil'na Ukrayina! Khay—*"

The bullets cut his legs from under him. He staggered and went down. He landed heavily on his knees, doubling over as though winded, leaning on his hands. Then he dove across the rocks. He slid on his stomach and snatched up the pistol. He pushed the muzzle under his chin.

Crack.

His head dropped, his body jerking.

And Tolya ran.

He flung himself up the bank, clawing at the black earth. He got a knee up on the rim and lunged for the cover of the trees. Bullets raced after him. Splintered wood stung his bare heels and the backs of his legs. Kicked-up leaves and dirt and detritus showered around him. He darted this way and that between the tree trunks, shoving through the underbrush, skidding and sliding over dry leaves. Branches tore at his face and hands, briars tugging at his trouser legs. He fell once, jamming his toes against a root and pitching headlong to the ground. The pistol flew from his hands. He staggered to his feet and went on, leaving the pistol, not caring. There were tears blurring his eyes, pricking on his face. His throat was closed. He couldn't see, and he couldn't breathe, and he couldn't think, and over the roar of blood in his ears he couldn't hear anything but Solovey's voice.

Run, Tolya.

So he ran.

21

HE RAN UNTIL HE COULDN'T RUN ANY MORE.

The moon had set by then. The wood was cool and dark and silent. He curled up on the pine needles, looping his arms around his knees, and he cried, without making any noise—eyes squeezed shut, shoulders shaking, face pressed to the dew-damp earth.

Then he was too tired to cry, and he lay numbly still, hugging his knees, listening to the nightingales.

His head cleared very slowly.

The trick was to focus on the immediate things, laying them out like playing cards in his head, and to go through them one by one.

So, first—his own pain.

He'd broken a toe. He couldn't see it in the dark, but he could definitely *feel* it. His left arm ached from shoulder to fingertips, and the ache sharpened to pain when he moved. The gash on the inside of his foot was bleeding again, and there was a new one, fairly deep, just above the ankle on the outside of his right calf, where a bullet must have grazed him. His hands bled and stung. He'd scraped the skin off his palms when he fell in the streambed. But he could walk; that was the important thing. He could run if he had to.

Second—what to do now.

He couldn't go to Hruszów. He didn't know what Solovey had expected to find there—more UPA?—but in any case the NKVD had probably guessed why Solovey had chosen this line westward through the wood. They would be going to Hruszów themselves—or they were there already, waiting, the way they'd been waiting at the cabin.

He couldn't go to the church on Ruska Street either. It didn't even matter that they would shoot him as a spy or a collaborator or a Pole. The point was that whoever had given up the cabin had probably given up the church too.

He could make Stryy in three or four days, if he risked open country—Stryy, the way Koval had wanted.

He needed a weapon. He could live off the land well enough, but there was a good chance that at some point between here and Stryy, it would come to shooting, not running, and he had no weapon now but Solovey's knife, tucked in his waistband. There was no question of finding his pistol again—not in the dark anyway—but there was another good chance that the NKVD hadn't taken the time to strip Solovey's body.

There was a very good chance that the NKVD weren't expecting him to backtrack.

Slowly, carefully, he uncurled himself and got up, brushing

the embedded sand from his raw palms, keeping his weight off his toes.

The machine gun picked up again.

He ducked low, sprawling on his stomach, but it was farther away than he'd thought—somewhere off westward. Five kilometers? Ten? The night air and the hills played games with sound. He waited, listening. There were other guns, answering guns, too distant to be distinct, but he recognized the *pop* of handguns and the quick, insistent *rat-tat-tat* of submachine guns.

They weren't friends, whoever they were—UPA, Poles, Germans. *Your chances aren't very good, Tolya.* But they were drawing the NKVD off.

He got up again and struck out eastward, the way he'd come.

* * *

He found the stream again a little before dawn. He was downstream from where he and Solovey had crossed. The water was slower and deeper here, the banks low and flat and wide. He walked along the western bank, upstream, until the bank was towering steeply over the water, the long slope of the ridge running away westward above him, the cut splitting off eastward below. From the top of the bank, he had a good, long view of the streambed in both directions.

The body was gone.

He slid down the bank in a shower of crumbly dirt. He

crossed the rocks. It had been just here. There was Solovey's blood on the dry, bone-white tops of the rocks. But the body was gone, and the pistol was gone.

Panic numbed his lips. He'd seen the shot. He'd seen the body jerk and go still. He was dead—he was *dead*—he *had* to be dead—*please, God, I wouldn't have left him alive*—

No. The body was there.

They'd taken him up on the eastern bank. They'd hung him by the wrists from the low branch of an alder tree on the edge of the bank. He was turning slowly back and forth in the breath of wind, bare feet dangling just off the ground. His uniform was in pieces around the base of the tree.

Tolya crossed the stream and went up the bank. There was a tightness between his shoulder blades, a cold lump of lead at the base of his throat. He took Solovey's knife in his hand and leaned into the tree trunk, standing on his good toes on an exposed root, stretching to his fingertips. He cut the rope from Solovey's wrists and eased the body down against the bole of the tree.

It had been cool enough in the night that the body wasn't swollen. With his head bowed in the half-light, you couldn't see the hole gaping under his chin, and with his eyes closed you could almost imagine that he was just sitting there very still against the tree, resting. Tolya tucked the knife back into his waistband. He picked up Solovey's jacket and put it over Solovey's body. He couldn't remember much of the akathist, but he knew the words of the funeral psalm.

"He who dwells in the shelter of the Most High," he said, aloud into the silence, "who abides in the shadow of the Almighty, will say to the Lord, 'My refuge and my fortress; my God, in whom I trust—'"

Then his throat closed, and he couldn't finish it.

He shut his eyes and said the Memory Eternal in his head. Then he took Solovey's boots and went a little way down the bank. He cuffed his trousers and washed his feet and lay looking up at the streaks of cloud in the dawn sky while his feet dried, the boots beside him.

* * *

He fell asleep, like an idiot.

He woke up to voices and booted footsteps coming toward him down the bank.

He grabbed Solovey's boots and slid up the bank into the trees, swearing in his head—Polish and Ukrainian—at his own stupidity. Midmorning sunlight was slanting across the stream-bed. He'd slept for hours.

The boots and voices came closer. They were speaking Ukrainian, not Russian. He could see them through the trees— two riflemen, wearing the green-gray jackets and trousers and side caps of the UPA.

He crouched low against the base of an old, gnarled oak, leaning his cheek on the mossy bark, listening. He heard them find

Solovey's body. He lifted his head a little and watched them lay him out gently on the black-earth bank. One of them knelt to look at the bullet wounds. The other was holding his rifle in the crook of his arm, looking at the ground. He found Tolya's footprints and came down the bank, following the prints. It wasn't going to take him much longer to find the fresh footprints going up into the trees, so Tolya slipped his feet into Solovey's boots and got up, holding up his hands, palms out.

"Don't shoot," he said. "Please, don't shoot. *Ya ukrayinets'*— I'm Ukrainian."

The rifle swung up. The rifleman sighted, finger ready on the trigger.

"Come down here—slowly. Keep your hands up."

Tolya stepped out from behind the tree. The other man came down the bank. He was about Solovey's age, tall and hard-faced, with fallow-brown hair shaven close to the sides of his head. There was oily black axle grease smeared in three-fingered streaks across his cheekbones. He was an officer. He wore a sidearm at his belt and the same bloodred stripes on his sleeves that Solovey had worn.

He slung his rifle over his shoulder and hooked his thumb on the sling. He looked Tolya over, pausing when he came to Solovey's boots.

He looked into Tolya's face.

"Explain," he said very coldly.

"I was with him," Tolya said, "with Solovey." His mouth was

dry, his heart pounding. He had to be very careful now. "My name is Tolya Korolenko."

"What happened?"

"They found our camp two nights ago—the NKVD. We were running. We were going to Hruszów." His throat had knotted tight again. He swallowed, blinking. "They caught up to us last night."

The officer came close. He put his hands in Tolya's pockets and brought out Solovey's spare clips.

"Where's the gun?"

"I lost it in the wood."

The officer shoved the clips into his own pocket. He took Solovey's knife from Tolya's waistband and turned it over in his hands, considering, holding the blade between thumb and forefinger and tapping the haft against his palm.

"What—did you come back to strip him?"

"No," Tolya said, through shut teeth. It wasn't really a lie. Solovey had told him to take the boots.

"*Sterv'yatnyk*," the officer said. "Vulture." He kicked Tolya's ankles.

Tolya didn't say anything. He knew how it was going to go, and there was nothing for it. The officer stuck the knife in his belt and returned to his search, more vigorously now. He knelt to pat down Tolya's trouser legs. He straightened again, running his hands roughly over Tolya's arms, feeling under Tolya's shirt. He brought out the rosary and held it in his clenched fist, looking at it.

He held it up in front of Tolya's face, dangling the crucifix.

"What is this?"

"That's a rosary," Tolya said, because there was nothing for it, and suddenly he didn't care.

Still, he knew better than to duck the fist. He couldn't win this fight, and he knew how it was going to go if he showed resistance. He felt every one of the officer's knuckles connect with the corner of his mouth. He spun and dropped, sprawling facedown on the bank—gratifyingly, he hoped, because he didn't want a rifle butt in his stomach, and he very much didn't want one between his legs.

The officer put a heavy boot between Tolya's shoulder blades. He unslung his rifle and pressed the cold steel muzzle to the back of Tolya's neck.

"I knew you were Polish shit," he said. He used the derogatory word—*lyakh* shit. To the other man he said, "Go get that rope."

Then he said, "No—wait."

He kicked Tolya's ribs. "Up," he said. He clipped the side of Tolya's face sharply with the nose of his rifle. "On your feet."

They went up the bank. Tolya stumbled ahead, blinking hot blood out of his eyes. The officer came behind, prodding him along with the mouth of the rifle, pushing him down to his knees beside Solovey's body.

"Dig," the officer said. He put his foot between Tolya's shoulder blades and shoved Tolya to his hands in the dirt. "Use your hands. That's what *lyakhy* are good for, isn't it?"

Tolya spit blood at the officer's feet.

That got him the rifle butt in the stomach. For a long moment afterward, he was curled over his knees, hugging his ribs and wheezing, while the wood spun around him and the breath trickled slowly back into his lungs. Out of the corner of his eye, he could see more UPA soldiers crossing the streambed, coming down the bank, crowding around to watch silently and solemnly, somewhat bored, as though this were one of Zampolit Petrov's political lectures.

He recognized one of the faces.

He lifted his head, blinking—dazedly, stupidly.

"Yakiv," he said.

Yakiv—alive and unhurt, leaning against the alder tree, smoking a cigarette, pretending not to hear him.

"Yakiv," Tolya said.

The officer's rifle was in his face. He caught the barrel in his hand and shoved it away. "Yakiv, look at—"

Then he was facedown in the dirt again, the officer's boot on his back, the mouth of the rifle kissing the base of his skull. He didn't care. He was too angry to care. He wrenched and twisted under the boot, fighting to raise his head.

"Look at me, Yakiv. You can tell them—you've got to tell them. Please, Yakiv. Tell them who I am."

Yakiv shifted against the tree. He took the cigarette out of his mouth and flicked the ash from the tip.

"They know who you are, *zradnyk*," he said. "Better start digging."

22

"I'LL MAKE YOU A DEAL," YAKIV SAID.

He was sitting against the alder tree with a *papasha* submachine gun across his knees, smoking and watching while Tolya dug in the crumbling black earth beneath the trees on the bank. The rest of the squad were making camp up in the wood. It was noon, and the sun was pouring through the trees. Tolya was sweating as he dug.

"Do you hear me?" Yakiv said. "I can get you out of here."

Tolya ignored him. He dug—head bent, teeth clenched. He'd dug with his hands first, scratching at the dirt until his fingers were torn and bloody. Then they'd gotten impatient or bored with the game, and somebody had brought him a trench spade.

"Squad Leader Vitalik thinks you're Polish Resistance— thinks you're an infiltrator, a spy." Yakiv was leaning back comfortably against the tree trunk, feet spread. "Why shouldn't he? You show up, and a day later the NKVD blow us to hell."

They would shoot him when he was done. Tolya knew that. Dig and then die. They would tell him to stand at the edge of the hole, or to lie on his face at the bottom, and they would give him the *genickschuss*, the single shot to the back of the neck.

"Do you know what Vitalik does to spies?" Yakiv said.

Tolya's shoulder was hurting badly, the lips of the wound pulling and cracking, but there was nothing for it. They would shoot him when he was done, and they would shoot him if he dawdled.

"Solovey was just going to shoot you," Yakiv said. "Bullet to the brain, nice and quick." He demonstrated with the *papasha* carelessly, lifting the muzzle to Tolya's face and mouthing the sound of the shot, *rat-tat-tat*, miming the recoil. "You know that, don't you? He was going to shoot you when he was done with you."

He was dead either way.

"He wanted a sniper," Yakiv said. "That was why. He wanted to take out Volkov. He was going to shoot you as soon as he was done with you. That's what he told the commander. That was the condition for getting you out."

Don't listen, Tolya.

"Don't believe me?" Yakiv said. "He told us later. It was all planned out. Of course he didn't know you were a Pole. Might have changed the plan a little. He hated Poles. He hated Poles more than he hated Volkov. He hated Volkov in theory. He hated Poles in practice." Yakiv smiled. "He never took Polish prisoners. He'd line them up afterward—walk down the line and plug them in the forehead. *Bang, bang, bang.*"

Don't listen, Tolya. Dig.

"I think that's the difference, you know?" Yakiv said. "He was a gentleman, Solovey. Bullet to the brain—*bang*—done, and he'd look you in the eye while he did it. Vitalik, now. Vitalik is an animal."

Dig, Tolya.

"I've seen him take all day on a Polish prisoner," Yakiv said.

Dig, Tolya.

"He doesn't use this," Yakiv said, lifting the *papasha*. "He uses this." He stretched out his leg and showed Tolya the knife in his boot.

Dig.

Yakiv slid the knife back into his boot.

"Whenever you want to talk, Tolya," he said, "I'll talk. Remember that."

Dig and die.

"Whenever you want to talk," Yakiv said, "while you've still got your tongue." He smiled and puffed his cigarette.

* * *

They didn't shoot him when he was done.

They pulled him out of the hole and tied his hands with the rope he'd cut from Solovey's wrists, and they made him lie on his stomach on the bank while they put Solovey in the hole and covered him with the black earth.

The problem, as he understood, was not *just* that he was Polish and not *just* that he was a collaborator.

The problem, as he understood, was that Vitalik thought he'd killed and stripped Solovey.

So—"We're going to talk," Vitalik said, "you and I, the two of us."

The rest of the squad had gone back up to the camp. They were alone on the bank, he and Vitalik, and Vitalik had pulled him up by an elbow and sat down cross-legged, facing him—closely enough that Tolya could smell the bittersweet, burnt-grass smell of makhorka on his jacket. Vitalik took a packet of the red-brown tobacco and a rolling paper from his breast pocket. He rolled a cigarette on his thigh, careful not to let any of the tobacco spill. His hands were like Solovey's hands—smooth, middle-class hands with long, slender fingers—except Solovey's hands had been whole. Vitalik's hands, both of them, were missing the tips of the little fingers, below the knuckle.

Vitalik folded the packet of tobacco and put it in his breast pocket. He stuck the cigarette between his teeth. He caught Tolya's eye and followed Tolya's gaze to his hands.

"A memento of the Brygidki," he said, "courtesy of your friends. Do you know the Brygidki?"

"The prison."

"Not always. They built it as a convent. That's where the name comes from: It was a convent of the Bridgettines. The Hapsburgs made it a prison." Out came a lighter—unhurriedly, methodically. It was a performance, all of it, done with the precision of long practice. "The Reds made it a slaughterhouse. It's a natural progression."

Vitalik brushed the tip of his cigarette against the flame.

"Here's how this is going to work," he said. "Very simple. I ask questions, you answer." He put the lighter in his pocket. He slipped Solovey's knife from his belt, leaned very close to Tolya, smelling of makhorka, and reached around to cut the rope from Tolya's wrists. He put the knife back in his belt and pulled Tolya's hands across his lap, turning the palms up. He pushed Tolya's left sleeve up to the elbow.

"This is what happens when you lie to me," he said.

He took the cigarette out of his mouth, blew the smoke into Tolya's face, and touched the burning tip to the inside of Tolya's wrist.

Tolya's hands jerked reflexively. Vitalik's fingers tightened around his wrists.

"Now that's clear," Vitalik said, "we'll talk."

Tolya bit the inside of his cheek. There was an angry purple welt bubbling up on his wrist. "I'm not Resistance."

"You inform for them."

"No."

Vitalik held the cigarette in two fingers, watching his face. "But you inform for the NKVD."

"Not if I'm Resistance. Make up your mind."

The tip of the cigarette dipped very close to his skin. "Why not? You're all Red collaborators, you *lyakh* shit."

"They're disarming them. They're sending the officers to the camps. They're shooting the rest—the ones who won't join the Front."

"How do you know?"

"Because I've seen it. They've been shooting them in the square outside the station."

"Is that why you killed your *zampolit*?" Vitalik said. "Didn't like to watch him shooting Poles?"

He couldn't answer. He blinked up stupidly into Vitalik's face.

Vitalik let go of Tolya's hand while he slipped the cigarette back into his mouth. He took a drag, breathing the smoke out softly through his nostrils.

"Yes—I know about Zampolit Petrov," he said.

"Solovey got me out." It burst out before he could stop it. He was furious suddenly. "Do you know that? Your own commander ordered him to get me out."

"Incorrect." Vitalik pulled on his cigarette long and slowly, working the tip to a red glow. "Command *advised of the situation*. Solovey made his own decision about trying to get you out—a stupid decision, but he wanted a sniper."

"No."

"No what?"

"That wasn't why. That wasn't his reason."

"I was there," Vitalik said. "I know it was his reason."

"Not his only reason. He didn't need a sniper after two nights ago. If he thought I was a traitor, he'd have shot me then, not run with me." Tolya's hands clenched. "Don't try to tell me he thought I was a traitor."

"The point of relevance here isn't whether you're a traitor," Vitalik said. "You were a traitor and a collaborator the day you put on the Reds' uniform. The point of relevance here is that Solovey is dead."

"I didn't betray him."

The tip of the cigarette touched his wrist again. Tolya shut his eyes.

"This goes one of two ways, Tolya," Vitalik said, "but you should know they both end in the same place."

"I didn't betray him. It had to be one of his own men."

The tip of the cigarette paused, hovering.

"So?" Vitalik said. "Explain."

"We weren't going to Hruszów, first. There was a cabin. Solovey said he'd been using it as a munitions dump. He was going to hold out there while things cooled down."

"So?"

"They were waiting for us—the NKVD. They knew to wait for us there. And Solovey said the only ones who knew about that place were the men of his squad."

Vitalik bent his head and put the cigarette back in his mouth, holding Tolya's wrist in his fingers. His face was expressionless.

"You're lying," he said. "You led him to them."

"You can think that if you want. I don't care."

Vitalik let go of Tolya's hand suddenly. He unholstered his pistol and pressed the mouth of the pistol to Tolya's forehead.

"And now?"

The metal bushing was cold on his skin, and Tolya flinched, despite himself. Vitalik's finger was ready on the trigger, his thumb clear of the slide, his hand steady—the precision of long practice. There was a knot in Tolya's throat, an aching hollow where his heart should be. There were the words of the kontakion fluttering through his head: *With the saints give rest, O Christ, to the soul of Thy servant, where there is neither sickness, nor sorrow, nor sighing, but life everlasting . . .*

He met Vitalik's eyes and shrugged.

"I don't care," he said. "Do it."

And Vitalik pulled the trigger.

For a split second that lasted an eternity, Tolya was frozen, waiting, his breath caught against the knot in his throat. There would be the *crack* of the shot first, then the flash of light, then the world to come—but instead there was the *click* of the bolt on an empty chamber, and Vitalik was tapping the mouth of the pistol gently, once, twice, on Tolya's shut lips. He holstered the pistol and tipped the ash of his cigarette onto the back of Tolya's hand.

"Not yet, Tolya," he said. "First we take care of your friends."

* * *

He spent the rest of the afternoon tied to a tree at the edge of the camp, watching them clean rifles and reload cartridges and prime grenades, wondering whether it was true, after all, that Solovey was going to shoot him once Volkov was dead—whether that had been the plan right to the end—or whether at some point between here and Lwów the plan had changed.

It must have changed. Maybe not the first day. Maybe not even that next morning on the ridge. Maybe that had only been a test—all that stuff about *options* and *educated choices*. Maybe Solovey would have put a bullet in his brain then, if he'd chosen wrongly. Maybe he'd been in a marksman's sights the whole time he'd been up on that ridge. But in the cut yesterday, when he'd asked for the truth, for Solovey's trust, and Solovey—the mathematics student, the night porter, *Aleksey Yevhenovych Kobryn, from L'viv*—had given it to him, surely it had changed by then.

Surely it had changed by the streambed.

They had a smoky wood fire burning on a strip of bare dirt beneath the trees. They fed it through the afternoon. At first he thought that Vitalik must not be as careful as Solovey when it came to smoke—either because he thought they were deep enough in the hills that it didn't matter or just because he was that stupid. Then he saw three of Vitalik's men taking a heavy machine gun, a *dashka*, up through the trees to the top of the ridge, wheeling the mount and wearing the cartridge belts looped on their necks like priests' stoles, and he realized Vitalik knew perfectly well about smoke.

Vitalik came and cut him loose toward dusk.

"I want you to see," he said.

They went up to the ridge. There was a breath of wind rustling the pine boughs. Through the gaps in the dark treetops, Tolya could see the moon waxing bright and clear in the twilit sky. He sat with Vitalik against the bole of a towering oak, just aside from where they'd mounted the *dashka*—Vitalik with his rifle across his knees, his right arm resting companionably on Tolya's shoulders. The rest of the squad were spread in a semicircle around the *dashka*. They waited in silence, watching the empty campsite.

Then somebody said, "Look."

Black shapes moved in the darkness below, coming up through the trees from the streambed.

Vitalik bent his head to Tolya's. His breath tickled Tolya's ear.

"One sound from you," he said softly. He slipped his hand under Tolya's chin, crooking his arm across Tolya's throat. He clenched his fingers to a fist. "Understand?"

Tolya watched, Vitalik's arm tight across his throat, while the NKVD squad set a perimeter and raked the campsite with a salutatory burst of submachine-gun fire. Some of Vitalik's men took advantage of the noise, fanning out quickly and silently into the trees to draw a loose cordon around the campsite. Vitalik lifted his free hand slowly, palm up, preparing to signal.

On the other side of the *dashka*, somebody opened up early— one short burst from a *papasha* as a finger twitched too soon on a trigger. Vitalik swore through his teeth, sliding his arm from Tolya's neck. He shoved Tolya down against the base of the tree and shouldered his rifle.

The slope exploded in gunfire. The *dashka* opened up, pounding like a sledgehammer—*thud, thud, thud*. Tracers streaked up and down the slope. Somebody lobbed a grenade. It tore through the trees—*bang*—and for a second the whole hillside was lit up red and white, burned onto the inside of Tolya's eyelids. Vitalik was on his feet, rifle shouldered, legs braced against the recoil, hand flying as he worked the bolt. He emptied his clip and lowered the rifle, planting the butt between his feet. He held up his left hand in a fist.

The *dashka* fell silent. Somewhere there was the *crack* of one more rifle shot, echoing away through the trees.

Somebody was whimpering in the darkness down the slope.

Vitalik slung his rifle furiously. He hauled Tolya up by an elbow and shoved him, kicking his ankles. "Walk."

Tolya stumbled down the slope. Vitalik followed, pistol in

hand. One of Vitalik's men was coming up to them from the camp.

"Your signal—"

Vitalik swore savagely.

"What do you want to do?"

Vitalik jerked his chin. "Get the weapons and ammunition. Then we're getting the hell out of here. They'll be back."

There were three NKVD dead. The fourth man, the wounded man, was kicking across the dirt at the edge of the thin firelight, trying to push himself away. He wasn't whimpering now. He was holding his throat in his hands, gurgling blood.

Vitalik holstered his pistol. He went over to the wounded man. He knelt, prying the man's trembling hands gently loose, speaking softly in Russian. He looked at the wound on the man's neck. Then he sat back on his heels.

"Tolya," he said.

The rest of the squad were coming down into the circle of firelight, spreading out to strip the dead. "Come here, Tolya," Vitalik said. He got up, slipping Solovey's knife from his belt. He put the knife in Tolya's hand and brought his pistol back out.

"Kill him," he said, and he lifted the pistol to Tolya's face.

Tolya didn't move. The NKVD soldier twisted and gasped on the dirt, pushing with his heels.

"Kill him, Tolya," Vitalik said. His voice was quiet. His finger was ready on the trigger, thumb clear of the slide, hand steady— the precision of long practice.

And there was a part of Tolya that knew this soldier was going to die anyway, and maybe it was better this way, better at his hand, because Vitalik would take his time.

And there was a part of him, colder and harder, that wanted to do it—for his mother, and for his father, and for Comrade Lieutenant Spirin, and for Koval, and for Solovey, and for everyone and for everything they'd ever taken from him.

And there was a part of him that said, *But they have not taken this.*

He looked in Vitalik's eyes and said, "No."

"Kill him, Tolya," Vitalik said again, quietly.

He dropped the knife.

"No," he said.

For a moment, Vitalik stood very still, looking at him—eyes narrowed slightly, as though he were working out a puzzle. Then he swung his pistol smoothly down and let off a quick shot, hand jerking back tightly with the recoil. The soldier gurgled and sighed, his body going slack. Vitalik let off another shot and another, and another, and each time the soldier's body shivered and jumped a little on the dirt. Vitalik stepped close, leaning over the body to empty the clip.

Then he straightened, turned the pistol in his hand, and smashed the butt across Tolya's face.

23

THERE WAS DARKNESS, FOR A VERY LONG TIME,
and the smell of damp earth.

He was in a root cellar. He'd figured that out pretty quickly.
It had taken him a little longer to figure out that he was blind-
folded. He was standing with his back to a wooden post, his arms
stretched above his head, wrists and waist and ankles roped to
the post. There was cool, smooth-packed earth under his bare
feet, and the groaning of floorboards above him, and sometimes
the soft crackle of a wireless and the murmur of voices.

Always when Vitalik came there was first the creak and scrape
of a door, then the slow *clomp, clomp, clomp* of Vitalik's boots
coming down wooden stairs.

The routine was always the same. First there would be
questions, all manner of questions. There would be the technical questions—about his training in Moscow and his orders
and whether there were any other infiltrators, and how many,
and where, and for how long. Then there would be the reflec-
tive questions, such as what it felt like knowing he was going

to die a coward and a traitor and a godless Stalinist whore and whether he thought anybody would care he was dead (because they wouldn't, Vitalik said, not even his masters in Moscow)— but of course it didn't matter, did it, because a godless Stalinist whore didn't need anybody to pray rest for his soul.

And if he didn't answer, or if he didn't answer satisfactorily, then there would be pain.

There was all manner of pain as there was all manner of questions. He was never sure which it would be beforehand because Vitalik never took off the blindfold for the questionings. Most basically, and most often, there were Vitalik's fists and boots and cigarette tips because when Vitalik lost his patience—which was regularly—those were his quickest resorts.

Sometimes Tolya was on his knees against the post while Vitalik savaged his back with electrical cables. That wasn't often because there wasn't much return from it relative to the effort involved—"inversely proportional," Solovey would say. He blacked out too quickly, and he couldn't remember things when Vitalik poured water over his face to wake him up—not the right things anyway, not the things Vitalik wanted to hear, just stupid things like the churchyard in Kuz'myn, and the closet in Ivan's apartment in Kyiv, and the way he used to think that if you clenched your teeth and held your breath and were very careful not to make any noise, then maybe people would forget you were there. It never worked, but that didn't stop him from trying.

Only very occasionally did Vitalik have patience and care enough to use the knife. Yakiv had been exaggerating about that.

* * *

He came down once, Yakiv. He sidled against the wall, smoking—not that he'd taken off the blindfold either, but Tolya could smell the makhorka on him.

"It doesn't have to be like this, Tolya. I can get you out of here. All I need is a name. Do you hear me? Just a name."

And because he'd already used up his reserves that day—that night?—facedown on the floor, biting the insides of his cheeks to bloody ribbons while Vitalik dressed his raw back with vodka, Tolya said, "What name?"

He could almost hear Yakiv smile, pleased with his victory.

"The source," Yakiv said. "The man in the Front—the one who gave your name to the commander. Who is he?"

And he was too long in answering, too busy trying to figure out the trick—because he was sure it was a trick—so Yakiv prodded him a little, impatiently.

"The source, the source. Who requested the extraction?"

"I don't know," Tolya said.

"Just his name."

"I don't know."

"Listen—sooner or later Vitalik's going to realize he's wasting his time on you, as much fun as he's having."

"Ask him. He was there."

"He doesn't know. None of the squad leaders know."

"Ask your commander."

"I don't think you understand," Yakiv said. "I'm not with the UPA anymore."

And Tolya didn't say anything because he *did* understand, all at once, in that moment—

Yakiv, who'd told Solovey they couldn't make the shot that night, because the hotel girl had said Volkov was up in Zhovkva.

Yakiv, who'd had the watch on the ridge.

Yakiv, whose finger had slipped on the trigger of the *papasha*, springing Vitalik's trap too soon.

Yakiv, now, leaning against the wall, smoking carelessly, saying, "She's still alive, you know—your girlfriend."

"No."

"Nataliya—that's her name, isn't it? The pretty little blond."

Tolya wrenched against the post, jerking his wrists. Yakiv laughed.

"Calm down. I said she's still alive."

"Where?"

"Where do you think? She was insurance. They want the source."

"I don't know."

"Somebody knew you shot Petrov that night. Somebody knew and didn't talk."

"I don't know. I swear I don't know."

"Maybe if you think really hard. Think about Natalka."

It was like a fist to the gut, hearing it on Yakiv's tongue—the pet name he'd never dared use for her even in the safety of his head, *Natalka, little Nataliya.* He swallowed bile and fury in a painful, solid lump.

"Please," he said.

And Yakiv was silent, breathing smoke softly into Tolya's face.

"Well," he said finally. "I've done in five minutes what Vitalik hasn't been able to do in three days. I've made you beg."

"I'll tell him. I'll tell him it was you."

"Go ahead," Yakiv said. He was going up the stairs—*clomp, clomp, clomp.* "See if you can make him believe you."

* * *

Later, of course, when the anger had run cold, it occurred to him that Yakiv had just been a test—part of the game, Vitalik's game.

Because it *was* Vitalik's game, all of it. It was Vitalik bringing him lukewarm, metallic water in a battered canteen, or heels of dry, tasteless black bread, and Vitalik untying him from the post and slipping off the blindfold and sitting and smoking and watching while Tolya ate and drank and pissed in the pot in the corner, and Vitalik tying him up and blindfolding him again afterward, and Vitalik kneeling beside him on the packed earth when the pain was done, speaking softly into Tolya's ear as his smooth, maimed hands cleaned and dressed and bandaged—carefully, very carefully, almost gently, because it wouldn't do for him to die just yet. Soon, but not yet.

It was Vitalik, once, sitting against the wall, smoking his cigarette and reading through a dossier by the light of the single electric bulb, saying, without looking up, "Why wouldn't you kill him?"

Tolya blinked stupidly in Vitalik's face. He was holding his bread in his hand, tearing it with careful fingers and putting it piece by little piece into his swollen mouth, packing it against his cheek and letting his saliva soften it until he could suck it down because he couldn't chew it. Vitalik's fists had turned his gums to bloody mush.

"That soldier," Vitalik said. He shuffled the papers and looked up. "Do you remember, Tolya?"

And Tolya remembered the NKVD soldier, with his life pouring out through the gash in his throat, kicking circles in the dirt at Vitalik's feet.

"Yes," he said. His voice had long ago stopped being his own. It came out in a whisper, low and clotted and rasping.

"Why wouldn't you kill him? It was stupid—blowing cover for him. He was dead anyway. You knew that."

There was, of course, no use protesting or denying or contradicting. There was no use pointing out that he had no cover to blow because he wasn't NKVD. He'd learned at Vitalik's fists and Vitalik's feet and under Vitalik's knout and under Vitalik's knife that it was easier to let Vitalik believe what he wanted to believe.

"Was he a friend?" Vitalik asked.

"Yes," Tolya said, because it was easier that way.

"What was his name?"

"Yura," Tolya said.

Vitalik smiled around his cigarette. He flicked the ash from the tip.

"Don't lie to me, Tolya," he said.

* * *

There was darkness, mostly.

His parents were there, sometimes, in the uneven stretches between the questionings, or Aunt Olena, or Father Stepan, who'd outlasted the famine only to disappear in the night during the purges, or Father Dmytro, who'd been shot in the church-yard and who would still say—Tolya knew he would still say—there was nothing for it but to love, only to love, as God only loved.

Sometimes it was Koval, cool and blond, putting cool, gentle fingertips on his swollen face, pressing cool, gentle lips to his swollen lips, and his eyelids, and his jaw, and his throat—and he was back in Kyiv, and it was December 1943, two weeks before Christmas and six hours before they were to cross the Dnieper on the new offensive, and the snow was falling new and clean and white on the ruined shell of the city, and they were watching it from the bell tower of Holy Sophia, warm and close under his greatcoat, finally unguarded enough to talk about *after*—because it had seemed then, for the first time in so many years, that there really would be an *after*.

Sometimes it was Comrade Lieutenant Spirin, sitting patiently beside him, just sitting, *being there*, not saying anything and not needing to say anything, the way he'd sat on the bank in Voronezh, letting Tolya eat every last one of his lend-lease tinned pork rations.

Sometimes, when the pain had been very bad, it was Solovey, putting his hands on Tolya's shoulders and leaning in close to say, *It's all right, Tolya, it's all right*—and it was.

Then he knew it wasn't just Solovey, but his patron, his name saint, the first Anatoliy, Anatoliy of Laodicea, Anatoliy the Peacemaker, Anatoliy the Mathematician, come to comfort and to strengthen in the hour of death.

* * *

There was gunfire.

He heard it distantly at first, then much closer. *That* was the *dashka*—thud, thud, thud. Voices shouted and doors slammed and boots pounded across the floor. The wooden post shuddered at his back. Mortar fire? A grenade? There was the heavy *thump* of a falling body somewhere above and another spattering of gunfire.

Then there was silence.

After a little while, there were slow, careful footsteps across the floorboards. The door creaked and scraped open. Voices floated down the stairs, unfamiliar voices—Polish voices.

Somebody was calling for a light.

Tolya waited.

They came down the stairs. One of them tripped and caught himself and laughed—and then abruptly stopped laughing, and Tolya knew they'd seen him.

Footsteps approached cautiously across the packed earth. Uncertain fingers slid over Tolya's throat.

"Alive?" somebody asked quietly from the staircase.

"I think so." The fingers went away from Tolya's throat. "Do you have your knife?"

Then there were hands on Tolya's ankles and fingers fumbling at the ropes. A knife blade eased between the loops.

"Ours?" the voice on the staircase asked.

"No."

"NKVD?"

"I don't know."

"I'll go get Janek."

"No, come here. Help me take him up."

They cut the ropes from his waist and wrists and laid him carefully on the floor. He lay holding himself very still, his cheek pressed on the cool, packed earth, while they debated how best to get him up the stairs. In the end, they carried him up like a sandbag between them, cradling his shoulders and knees. They put him facedown on the floorboards at the top of the stairs.

"Holy hell, it's bad," one of them said.

Tolya felt somebody bend over him.

"Can you hear me? I'm going to take off the blindfold. Shut your eyes. The light might hurt."

Tolya squeezed his eyes shut. Fingers slipped under the blindfold, loosened it, and tugged it off.

"You stay here with him," one of the voices said. "I'm going to get Janek."

Booted footsteps went away across the floorboards. Hands lifted Tolya's head gently. Water trickled over his face. The spout of a canteen pushed between his cracked lips.

"Here—try to drink," the voice at Tolya's ear said.

Water ran over Tolya's teeth, cool and soft on his swollen gums, washing over his tongue and down his aching throat.

"Can you hear me?" the voice said. "*Czy rozumiesz po polsku*— can you understand Polish?"

Tolya swallowed. He wanted to laugh. He wanted to cry. He turned his head away from the canteen.

"*Tak*," he said hoarsely, in the voice that wasn't his own.

"How long have you been down there?"

And then he *was* crying, shivering as with cold. "I don't know."

"What are you? NKVD?"

"No."

"Are you Polish? Russian? German?"

"I don't know," Tolya said. "I don't know."

IV

ALEKSEY

Sunday, June 29–Thursday, July 3
1941

24

IT WAS DARK WHEN I WOKE UP. I WAS A LITTLE
surprised Mykola had let me sleep so long. I sat up to tell him
so and flopped right back down, wheezing. I wasn't quite so
blessedly numb now.

Neither was I under the old castle wall.

I was in a bed. Those were feather pillows I'd flopped down
against—*pillows*, as in more than one pillow. The mattress was
feathers too. The sheets were cool and slippery. My left thigh
had been bandaged—really bandaged, I mean, not wrapped with
the ripped-up, bloody bits of my shirt—and there was a heavy
plaster casing around my right calf. I was wearing a nightshirt
that certainly wasn't mine.

I lay blinking up at a high, molded ceiling, waiting for everything to start making sense. I wasn't tied to a chair in a wine
cellar, and I wasn't dead. Either of those would have been
understandable. Satin sheets and featherbeds were beyond my
capacity at the moment.

I started experimenting. I couldn't move my legs without

considerable pain, but I could reach the bed table with one hand if I stretched. I fumbled blindly over the tabletop. I knocked over a glass that hit the floor with an odd, meaty thump. Somebody swore. I found a lamp and tugged the pull chain. Electric light flooded the room. Mykola was sitting up on the floor, wiping water from his face with the back of his hand.

"I guess that wasn't the floor," I said.

"No, just my head."

"Glad it wasn't anything important."

"Of course I'm all right," he said. "Thanks for asking."

He'd been cleaned up too. There was still a line of ripe, purple, knuckle-sized bruises across his cheekbone, but the blood was off. He was wearing a pair of striped pajamas big enough for three of him. The ends of the sleeves hung past his fingertips. He had to hold the pants bunched at the waist to keep them from slipping down when he stood. The hems trailed behind him like streamers.

He took the glass and vanished through a doorway to the right. I heard a tap running. He came back with the refilled glass and put it back on the bed table.

"Historically, that's been a bad idea," I said.

"You can take another codeine tablet if you need to. It's been more than three hours." He showed me the pill case—silver, engraved with a curling monogram in Latin letters I couldn't untangle just then. "And there's some dinner left in the refrigerator. We couldn't keep you awake long enough to feed you."

"Who's *we*? Where are we, anyway?"

He didn't look at me. He picked up his duvet from the floor, wrapped himself in it, head to toe, and sat down in the armchair, looking something like a sausage rolled up in a puff pastry.

"The Kijeks'," he said.

"What?"

"The nurse—Mrs. Kijek. The one with the card."

"No, I know. I meant *what*?"

"I didn't know what else to—"

"Damn it, Mykola. Did you try thinking?"

His face paled. "Must have been too busy saving your life. Sorry."

I sank back against the pillows, defeated, digging the heels of my hands into my eyes.

"I didn't know what else to do," Mykola said again, miserably.

"I know," I said. "I know. I'm sorry. I didn't mean to yell at you." I dropped my hands. "How'd you get me here, anyway? You didn't carry me, did you?"

"You don't think I could?"

"It's not about whether I think you could. It's about the fact that I wasn't wearing any pants."

That got me a ghost of a smile. "We brought you in Mr. Kijek's car."

"Nobody saw me."

"No."

Maybe this wasn't so bad. Unless somebody saw us and

talked, or unless the Kijeks found out about the price on my head and took an opportunity to curry favor with the new regime, the Nachtigallen would never think to look—

Wait.

Oh, merciful God.

"We've got to go," I said.

"What?"

"We've got to go now."

"Aleks, nobody saw you. Nobody knows we're here."

"Andriy was there when she gave me the card," I said. "He heard me tell you the address."

25

"THAT LEG IS BROKEN," MRS. KIJEK TOLD ME
bluntly. "You're not going anywhere."

She'd heard us talking and seen the light under the door and
come in with a plate of warmed-over pork roast and potatoes. It
must not have been quite as late as it seemed. She and her husband were both still in dinner dress. Mr. Kijek leaned against the
doorframe with a cigarette and a snifter of cognac or Scotch—
something amber-colored and expensive anyway. Something
about him seemed oddly familiar—maybe his face, maybe the
way he leaned on the jamb, exuding a vague, aristocratic care-
lessness. Maybe I'd seen him at the Hotel George? I couldn't
put a finger on it. He seemed content to let Mrs. Kijek do the
talking. I realized when she directed a remark to him in Polish
over her shoulder that he must not understand Ukrainian.

I pushed potatoes around the plate, wondering how much
I should explain. I could tell them about the price on my head
and hope they'd be *principled* enough just to turn us out, not
to hand us over. My hopes weren't very high. Anybody who'd

done this well through two years of Soviet occupation had either paid protection money or collaborated. They'd hand us over to the Nachtigallen to save their own necks.

"We've got enemies," I said. "You're in danger as long as we stay."

She sat on the edge of the bed and pulled back the duvet to check the bandage above my knee. "They're not going to find you here."

"They've got the address."

She paused.

"I trusted the wrong person," I said. "I'm sorry."

She lifted the edge of the bandage with a fingertip. Then she smoothed it down, satisfied, and draped the duvet back across my legs. Her face was expressionless.

"German or Polish?"

"Ma'am?"

"Your enemies. German or Polish?"

"It's not political," I said.

I said it a little too quickly, and I'd hesitated a little too long. The lie sounded thin. Out of the corner of my eye, I saw Mykola shift in the armchair. Mr. Kijek was swirling his cognac in the doorway, head tilted, studying me. He was scowling. He didn't need to dance the dance to know I'd just put a foot wrong.

Mrs. Kijek looked at me very hard for a second—just long enough to make it clear she knew I was lying.

"We can move you tomorrow," she said. "The car's on loan to a

friend tonight. You're safer here than out on the streets for now."
She patted my arm. "Eat, Aleksey. You've lost a lot of blood."

I was pretty sure anything I put in my stomach was just going
to come right back up again, but I managed three bites of potato
and a mouthful of pork, which was a good enough start to convince them I'd finish the rest on my own. I put the plate down as
soon as they'd shut the door.

"There'll be Germans all over the place tomorrow," Mykola
said bleakly.

"We're not going to be here tomorrow," I said. "We're getting out tonight."

"You heard what she said."

And I'd seen what she hadn't said. That look had told me all
I needed to know.

"She was lying."

"What?"

"You really think the car's *on loan to a friend*? Who borrows a
car at this time of night? She's buying time so they can get a message off to the Polish Resistance. They think that's who we're running from. They think we're UPA. They're going to give us up."

Mykola was silent.

"This is their front—all of this." I waved at the room in general. "Live like rich suck-ups and fund their Resistance right
under the Reds' noses."

He didn't look convinced. "Why would they think we're
UPA? They don't know who we are."

"They know *what* we are. The Resistance will figure out *who*."

He pulled his duvet tight and looked at the wall. "Maybe you're wrong," he said.

"When have I ever been wrong?"

He cast a disdainful glance at my legs. "I can think of at least once."

"When have I ever been wrong about Poles?"

"You trusted Andriy *just because* he's Ukrainian. What does that say about distrusting people *just because* they're Poles?"

"It says one of us pays attention to history."

"It wasn't Poles who shot you," he said. "You're just a fascist bigot. You're like Papa."

"We're leaving tonight," I said.

He scoffed. "You can't even walk."

"I can walk."

"You can't walk. You think you can because you're doped up on codeine."

I swung my legs off the bed to prove him wrong, deposited my weight on my left foot, and sank promptly to the floor as my knee buckled.

He looked down at me indifferently.

"Twice," he said.

I pulled myself awkwardly back into the bed. That had hurt like hell, but I wasn't going to let him see it. I wasn't going to concede total defeat either.

"Well, you're going, even if I'm not," I said.

"Make me," he said.

"Listen to me, Mykola."

"What are you going to do—throw a pillow at me?"

"Think about what happens if I'm right," I said.

I knew he must have been thinking about it because he didn't fling that one back at me. He shrugged.

"I'd stay anyway," he said. "But you're wrong."

* * *

I spent a long time lying awake in the dark, listening for booted footsteps and watching the door, waiting for it to burst open and gunmen to rush in, the way they'd come for Papa. But when the door did finally open it was just Mrs. Kijek with a breakfast tray and her nurse's bag and my coat, laundered and neatly pressed, and a shirt and trousers and pair of shoes that must have been Mr. Kijek's. There was sunlight poking in through the tiny holes in the window blinds. The clock on the bed table said half past ten.

Mykola was gone.

I sat bolt upright.

"Where is he?"

It came out in a snarl, but she didn't seem to notice. She put the tray on the bed table.

"He found the bookshelves in the study," she said.

My mouth moved faster than my brain. "He can't read Polish."

She must have heard that without really listening. She was holding my wrist in her fingers, feeling the pulse.

"I think he was looking at the atlases," she said. "I think he's also made friends with the cat." She laid a cool wrist on my forehead. Then she pulled back the duvet and looked at my legs. There were two dull red stains on the wrapping above my knee. She peeled the wrapping back, making a disappointed *tck* against the back of her teeth. "I thought we'd gotten that bleeding stopped."

She didn't ask for an explanation, which made me wonder what exactly she thought I'd been doing to open it up again. She cleaned it without a word and rewrapped it and washed her hands in the bathroom.

"We might not be able to move you this morning," she said when she came back in. She took the cozy off the teapot and poured steaming tea into a milk-white porcelain cup. "The Germans have got the streets blocked off for their victory parade. Adrian went to see if he can find a way around." She handed me the teacup and saucer. "Sugar and no milk, Mykola said."

The tea was too hot to drink. I held the cup on my lap. I had that same terrible feeling that she could see right through me.

"Mykola talks too much," I said sourly.

She uncovered the plate and waited a second for the steam to dissipate. "Trusts too easily, you mean."

That was what I'd meant. It irked me that she knew. I tried

to sip my tea carelessly and burned my tongue so badly that I nearly choked.

She chipped the top neatly off the soft-boiled egg, ignoring my difficulties. "Don't discredit him," she said.

"Ma'am?" I gasped hoarsely.

"This wasn't easy for him—coming to us for help. He's not naive. He knew the risk he was taking. But he loves you that much."

That stung. I wondered whether she'd meant it to. *I hadn't been willing to take that risk. We've got an uncle in Kraków*, I'd said. *I don't need your help*, I'd said.

I looked away. There was a knot in my throat, and not just because I'd almost swallowed my tongue.

"Innocent," I said, "not naive. Please let him go."

"Eat this egg before it gets cold," she said.

I fought the urge to throw the teacup at her. "Please. He's never had anything to do with—"

"Aleksey," she said.

I shut up. Half of me was so angry that the teacup was rattling. Half of me wanted to curl up against the pillows, pull the duvet over my head, and sob.

She took the teacup away from me before any form of disaster could strike.

"The less you tell me," she said, "the less I have to lie when I'm asked. But if you could go to the Germans, you wouldn't have come to us. I can put that much together myself."

I braced myself, swallowing the urge to beg.

"We can't go to the Resistance either," I said.

I don't know what I was expecting—a sharp intake of breath, a gun in my face, booted footsteps on the stairs—but what I got was a spoon.

"If you could go to the Resistance," Mrs. Kijek said, "we'd have sent you with our friend last night. Eat the egg."

26

IT WAS MIDAFTERNOON BEFORE MR. KIJEK
thought the streets were clear enough to try taking the car out.
I had no idea what he thought about all of this. His cold, well-
bred face was about as expressive as a boiled potato. He didn't
talk except for one or two words in Polish to Mrs. Kijek every
now and then. He and Mykola slung me between them and carried me down to the car like a sandbag, draping me across the
back seat with my legs stretched out. Mykola sat on the floor,
folded up small and tight with his arms looped around his knees.
The car was a coupé, and slumped as I was, I couldn't see much
through the tiny windows except the fronts of buildings going
by in a blur. I tried to follow the turns in my head, but I got lost
around Piekarska Street. We were somewhere on the east side,
that was all I knew.

I thought I'd be able to get my bearings when we finally
stopped, but all I saw when they lifted me out of the car was the
shabby, overgrown concrete courtyard of an anonymous brick
apartment block. It looked like the kind of place where people

got bullets in the backs of their heads late at night in the glare of car headlights. I tried to console myself with the thought that if the Kijeks wanted to put bullets in the backs of our heads, they wouldn't have needed to bring us here to do it. Then I remembered that they wouldn't be putting bullets in the backs of our heads anyway, if they were going to give us to the Resistance.

So I was half expecting Polish gunmen to be waiting for us when Mrs. Kijek unlocked the door of the flat, but it was just a drab, dark room, about the size of our own place in Zamarstynów, stuffy and sour with the smell of rot, empty except for some sheeted furniture and a pile of old mattresses. Boards were nailed over the windows, shutting out light and air. Exposed pipes ran in tangled clumps across the ceiling and down the walls. Some sort of animal—small cat or very large rat—had been in here recently, leaving a trail of faint, brushy pawprints through the dust on the floor. I saw Mykola eyeing the prints with grim resignation, like a gladiator facing down a tiger.

"We'll come as often as we can," Mrs. Kijek said quietly. She'd shut the door behind her. The only light was the little bit coming in through the thin cracks between the window boards. "I have a patient in this block. People are used to seeing me here. But this unit is supposed to be empty, so we'll need to be careful."

"No lights," Mr. Kijek added in Polish. He must have understood more Ukrainian than he let on. "No noise."

They dragged one of the mattresses off the pile and laid me

down in a soft shower of dust. Mr. Kijek went out to the car and came back with a cardboard box. He placed the box gently on the floor, careful not to let it bump, and brought out a pair of pistols from somewhere under his coat. He gave one pistol to Mykola, one to me. He put a cartridge box beside me on the mattress.

"Ask them if they know how to use them," he said to Mrs. Kijek.

He made both of us show him that we could fit the magazines in and take them out to reload. I don't think he was happy even then—they were good pistols, much too good for us—but he seemed satisfied that we weren't going to shoot each other by accident or slice our thumbs off with the slides. Mrs. Kijek took one last look at the dressing on my thigh to make sure the bleeding had stopped. Mykola knew the medicine dosages. He could change the dressing if he had to. There was food and water in the box, and an electric torch to be used only in an emergency. She would be back in the morning, around eight thirty, and she would knock four times when she came, *short-short-short-long*, so we would know who it was.

They locked the door from the outside when they left. They had to do that, I knew, but it was damn nerve-racking to hear the lock click and realize we were alone and trapped in the dark until the next time they came—the next time they *decided* to come. There was a part of me screaming that they weren't going to come back at all. I didn't really think they would deliberately leave us here to starve—I wasn't at that point of panic, yet—but there were plenty of other, perfectly rational scenarios that were equally terrible. Maybe the streets would be too dangerous. Maybe they'd be forced into hiding themselves. Maybe they'd change their minds and sell us to the Resistance or the Nachtigallen after all.

Any which way, we were powerless.

I worried about it for a lot longer than I normally would have, mostly because there was nothing much else to do. It was too stuffy in that room to sleep. Mykola had pulled down another mattress and spread it out beside mine—strength in numbers against the rats. We were just lying there in the dark, not moving and not speaking, listening to the silence. I had time to worry through everything, rational and irrational. That door was too heavy to kick down—or *I* certainly couldn't kick it down, and I doubted Mykola could. Easier to pry off the boards and go through the windows. If there was a fire, we probably wouldn't have time to do either. Mr. Kijek was a puzzle, that was for sure. How much must he detest Ukrainians, if he pretended not to understand our language just to avoid speaking to us directly? Maybe he would hand us over without Mrs. Kijek knowing. All right, but why leave us the pistols? Maybe he'd taken out the firing pins. Maybe the bullets were blanks.

Screams broke the silence.

The first one made me jump. I must have been closer to falling asleep than I'd thought. Beside me, Mykola sat straight up as though he'd had an electric charge shot through him. Somebody was screaming out in the street—long, ragged screams of pain, wordless but horribly human, choking off into whimpering sobs. I'd never heard screams like that before—not yesterday at the Brygidki, not any of the times I'd seen the NKVD pack some poor beaten, bloody soul off into one of their dreaded black vans.

A door flew open with a bang somewhere down the hall. It must have been the street door because the screams were suddenly louder. Booted footsteps tramped across the floor. Voices shouted indistinct commands. I could pick out words here and there. Whoever they were, they were shouting in Ukrainian.

Mykola hauled me off the mattress and dragged me by the arms over to the wall, behind one of the sheeted pieces of furniture. We huddled there, holding our pistols and our breaths. There was a burst of submachine-gun fire and a loud *crash*. They'd shot open the door of the flat next to ours. More screams now and the heavy *thump* of blows. Something or somebody was being dragged across the floor into the hall. Footsteps pounded up the stairs. The sequence was repeated on each floor in succession— submachine-gun fire, the *crash* of a door, screams, the muffled sounds of a quick and useless struggle.

The screams in the street had died away by the time the raiding party came back down. I didn't want to think about why. We sat frozen against the wall, listening to them kick and drag their prisoners through the hall and into the street. Another scream tore through the air, muffled abruptly when the street door slammed shut.

Mykola let out a long, shuddering breath. His hand was on my shoulder, his fingers clenched so tightly that it hurt.

"Nachtigallen," he said.

"Or just Germans."

"Speaking Ukrainian?"

"Maybe those were translators."

"Do you think they were looking for us?"

"I think they found whoever they were looking for. Otherwise they'd have knocked down every door." I pried his hand off. I was shaking, and I didn't want him to feel it. Those screams were going to stay with me. "Let's see what we've got to eat. Everybody's going to be lying low for a while after that. We can move around a bit."

Mykola took the food box over to the window and held up the tins one by one against the light, trying to read the labels. "It's all in Polish."

"What did you expect, idiot?"

"This is milk," he said. "I know that one. And fish. We've got fish."

"Just 'fish'?"

"That's what it says. *Ryba*."

"I find that worryingly vague."

"What is *w-i-e-p-r-z*—oh, pork. I knew that. *B-u-r-e-k* . . . *bureki* . . ."

"Beets," I said. "*Buraki. Burek* is 'bastard.'"

"Tinned bastard. My favorite."

"This is painful. We're going to be here all night, the rate you're going."

"We're going to be here all night anyway. It's not like you have anything better to do."

"Eat," I pointed out.

He squinted at another tin. "I'm sorry for calling you a fascist bigot."

"That comes in a tin?"

"I didn't mean it," he said.

It was an odd time to be making an apology, and an odd apology for *him* to be making at any time. I couldn't remember the last time he'd come straight out and said *I'm sorry* about something.

"I know," I said.

"Do you think they knew? The Kijeks?"

"What, that there'd be a raid?"

"Mm."

"I don't see how they benefit, if that's what you mean."

He shrugged. "They get rid of us. Nobody asks any questions."

"I think there were easier ways to do that, if they wanted to do that," I said.

27

"THERE WAS A RAID LAST NIGHT," I TOLD MRS. Kijek, when she'd taken the thermometer out of my mouth. "Ukrainian militia, or Germans with Ukrainian translators."

She took the thermometer over to the window and held it up to the light. "Yes. I know."

"I think they had specific targets," I said. "They didn't even try our door."

"Did you just wake up?"

"Ma'am?"

"Your temperature is a little high."

"He's been awake," Mykola supplied unhelpfully. "We didn't sleep much."

I shot him a death glare, which he probably didn't see. "Ma'am, if they've got this block marked as a Resistance cell, it could be dangerous for you to keep coming. They'll be watching to see if they missed anybody."

She wiped the thermometer and put it back in its case. "They weren't looking for a Resistance cell. They were looking for Jews."

My head was hurting more than I was going to admit. It took me a second to grasp what she was saying.

"A pogrom?"

"Yes."

"Who is it? The Germans?"

She brought me one of the water bottles. "Drink. We need to bring your temperature down."

"Ukrainians?"

"Drink, Aleksey."

"Is it Ukrainians?"

"You can drink this now," she said, "or you can come with me to the hospital and take an intravenous solution. Do you know what that is?"

"Something unpleasant," I guessed.

"Fluids pumped directly into your veins through a tube. It's your choice."

She wet a cloth with what was left in the bottle afterward and made me lie down with the cloth on my forehead. She slipped a spoonful of something syrupy onto my tongue.

"Four hundred milligrams," she said, showing Mykola the bottle, "every four hours until the fever breaks." She unfastened her wristwatch and gave it to him. "Make sure he drinks."

"She didn't say when she'd be back," Mykola remarked quietly, when the *click* of her heels had faded away. He slid her watch gravely onto his own wrist. It hung loose around the top of his hand.

"Slipped her mind," I said. I was bitter and aching, and I was pretty damn sure things didn't slip Mrs. Kijek's mind. She wasn't going to be back. Ukrainians were dragging Jews out of their own homes and killing them in the streets. She wasn't going to be back.

"I meant to ask her if you could still take the codeine while you're taking this." Mykola studied the label of the syrup bottle. "You're not hurting too bad, are you?"

"No," I lied.

* * *

I spent the rest of that day drifting in and out of sleep. Mykola woke me up every four hours to give me the syrup and make me drink. I woke up once to gunfire—a lone submachine gun, somewhere off in the distance—and once to the rapid patter of footsteps going up and down the stairs. Scrapes and crashes and thumps echoed through the walls.

"Looters," Mykola said softly. He was sitting up facing the door, pistol in his hand.

I woke up once in absolute darkness and silence, sweating. Mykola was asleep beside me, curled up tightly on his mattress with the corner of another mattress pulled over his head. I don't know how he did it. I was dripping sweat as if I'd just come off my shift on the ice for Czarni. I tugged his arm over to look at the time.

"What is it?" His voice was thick with sleep.

I held his wrist up in front of my face, trying to catch enough light on the face of the watch to read the hands. Not quite midnight. I let go of his arm.

"Fever broke," I said.

"That's good." He was too tired to make a joke about it.

"Did Mrs. Kijek come?"

"No."

I wiped sweat from my face with the backs of my hands. Stupid to ask. I knew she wasn't going to come.

"Sorry for waking you up," I said, but he was already asleep again.

* * *

"We're going to be out of water tomorrow," Mykola said, the next night.

"How about food?" I asked.

He took a quick count, tipping the box toward the window as he rummaged. "Two tins of mystery fish, a tin of pork, a tin of carrots, a jar of apples, and three more tins of milk."

"So four or five days. A week if we really stretch. Two weeks at most until we're drinking piss."

"Something like that."

I kneaded my temples. The fever came and went—worse during the day, better at night—but my head and throat ached perpetually. I suspected the only reason we hadn't run out of water already was because Mykola hadn't been drinking his share, since I was pretty sure I'd been drinking more than mine.

"All right," I said, "three options. One—we stay here, ration everything as carefully as we can, and wait for things to settle down. The Germans keep rolling eastward, the Nachtigallen roll right along with them, and all we've got left to deal with in a couple weeks is the occupation. The downside is we've used up our entire food supply in the meantime, which means we've got to run the risk of resupplying here in Lwów before we even think about the mountains."

He was perched on the corner of a sheeted table, swinging a foot thoughtfully. "Second option?"

"We make a break for it now."

"How?"

"Same as we would then. The windows."

"They're stationary. They don't open."

"You're sure?"

He nodded. "I think this used to be a furnace room. Something that didn't need open windows anyway. We'd have to break them."

"So let's hypothesize. What's the worst thing that happens if we break them?"

"Nachtigallen catch us, torture us, and shoot us."

"All right. What's the *first* worst thing that happens if we break them?"

"Somebody hears us."

"But probably not Nachtigallen. We could be three blocks away before somebody figures out what's going on and finds some Nazis to tell about it."

"*I* could be three blocks away," he said.

"And that's assuming they even want to turn us in."

"You've got a price on your head."

"How would they know?"

"The Germans have probably got your photograph up. And anybody who looks at you is going to know you're on the run. You've been shot. You're wearing somebody else's shirt. Anyway, if they're Jewish or Polish, they might just kill us themselves."

I played my trump card.

"Third option, then," I said. "You go."

For a second, I thought he was going to kick me in the face. I think the only reason he didn't was because he was worried about the noise. He hopped off the table.

"We're done," he said.

"Listen to me."

He kicked his mattress instead. He kicked it away from mine and flopped down on it, his back to me.

"Listen," I said. "You've got enough food to get you to Stryy, maybe to the border—someplace where it's safe to use the money. There's no point in both of us staying. There's no guarantee we'll make it out even if we wait. This is your best chance."

He sat up without a word, reached across me, took my pistol from beside the mattress, and lay back down with both pistols cradled protectively under his arm.

"Mykola," I said, "listen to me."

"You can keep saying that. It's not going to work."

I couldn't even get him angry. I tried a less nuanced approach.

"You're an idiot," I said.

"And you're sick."

"Dying," I said viciously. "I'll be dead by morning, so you might as well—"

"I'm not leaving you," he said, "so shut up."

I tried one last tack.

"I'd leave *you*," I said.

"Aleks," he said peacefully, "shut up and go to sleep."

* * *

The knock made both of us jump.

It was either very late or very early. The room was still pitch-black. Mykola must have been lying there awake as I was; I don't think the knock would have woken us up if we'd been sleeping. The pattern was right, *short-short-short-long*, but it wasn't Mrs. Kijek. She'd tapped lightly with one fingernail. This person was using a knuckle.

Mykola nudged my arm in the darkness and handed me my pistol. There was a rattle and a soft *snick* as the tongue of the lock depressed. The door eased open. I had a glimpse of a tall, oddly bulky figure in coat and fedora, silhouetted against the light from the streetlamps. Then the door slid shut again.

"Don't shoot," Mr. Kijek said, in Polish.

He came over from the door, unbuttoning his coat. I heard the rustle of paper packages and the *clink* of bottles.

"Vodka?" I said, also in Polish.

I couldn't tell whether he knew that was a joke. He didn't laugh.

"Water—four bottles. Sausage, cheese, bread, jam, two bars of chocolate." He set them out on the floor, one by one. He spoke in a low, level voice. "We'd have come sooner if we could. They've been watching us—the Gestapo. Tailing us. Has anybody tried the door?"

I felt stupid and selfish and ashamed all at once. My face heated up.

"No," I said.

"Two days ago," Mykola said.

I rounded on him. "What?"

He spoke in Ukrainian. He'd always been shy about trying to speak Polish.

"The first," he said quietly. "The afternoon of the first. Aleksey was asleep. I think it was just looters."

"You didn't tell me," I accused.

I couldn't see it, but I knew he shrugged.

"What were you going to do about it?" he said.

"And since two days ago"—Mr. Kijek, in Polish—"nothing?"

"Nothing," Mykola agreed in Ukrainian.

"My wife has an estate outside Zarudce," Mr. Kijek said, "too far outside the city to be requisitioned as an officer's billet, thank God. We're going to try to move you there." He hesitated. "The trouble is they've impounded our car, so we won't be able to move you, Aleksey, until you can walk it. Mykola can go sooner, of course."

I felt Mykola stiffen. "No."

"When is *sooner?*" I asked.

"We can move him today."

"No," Mykola said again, more sharply.

"The longer we wait," Mr. Kijek said quietly, "the greater the risk—for all of us."

He was talking to me, not to Mykola. I knew what he was really saying. Mykola had a chance. I didn't. He was counting on me to be sensible about it.

"It's Mykola's decision," I said. No use pretending otherwise.

"I don't go without him," Mykola said flatly—in Polish, as if to make sure Mr. Kijek heard him this time.

Mr. Kijek was silent for a moment, probably trying to figure out how to explain tactfully that we were both idiots.

"There is another option," he said finally. "We have friends who can get you out in their car—both of you, today."

He waited for us to grasp the implication.

"Resistance," I said.

"On my orders," he agreed.

I was an idiot, all right.

He'd backed us into a corner, and he knew it. He'd known Mykola wouldn't leave me. The infuriating thing was that he didn't need to do it. We were powerless. He could do whatever he wanted with us, and he could do it without a word. He'd just wanted to hear us admit it.

If I hadn't been so angry, I might have conceded it was neatly done. As it was, I put my pistol to his forehead.

"How about this? We give you to the Germans, and they give us amnesty."

"Aleks," Mykola said.

"They won't give you amnesty," Mr. Kijek said. Except for the fact that he was sitting very still, you'd never have guessed he had a gun against his head. His voice was maddeningly calm. It made you wonder whether he was used to talking down angry Ukrainians brandishing pistols. "You killed a Nachtigall officer. The best you'll ever get from them is a bullet in your skull, and I wouldn't count on that. They want you alive. They'll make an example of you."

I wondered how he'd known, and how *long* he'd known, but I wasn't going to give him the satisfaction of knowing he'd caught me off guard.

"As if we'd get any better from your people," I said.

"Aleks," Mykola said again.

"I'm asking you to trust me," Mr. Kijek said.

"And I'm answering."

"Tell me why we'd betray you now," he said, "*now*—after all this. We could have handed over the two sons of Yevhen Kobryn five days ago."

I was too truly startled this time to care if he could tell, and too exhausted suddenly to be angry. I lowered the pistol.

"You told him?" I asked Mykola, in Ukrainian.

"He didn't say a word," Mr. Kijek said, in Ukrainian that was better than mine.

"Who told you? How'd you know that name?"

He shook his head. "I remembered your names—Aleksey, Mykola. Your ages were right. Neither of you was carrying identification. I could put it together."

"You were there."

"I was there," he agreed. "It was my case—my operation. My arrest."

And I remembered him.

I remembered the way he'd leaned silently against the door after they'd taken Papa out, smoking his cigarette and watching while the police pulled books off shelves and rifled through papers, while they slit mattresses and ripped up floorboards, looking for anything that might so much as hint at treason. I remembered him thumbing idly through the fresh-printed stack of UPA pamphlets that Papa hadn't had time to stuff into the stove. I remembered him bending his head to speak into an underling's ear, and the underling coming over with a photograph of Shukhevych and asking whether we remembered seeing that man before—asking Mykola and me, not Mama. They wouldn't let Mama speak while they questioned us. I'd shaken my head and said no and wondered whether that was a lie I would have to confess or whether God understood when you lied to protect somebody. Mykola hadn't said anything. He hadn't said anything the whole time. The underling had prodded him with a booted foot and dragged him up by his hair—"Please," Mama had said in Polish, "please don't hurt them." I had never heard her speak Polish before, but she'd spoken Polish then. The underling had laughed and called Mykola an inbred runt, at which I'd lunged at him and bitten his hand hard enough to draw blood, at which he'd cracked me across the face with his pistol butt.

I'd had the welt and a swollen-shut eye for three weeks, and Mama had said to tell people at school that I'd tripped on the stairs. I still had the scar—a tiny, silvered divot under the corner of my right eye, on the cheekbone.

"You weren't police," I said. I remembered. He'd worn plain clothes—suit and fedora, his overcoat folded over his arm.

"No," Mr. Kijek said.

"Border guard?"

"Second Department," he said.

Polish counterintelligence. He'd been an undercover agent—an infiltrator into the Ukrainian underground. Papa would have known him before that night. Papa would have trusted him.

"You're lucky to be alive," I said. The Reds hadn't bothered sending captured Polish intelligence agents to the camps, the way they'd done with army and police. They'd tortured and shot them right here in Lwów.

"I left the department," Mr. Kijek said. "That was the last assignment I took."

"Got what you were after?"

He didn't say anything.

"Good thinking," I said. "Quit while you're ahead." My throat was tight. I was dangerously close to sniffing. I dashed my hand across my nose and hoped he and Mykola didn't see.

He put out a hand suddenly, and I jerked back. I thought he was going for my throat. Instead he laid the backs of his fingers on my forehead.

"You've been taking the acetaminophen?" he asked.

The question was so unexpected that I just blinked at him for a second.

"The medicine for the fever," he prompted.

"Yes." His fingers were cold against my skin. I resisted the urge to squirm away.

"The full dose?"

"Yes."

"Is he telling the truth?" That was to Mykola, the trustworthy one.

"Four hundred milligrams every four hours," Mykola recited.

Mr. Kijek let go of my head. I heard him release a long, low breath.

"He hasn't been taking the codeine," Mykola said. "I didn't know whether he was supposed to keep taking that when he was taking the—other stuff."

Mr. Kijek put a hand on my knee. I flinched reflexively. I tried to swallow the groan and ended up sounding something like an asphyxiating duck.

He let go of my knee and pushed me down against the mattress.

"Acetaminophen," he said. He sounded distracted. "Yes, he can take the codeine."

"Is he all right?"

Mr. Kijek hesitated, long enough that I could guess at what he wasn't saying.

"Infected?" I said.

"The knee doesn't look too good," he said quietly. "We can make you comfortable, keep the fever down, keep you hydrated and rested—but you need antibiotics, not painkillers."

"Can you get them?" Mykola asked. His voice was level, but he'd stiffened again.

"I don't know," Mr. Kijek said.

Mykola fumbled in his coat and pulled out the twenty marks. He held the wad out to Mr. Kijek.

"Please," he said.

Mr. Kijek shook his head. He pushed Mykola's hand away gently.

"We've been trying," he said. "We'll keep trying. The problem is that the Soviets cleaned out everything when they retreated. The hospitals, the black market—all the sulfa antibiotics they could get their hands on. If we're going to get them, we're going to have to get them from the Germans."

28

THEY WOULD BRING THE CAR AT SEVEN, MR. KIJEK
said—he and his *friends*.

I could tell he wasn't very happy about it. There was a curfew
at sundown, and neither Mykola nor I had identification. My fake
passport had been in the pack we'd lost in the tunnels, which
meant the Nachtigallen had it now, which meant the Gestapo
and the SS had it too. I would be identified straightaway if we
were stopped, and we would almost certainly be stopped if we
took the car out after dark. But they were making another ship-
ment today—that was the word he used, *wysyłka*, exactly as if
we were packages—and that was the earliest they could make it
back with the car.

At half past seven, Mykola said, "What time is sundown?"

"About nine thirty," I said.

"Maybe they decided to wait until tomorrow," he said.

The lock finally rattled at a quarter to nine. I think we'd both
accepted by then that the car wasn't coming tonight. The noise

caught us off guard. The door swung open before it occurred to me that there hadn't been a knock first.

It shut again before I'd registered anything but the steel Wehrmacht helmet and the bayoneted rifle.

I snatched up my pistol, snapped the slide, and aimed for the middle of the intruder's chest. Mykola's hand shot out to catch my arm. My brain caught up with the rest of me. Somebody would hear a gunshot. His rifle was slung. He was as off guard as we were. Maybe he was alone. Maybe he hadn't seen us. Maybe he was just looking for a place to sleep, and if we kept very quiet—

"Aleksey," Andriy said.

Maybe not.

I retrained the pistol. "Who's there?"

"Andriy. Please don't shoot."

"Oh, yes. I remember. Andriy of Proskuriv. Didn't recognize you in the uniform. Almost shot you by accident."

"Please, I've got to talk—"

"Which would have been ironic," I said, "because when I shoot you it's definitely going to be on purpose."

"Please," he said. "I've got to talk to you."

"Hands up, bastard. Come over here."

He came over quickly and wordlessly, holding his arms out like a scarecrow. The bulky wool coat looked ridiculously big on him. The deep brim of the helmet hung down low over his eyes. You could see a mouth and a chin and the tip of a nose, that was about it.

"Enjoying your two thousand marks?" I asked.

He didn't say anything. He dropped to his knees beside my mattress. He darted a glance over my legs. I yanked the rifle off his shoulder and gave it to Mykola.

"Alone?" I asked him.

"Yes. Aleksey, they—"

"Who else knows?"

"What?"

I shoved him down to the floor and pinned him, digging the muzzle of the pistol between his eyes.

"Who else knows we're here? Marko? The Gestapo? Who else?"

"V-Vitalik. Just Vitalik, I swear."

That gave me pause.

"Vitalik sent you?"

"And these. Anti-b-biotics." He dug a small paper packet from somewhere inside his coat and held it out, hand trembling. "G-good faith."

I snatched the packet away from him. "How'd you find us? Lucky guess?"

He shook his head doggedly. "I followed them—the Kijeks."

Realization dawned.

"You were the tail."

"You've got to listen—"

"That was you trying the door the other day."

"Please," he said, "you've got to listen to me."

"They thought you were Gestapo. I could have told them you were just a sneaky, cowardly, greedy little rat."

"Aleksey—"

"Stop saying my name." I dug the muzzle harder against his forehead. "Give me a reason not to, rat. Go on. Nobody's going to hear this in time to do you any good."

"I'm sor—"

"Not going to cut it. Try again."

"Please, just listen to me. They shot him—Kijek."

My stomach jumped as though I'd been kicked.

"What?"

"They shot him. They went to the house. T-took him out to the Wulka Hills and shot him."

"Who? Gestapo? SS?" From everything I'd heard, the Germans' secret police were just as bad as the NKVD—and the SS, the devils responsible for keeping us subjects of the Reich properly in line, were much, much worse.

"SS and Nachtigallen." He swallowed. "I'm sorry, Al—I mean, I—"

"You gave them the address?"

He blinked at me, his mouth open. Clearly he hadn't anticipated the question.

"You gave them the address," I hissed. "You told them they were with the Resistance."

"No, I sw—"

I shook him so hard that his teeth snapped together. *"You told them they were with the Resistance, didn't you?"*

"N-no, I didn't t-tell them anything, I swear. It's not b-because of the Resistance. It's because of the university."

"What?"

"They've got a list—the SS. Vitalik showed me. Names and addresses of university faculty, academics. Like the Reds. They took him because he lectures at the university."

Mykola lifted his head. He hadn't said a word this whole time—just sat hunched with the rifle across his lap, deliberately avoiding looking at Andriy. "If they'd known he was with the Resistance," he said quietly, "they'd have kept him for interrogation, not shot him." I was pretty sure he was crying, but his voice was steady.

"Please," Andriy said. "I didn't tell them anything."

"Weren't they paying well enough this time?"

"It wasn't for the mon—"

"Shut up." I nudged him sharply with the pistol for emphasis. "You said they took Mr. Kijek. What about Mrs. Kijek? She wasn't on the list?"

"N-no—I mean, yes, she's on it. That's what I c-came to—"

"Where is she?"

"At the hospital. N-night shift." He gulped a breath and rushed to get the words out before I could clobber him again.

"That's what I came to t-tell you. Mr. Kijek t-told them she was up in Zarudce. Bought some ti—"

I took the pistol away from his forehead. "Give me your uniform. Now."

Mykola looked up again. "What are you doing?"

I ignored him. "Come on, move it," I said to Andriy, who was fumbling at the buttons of his coat.

Mykola sprang to his feet suddenly, shoving the rifle off his lap. "You're not going. I'm going. Give me the uniform."

"Not a chance."

"I can move faster."

"I know the tunnels. You don't."

"You've got to *get* to the tunnels, and anybody who sees you—"

"Is going to know I've been shot," I said. "Yes, I know. I'm the one who needs to go to the hospital."

29

WE COMPROMISED. LATELY, THAT SEEMED TO BE
the best I could expect from arguing with him.

The Nachtigallen would probably be looking for Andriy, he
pointed out. Somebody might have noticed a Nachtigall soldier
coming in here from the street. Besides, he'd forced the lock,
and we didn't have any way to relock it—and anyway we still
didn't know for sure that we could trust him, so it would be
better to take him along as a hostage, just in case.

Andriy didn't raise any objections. I think he'd been fully
expecting us to shoot him, so he was coming out ahead, comparatively speaking.

The end result was we all went together—just like old times,
except I was in a Wehrmacht uniform and floating happily along
on sixty milligrams of codeine, and Mykola was holding his pistol
against the small of Andriy's back.

The apartment block, it turned out, was on Krupiarska
Street—barely a kilometer from the hospital, going by the sewers. The hospital's oldest, lowest cellar, the old, vaulted brick

one that looked like it had been a torture chamber at some point, opened right into the sewer tunnels. I knew that because I'd broken in before, back when Mama was still alive—back when this was still the General Hospital, not the properly Soviet-sounding State Medical Institute. They didn't keep medicine down here, or anything plausibly sanitary like linens and blankets. I'd been disappointed at first, since that's what I'd been after. But there was plenty of other stuff that went for good money on the black market—old electronics that could be stripped for parts, spare wall tiles and light bulbs, rubber tubing, tools—and there was a gold mine of filing cabinets full of musty old medical records, perfect for fuel. We probably burned through twenty years of General Hospital records that winter, 1935.

The cellar doors opened inward and were easy to kick in— easy for Mykola anyway, and he was gracious enough to spare me any gloating about how it was a good thing he'd come along after all. He and Andriy waited just inside while I found my way up the stairs and sidled casually into the corridor. We'd been living pretty much in constant darkness for the better part of a week, and I spent the first few seconds staggering like a drunk in the bright fluorescent lighting, blinking tears out of my eyes. I recovered just in time to slip into a custodial closet while some nurses went by with a cart.

I had no idea where the pediatrics ward was. There was a long *corps de logis* and two long wings, each three stories high: The hospital was shaped something like a letter *pe*, П, with the legs pointing north. I was in the west wing, ground floor. That was a miracle, honestly. Most of the main *corps* seemed to have been commandeered by a bunch of Germans—either as a hospital or just for billeting, I don't know. I caught a smattering of German voices and a glimpse of steel-gray uniforms through a thick smoke fug when I peered cautiously around the corner into the *corps*.

I think I must have spent ten minutes skulking about the floor, flitting in and out of closets and empty examination rooms, before I grudgingly admitted to myself that I'd probably rouse less suspicion just limping down the corridor, looking wounded and German, than I would if somebody found me trying to hide among the brooms and ammonia bottles. There was a stairwell at the end of the wing. I decided to head upstairs.

It was after eleven o'clock, and the first-floor corridor was pretty empty. I spent another five full minutes wandering the length of the wing before somebody finally noticed me. A nurse came out of a room with an armful of linens, saw me, swallowed just perceptibly, smiled brilliantly, and asked if I was lost—this was the maternity ward. She spoke in Ukrainian, eyeing the blue-and-yellow Nachtigall band on my arm, but I could tell she was Polish.

"I'm looking for Renata Kijek," I told her. Afraid that that had sounded a little too ominous, I added, "I've got a message for her." That sounded ominous when it came out too, so I fell back on the old standby and just grinned at her charmingly, like an idiot.

She seemed too relieved to notice. "East wing," she said,

pointing down the *corps*. Her fake smile was suddenly a lot more genuine. Whatever my business was, it wasn't *hers*.

Coward.

There didn't seem to be any Germans up here. I didn't know whether that was a good thing or a bad thing. It meant I was less likely to be questioned by random passersby—or more likely to be believed if I *was* questioned anyway—but it also meant I was more conspicuous, and I was moving a lot more slowly than I had been. The codeine was starting to wear off. I ached all over. I was holding on to the wall by the time I reached the end of the *corps* and rounded the corner into the pediatrics ward. I wasn't going to be able to run if it came to that, and the slower I went the more likely it would.

I found her office. She wasn't in it. The door was closed and locked. I held on to the wall and limped the length of the wing, looking in through all the open doorways. There was a tall sash window at the northern end of the wing that looked down onto the street. I watched three Mercedes-Benz sedans pull into the drive, just below. There were pennants on the fenders—black triangles with two jagged white lightning bolts in the center.

SS.

I hobbled back up the corridor. A nurse had come out of a room just ahead and paused to write something on a clipboard, her back to me. I drew myself up straight.

"Excuse me, ma'am," I said—growled, more accurately. My teeth were clenched. "I'm looking for Renata—"

Her head whipped around. I stopped in midsentence, wincing reflexively. I should have recognized that sleek, dark plaited bun. Everything about her, in fact, was exactly the way I remembered—the lift of her chin, the stiffness of her shoulders, the sudden flush of fury in her cheeks.

She inspected me, helmeted head to booted foot, in much the same way I imagined she might inspect an especially disgusting burst boil. Then she turned without a word, bent her head to her clipboard, and walked away.

I hobbled after her.

"Listen—it's urgent."

"Get away from me."

"Please."

She spun on one heel, reaching under her apron. She brought out a pistol and pointed it at my face.

"I said get away."

I held my hands up, palms out. "Please. I need to talk to Mrs. Kijek."

"She's not here."

"The nurse in the maternity ward—"

She jerked her chin, her gun hand never wavering. "Out. *Now.*"

"Aleksey," Mrs. Kijek said.

I don't know where she'd come from. Somewhere behind me—one of the rooms, must have been. She looked tired. For a second, I just gaped at her. I'd been so singularly intent on finding her that I hadn't really thought about having to explain *why* once I did.

What had Father Yosyp said, I wondered, when he told Mykola I was dead?

Mrs. Kijek filled the silence.

"You shouldn't be here," she said levelly. "Where is Mykola?"

That jolted me back to my senses. Mykola—the tunnels. We needed to move.

"There's an SS squad downstairs with a kill order for you," I said. "I can get you out, but we need to go now."

"He's lying," the dark-haired nurse, Anna, said sharply. "He's with them."

"We need to get to the cellar," I said to Mrs. Kijek, pretending not to hear. Panic fluttered in my stomach. I felt a sudden rush of sympathy for Andriy—damn it, why wouldn't anybody just *listen*? "We're going to get cut off in this wing if we wait much longer."

"He's with them," Anna repeated. "He's Nachtigall. This has to be some kind of trick."

Doors slammed down the hall. Another nurse, a lanky, athletic-looking girl with a boyishly short, sandy bob, had shut and bolted the doors to the *corps*.

"SS?" Mrs. Kijek asked her.

"Asking about you," the bobbed nurse said.

"Go home," Anna said to Mrs. Kijek. She was still holding the pistol on my face. "We'll take care of this."

"She can't go home," I said. "They're probably watching the house."

"And how do *you* know?" she snapped.

"Open the doors, Janina," Mrs. Kijek said to the bobbed nurse. "Tell them I've gone out on a call if you need to. Cooperate as much as you can." She pushed Anna's pistol down and brushed past her. "Aleksey," she said, over her shoulder.

Anna caught my sleeve. "If you're lying, *Aleksey Shevchuk*, I swear I'll kill you."

"You'll have to get in line, Anna Kostyshyn," I said.

* * *

We took the service elevator at the back of the ward down to the cellar. It was one of those exciting last-century elevators— agonizingly slow, ominously creaky, and one snapped cable or rusted pulley away from delivering you to your destination a lot sooner than you'd anticipated.

Mrs. Kijek turned to face me in the half-light as we lurched slowly along.

"Where is Adrian?"

She wasn't wasting time on stupid questions. She wasn't going to suffer stupid answers.

"Your husband's dead," I said. "Shot. SS and Nachtigallen."

She closed her eyes.

"They've got a list," I said. "Your name's on it too."

There was an unbearably long silence. The elevator car cranked laboriously down the shaft. I leaned against the wall, trying my best not to whimper when the car jolted.

"They suspect our Resistance work?" Mrs. Kijek said at last, opening her eyes. Her voice was low and level.

"I don't know. At least one of the Nachtigallen has been watching you for a couple days. Andriy—you met him. He was with us at the Brygidki. He's the one I spilled your address to."

"You think he knew we were hiding you."

"I know he did. He came to the flat tonight and told us everything. He could have tipped them off. He swears he didn't. Says they're going after academics, not Resistance. Says he's trying to help us."

"Do you trust him?"

"I don't know," I admitted. "He told us about the list, and he told us you'd be here."

The elevator groaned unsteadily to a stop.

Mrs. Kijek reached out a cool hand and laid it gently on the side of my face.

"Thank you," she said.

"I'm sorry," I said. I didn't know what else to say. What *had* Father Yosyp said to Mykola the night he told him I was dead in the Brygidki?

Mrs. Kijek opened the grating and the shaft door. Electric torchlight flashed in our faces.

Five Nachtigallen waited for us in a half circle at the cellar doors.

30

"YOU LYING BASTARD," I SAID TO ANDRIY.

He flinched. He was sitting very still against the doors, his shoulders hunched. Mykola was in a heap beside him, facedown on the floor, gagged with a wad of dressing gauze and wrapped up like a mummy with electrical cord—hands tied behind his back, ankles lashed together. He squirmed furiously when he saw me, making incoherent noises behind his gag. One of the Nachtigallen jabbed him between the shoulder blades with a rifle muzzle.

"Take it easy, Aleksey." One of them—the officer, judging by his collar tabs—had dragged over a chair from somewhere and was sitting with his legs stretched out, one booted foot propped on an upturned crate. "You're not the only one who's ever gone exploring down here. He didn't rat on you—this time. Just made one or two fatal errors in judgment." He leaned his head against the chair back and smiled at me.

Vitalik.

He tipped the chair lazily, then let it fall forward with a *thump*.

"He brought it on himself, in case you're wondering," he said, reaching with his foot and prodding Mykola roughly in the ribs. "He's a tiger. It took every one of us to get the gun away from him, and he was still trying to bite." He showed me the pistol in his lap—Mr. Kijek's pistol. He lifted it to my face.

"Rifle," he said.

I slid Andriy's rifle off my shoulder and dropped it on the floor.

"Now the pistol," Vitalik said. "Kick it over here."

I'd been hoping he wouldn't notice the bulge under my coat. I pushed my pistol to him across the floor. He caught it neatly under the toe of his boot. He jerked his chin at Mykola.

"Untie his feet. We're going to take a walk."

I limped over to Mykola. Vitalik's pistol followed me. I sat down with my back to Vitalik, my legs folded up like a misshapen pretzel—dear God, they were hurting now. I unwound the tangle of cords from Mykola's ankles unhurriedly, trying to think. None of their rifles were trained. I could yank the door open and shove Mykola out before anybody but Vitalik had time to react, and Vitalik wouldn't shoot to kill—not at me anyway, since they wanted me alive, and I was between him and Mykola. It wasn't much of a chance for Mrs. Kijek, but it would at least give her time to make a break for the stairs.

Mykola must have seen the look on my face. He shook his head just perceptibly, his eyes urgent—*don't*.

"Hurry it up," Vitalik said. "He's extra baggage, at this point. That means I kill him if he's slowing us down or if he's getting on my nerves or if any of you aren't cooperating or maybe just for the hell of it, because I can."

I cleared the last of the cords away and lunged for the door.

Crack.

I froze at the sound of the shot, my muscles seizing up involuntarily at the memory of pain.

Crack, crack, crack—three more shots in quick succession, echoing deafeningly around the close brick walls.

Four Nachtigallen were sprawled over the floor before it occurred to me that Vitalik wasn't trying to hit me.

I pulled myself up against the door. My heart was pounding.

"Whose side are you on, anyway?" I demanded.

Vitalik was up from the chair. He leaned on his left hand against the wall, keeping his weight off his leg. He nudged one of the bodies with the toe of his boot, eliciting a groan. He put a bullet in the man's head.

"My own," he said, "same as you."

He picked up the rifle I'd dropped and slung it over to Andriy. He picked up my pistol and held both pistols out to me, grip first.

"Shoot me," he said.

"What?"

"Shoot me and take the pistols. Get the hell out. Don't go to Zarudce."

I swallowed. "You know, there's a solution here that doesn't involve—"

He gestured impatiently. "I'm not asking you to shoot me in the head. And nothing humiliating. Just something that doesn't scream *self-inflicted*. These are SS, not thickheads like Marko. They'll be able to tell."

"Come with us," I said.

He pretended not to hear. "Might be good if you lay me out too. Give me an excuse for not sounding an alarm."

I pushed the pistols away. "Come with us."

"Stop wasting time."

"Vitalik—"

He shoved the pistols into my hands and stepped back.

"Come on," he said. "The Fritzes will have heard those shots."

V

TOLYA

Sunday, August 6–Sunday, August 13
1944

31

HE'D BEEN DOWN THERE IN THAT BASEMENT FIVE days, it turned out.

It was Sunday, the sixth of August, the feast day of the Trans-figuration, and Vitalik's squad had found him on the stream bank on the morning of the thirty-first.

He was on his stomach on the table in the kitchen, drowsy with codeine and comfortably warm in the crisp, early sunlight through the open kitchen door, watching through half-closed eyelids while they searched and stripped the dead out in the yard—UPA dead, NKVD dead. The NKVD had circled the house just before dawn, and this Polish Resistance patrol had heard the gunfire and come over and circled the NKVD.

Voices drifted over him.

"Can he be moved?"—a girl's voice, familiar somehow. Tolya tried to lift his head to look. Somebody pushed his head back down. "We need to move," the girl said. "They'll be back."

"He's not walking out of here, if that's what you're asking."

"So—look. We use the tabletop for a stretcher." That was the one called Jerzy. His was the voice that had spoken in Tolya's ear earlier. "Easy enough."

"All right," the girl said. "And take that radio too."

They put him down on the floor while they broke off the table legs. Then they put him back on the board and carried him out to the yard. The house was a little thatched farmhouse of lime-washed clay, pock-marked with bullet holes. There was a wicker fence running around the yard. They put him down on the grass by the open gate while they sorted out the captured weapons, and he lay feeling the sunlight and the wind, listening to the bird songs, looking at Vitalik's body across the yard.

He was sprawled on his stomach across the gate path, Vitalik, his head turned on his cheek, facing Tolya. His eyes were half-lidded and dark and empty, his pale lips rimmed with blood. His maimed hands were spread palm-down on the dirt, as though he'd tried to push himself up at the last, in defiance, but he didn't look defiant in death. He looked thin and tired, so very tired—and who was there to pray rest for *his* soul?

One, at least. That was what Father Dmytro would say.

I can't, Tolya would say, because he wouldn't dare say what he really meant, which was *I won't*.

You must, Father Dmytro would say. *You must forgive as our Lord forgives.*

And Tolya would say nothing for a little while, trying to find the words, and then in the end he would say only, *It's hard.*

And Father Dmytro would say, *Hate is harder.*

No.

Always.

And Tolya would be angry by then, and he would say, *Hate is the easiest thing in the world.*

Hate is like hogweed, Father Dmytro would say, *easily seeded, easily spread—but have you ever tried to root out hogweed? And you've got to root it out, because it chokes everything else.*

I don't care, Tolya would say. *I hate the men who killed Papa, and I hate the men who killed Mama, and I hate the men who killed you.*

But he knew he'd lost.

* * *

The girl was coming over to him across the yard.

He remembered her. The sunburn had gone to tan, but he remembered the freckles on her nose and cheeks, and the short, tight chestnut braids behind her ears, and the bulky soldier's jacket belted over her skirt, and the monstrous soldier's boots swallowing her feet.

She knelt by the board, shifting her submachine gun on her shoulder. She took Tolya's hand in her slim, brown hands, uncurled his fingers, and spooled his rosary onto his open palm.

He looked at the beads. He peeled his tongue off his teeth.

"How?"

"He was still alive when we got to him—the officer." The girl jerked her chin at Vitalik. "'The boy is yours,' he said, 'and this is his'—as calmly as that, though he must have wanted pretty badly to make sure we knew. Usually they kill themselves before they risk capture." She closed Tolya's fingers over the crucifix. "Are you Yakiv? He kept saying 'Yakiv.'"

* * *

He'd been so sure, so very sure, that it was Vitalik's game.

To be fair, so had Vitalik.

Then again, it wasn't Yakiv's game either, not really.

His body was outside the gate. Tolya saw it when they lifted the board. He was curled on his side, facing the pine wood. Vitalik had shot him in the back as he'd tried to run.

Really, anybody in the yard could have shot him, but in Tolya's mind it had been Vitalik.

He said the prayer the same as he'd said it for Vitalik, and he tried to mean it. In some ways, it was easier. He understood Yakiv—one traitor to another. He understood Yakiv's hatred and contempt. You didn't hate so much and so strongly unless you were hating part of yourself deep down—unless you saw part of yourself in the thing you hated. That was what Father Dmytro would say.

In some ways, it was harder. He wasn't sure how to forgive Yakiv because he wasn't sure how to forgive himself.

They went into the wood above the little farmhouse. Two

of them carried the board by the corners. He bumped and slid and gripped the edges of the board tightly, trying not to slip off.

Jerzy walked beside the board, his hand on Tolya's arm. "Careful," he said.

"How about *you* carry him?" one of the stretcher bearers said, grunting.

"No strenuous activity. Ask Janek."

"How about you be quiet, all of you?" the girl said from somewhere up ahead.

The wood tilted and spun. Tolya shut his aching eyes. He was back in darkness, waiting for the creak and scrape of the door, and the *clomp, clomp, clomp* of boots, and Vitalik's fists, and Yakiv's voice, taunting.

She's still alive—your girlfriend.

But of course he would say that. He would have said anything. He needed the name of the source, and he thought Tolya knew it.

Solovey had said she was dead. Solovey wouldn't have lied.

At least, he wouldn't have had any reason to lie.

Unless—

He was going to shoot you when he was done with you, Yakiv said. *You know that, don't you? He didn't take Polish prisoners.*

You've got to trust me, Solovey said.

It was all planned out, Yakiv said.

You've got to trust me, Solovey said, unholstering his pistol and pressing the muzzle to Tolya's forehead.

Bullet to the brain, Yakiv said, *done*.

"No," Tolya said, "no, no—"

He tried to tear away. He wrenched and twisted and fought, thrashing his legs, flinging out his arms. Hands held him down against the board.

And Solovey pulled the trigger.

Tolya jerked, gasping. The hands held him down tightly.

"You're safe," a voice said into his ear. "You're safe—with friends, all right?"

He recognized Jerzy's voice—Jerzy's voice, Jerzy's hand on his head. He was in the pine wood. There were shafts of warm, dusty sunlight coming down through the trees. He lay still. His throat was closed, his heart pattering frantically on the board—*thump, thump, thump*.

"Can you give him another dose?" the girl asked, distantly above.

"I'm out of codeine tablets." That was Janek, the medic. "He can't take another one for three hours anyway. I gave him sixty milligrams the first time."

"All right," the girl said, "change of plans. Jerzy, get this stuff back to camp. Kostek, Ryś, and Janek with me."

"She's not going to like it," Jerzy warned.

"She won't care about *him*," the girl said. "She just doesn't like *you*."

32

THEY TIPPED CRUSHED ASPIRIN ONTO HIS TONGUE
before they set out again, all the aspirin Janek had, to keep him
quiet. There were only the five of them now, and they went
more quickly than before. He lay watching the pine trunks slip
by in blurry streaks, trying hard not to make any noise when they
jolted him, biting his tongue and digging his fingernails into his
palms and blinking away the darkness—fighting it and fighting
it, until he was too tired to fight it anymore.

He shut his eyes. He didn't mean to sleep, but when he
opened his eyes again, there were white clay walls around him,
and a sloping, raftered roof above him, and a yellow plank floor
below. He was on his stomach on a soft, fat mattress, a cool pillow under his cheek. There was embroidery in scarlet thread on
the edge of the sheet and on the pillowcase, and the smell of fresh
rye bread drifting from somewhere, and just for a second—just
for a *second*—he thought he'd woken up in his bed at home in
Kuz'myn, and today was Obzhynky, the last day of the harvest,
and he was smelling the harvest loaf they would put out with salt

under the uncut grain at the corner of the field while Papa prayed the blessing on next year's crop.

Then he thought he must be dead.

Then he tried to move, and he knew he wasn't dead because it *hurt*.

"Lie still," somebody said.

A tall, straight-shouldered, striking blond woman, perhaps Aunt Olena's age, was sitting beside him on a stool, uncapping a syrette. There was a drip bag hanging from a pole by the bed and a thin intravenous tube taped to Tolya's forearm.

"Antibiotics," the blond woman said, holding the syrette up and pressing the tube carefully between her thumb and middle finger. "Preventative. We're not going to take chances with your back. You'll have the scars—nothing much to be done about that. But scars are to be preferred to septicemia."

She leaned over him, cool and businesslike and smelling faintly of lavender. There were tiny, creamy pearls at her ears and throat. She held his upper arm in strong fingers and slid the needle into the muscle. Her well-tended fingertips brushed the bullet hole in his shoulder lightly.

"*This* is coming along nicely. No damage to the bone or the brachial plexus. You've had treatment, haven't you? I mean proper treatment, not salt and vodka."

"Yes," he said, thickly, dazedly, in the voice that wasn't his own.

She withdrew the needle.

"You've got some broken ribs, judging by the pattern of the bruising. Three broken toes on the right foot; superficial to moderate lacerations on face, arms, hands, and feet; second-degree burns on arms and neck; malnourishment; dehydration—the list goes on, but I won't. How do you feel?"

He couldn't answer. His throat was closed, his heart clenched like a fist.

"You'll be feeling pretty good in a minute," she said. "That was thirty milligrams of morphine." She patted his arm briskly. "Try to sleep."

* * *

He didn't sleep this time, though his head was bleary with the drug. He lay awake, sweating in the heat. Afternoon sunlight slanted in through the dormered window above the bed, and though the window hung open there wasn't much of a breeze. He lay very still, his cheek on the pillow, listening to the chatter of the swallows up in the eaves and the murmur of voices coming up from below, through the opening in the plank floor. He could hear the woman's voice, and the girl's, and Janek's, and other voices that must be Kostek's and Ryś's. He couldn't hear what they were saying, but he could hear enough to know they were arguing.

They must have settled it, or agreed to put it off, because their voices went quiet. He heard the clatter of pans and the scrape of chairs and the whistle of a teakettle. Then he heard boots coming up the stairs—*clomp, clomp, clomp*—and just for a second they were Vitalik's boots.

He was off the bed before he remembered the tube in his arm.

He sprawled facedown on the floor, the tube tangling around his ankles. The drip pole crashed down across the backs of his legs.

Janek came up through the opening in the floor. He had tea and bread and jam on a tray. He took in Tolya and the toppled drip pole in one long, blank glance.

"It's just tea," he said. He put the tray on the stool. "Let me see that catheter."

Tolya pushed up slowly on his hands. He sat back on his heels. His heart was pounding.

"I'm not NKVD," he said.

"Let me see the catheter," Janek said.

He took a step toward Tolya, and Tolya backed away, kicking across the floor until he came up against the bedframe.

"Calm down," Janek said.

"You think I'm NKVD." It was very clear in his head, but he couldn't seem to get the words to say what he meant. Janek didn't seem to understand anyway. "That's why you're k-keeping me alive."

Janek crouched to tug the tube away from his ankles. "We can talk about that later."

"Now."

"Look, I don't know if you're NKVD. I know you'll be dead without antibiotics, so unless you *are* NKVD, that's probably what you should be worrying—"

"Janek," the girl said.

She'd come up silently. She was leaning against the wall at the top of the stairs, her arms folded. She wasn't carrying her submachine gun, but her pistol—Zampolit Petrov's pistol—peeked out from under her jacket.

"I'll take care of it," she said.

Janek picked up the drip pole and set it back up by the bed. He didn't protest, but Tolya heard what he said to her under his breath as he brushed past her: "Careful."

She ignored that. She waited until he'd disappeared through the opening. Then she came over and sat down beside Tolya on the floor. She took his arm across her lap and turned it up, holding it gingerly by the wrist and elbow. She pressed the tape back down with her thumb. Her fingers searched over the scabbing, purple welts on the inside of his wrist, following the marks of Vitalik's knife along his forearm.

She let out a low, sharp breath between her teeth.

"They did a job on you, didn't they?"

"I'm not NKVD."

"I know, Comrade. *They* know better than to leave witnesses when they murder somebody." She lifted her head to look him in the face. "Did you think I forgot?"

He didn't answer. He wasn't going to say what he really thought—that she'd pretended to forget, so she wouldn't have to explain to the others why she'd left him alive that day in the alley in Lwów.

"I didn't forget," she said. "We didn't introduce ourselves properly last time. I'm Lena."

He shut his eyes, swallowing. His teeth were chattering, though he wasn't cold.

"Your war n-name?"

"Really Lena. It'd be a boring war name." She turned his arm back over and held it across her lap. "Yours?"

"My war name?"

"If you want. Right now you're 'kid'—or 'poor kid,' if it's Jerzy. He's the softy."

He leaned his head back against the mattress. "Anatol," he said. That was how his mother had said it, in Polish.

"All right. Anatol. So, what—you deserted and ran right into the UPA?"

"Yeah." He didn't want to talk about Solovey.

"I'd say they got the better of it, except you're the one still alive." Her hand was firm and steady on his trembling arm. "You met Mrs. Kijek?"

"Your m-mother."

She looked at him sharply. "Did she tell you?"

"A guess."

"A lucky guess. We don't look anything alike. Sometimes I'm jealous. She got mistaken for Lidia Wysocka once, on the tram."

The name didn't mean anything to him, and she must have seen it.

"The actress," she said. "Lidia Wysocka. Did you see *Gehenna?*"

"I don't think so," he said, because that sounded better than no.

"Nobody will ever mistake *me* for Lidia Wysocka, is what I'm saying."

"No nonsense," Tolya said.

"What?"

"Both of you. Exactly alike. No nonsense."

"Yes—well. Everybody is, I suppose, these days. Anyway, keep it to yourself. Janek's the only one in the squad who knows, and that's just because we knew each other before the war." She folded his arm carefully over his stomach. "You've got two weeks on this round of antibiotics. It's easiest if you're here. Mama doesn't mind, really. It just means we've got to be careful. They've been coming up to the house every couple days— the NKVD. There's a guard post in Zarudce, and they come up to get eggs. So, just in case . . ."

She showed him how to clamp the intravenous tube, take out the catheter, and fit the drip pole into the space under the floorboards. Then she showed him how the dormered window swung open onto the roof, and how if he followed the roof down, he could drop into the backyard, toward the western wood. That was in case the NKVD came into the house. Usually they just came to the kitchen door, asking for eggs, but they always came looking for wounded and stragglers after there'd been a firefight in the woods.

"But nothing ever happens," she said. "We had Jerzy here for almost a week after we got him out, and nothing happened."

"Got him out?"

"That prison camp at the train station. We raided it. Managed to pack most of them straight off into the woods, but they'd, um—given Jerzy some special attention. He's got a couple of broken ribs, and he won't let anybody forget it."

"Oh."

"Your tea's gone cold," she said. "I'll bring you another cup."

He watched her go. His throat was tight.

"What happens after two weeks?"

"Depends on how you're coming along. Maybe another round of antibiotics. Maybe not. We'll see."

"If not?"

"We could use a sniper," she said.

* * *

He lay awake in the dark, listening to them at dinner.

He could hear the *chink* of silverware on porcelain plates, and the *thump* of a wine bottle on the board, and the mellow ripple of piano keys, and their voices, and their laughter—and he pressed his face into the mattress and put the pillow over his head to shut out the sounds because just then he knew exactly what he'd lost in the Soviet prison at Proskuriv and against the garden wall in Kuz'myn. On the muddy road out of Voronezh two years ago, when the Luftwaffe planes had strafed the refugee columns, and before a firing squad in a rubbled alley in Tarnopol. With one pistol shot in Lwów and with another in a streambed in the hills, where the bank ran down.

Lena came up later, bringing dinner on a tray. Tolya pulled the pillow off his head and pretended to be asleep. He could see her through mostly shut eyes—standing there in silhouette against the soft, yellow lamplight from below, the tray in her hands, then turning and going back down the stairs.

"What's wrong?" Mrs. Kijek's voice, at the bottom of the stairs.

"Nothing. He's out like a log."

"Finally," Mrs. Kijek said.

33

THE NKVD CAME THE NEXT MORNING.

Lena and Janek and the other two were already gone. Tolya had heard them leave in the cool, gray half-light before dawn. He hadn't been able to get back to sleep, so he was already sitting up in bed, fumbling with the tube, when Mrs. Kijek came up the stairs with a pair of trousers and a shirt and told him there was an NKVD staff car coming up the road from Zarudce.

She helped him take out the catheter and put the drip pole down between the joists under the floorboards, and she straightened the bedclothes and plumped the pillows while he dressed. Then she went back downstairs, and Tolya opened the window and sat on the sill to listen.

He heard the car pull into the yard, and he heard the engine cut off and three doors slam in succession. It didn't take three people to ask for eggs at the kitchen door. He swung his legs over the sill, pushing the window shut behind him.

The sun wasn't over the rooftop yet, and the mossed shingles were slick with dew. There was a breeze along the pitch and the smell of woodsmoke. There were voices and footsteps coming around the corner of the house, just below.

He sank quickly into the shadowed nook between the kitchen chimney and the dormer. He curled up against the side of the dormer, arms looped tightly around his knees, while two NKVD riflemen made a loose circuit of the yard. They opened the barn and the henhouse and the toolshed, flashing an electric torch. They fumbled for a second with the padlock on the cellar doors. Then one of them unslung his rifle and shot the lock away. They threw open the doors and flashed the torch down the steps.

Somebody opened the dormer window. There were Russian voices very close. Boots tramped over the attic floor. Mrs. Kijek's voice came indistinctly up the stairs. Then the window swung shut again. The riflemen kicked the cellar doors shut and moved to the far side of the house.

Tolya waited, shivering. Finally, he heard the car doors slam and the engine catch. The car swung a wide loop around the yard and rumbled away, back toward Zarudce.

Mrs. Kijek opened the window.

"You can come back in," she said.

He sat on the edge of the bed while she brought out the drip pole and swabbed the inside of his arm with ethanol. She worked in silence, not looking up.

"I'm sorry," he said, because he was ashamed and afraid of that silence.

She held his elbow in her hand and pressed a new catheter

into the vein in the crook of his arm. "There are guns under my floorboards," she said. "There are explosives buried in my vegetable garden, and there are timing pencils in my kitchen drawers." She took out the needle and fitted the intravenous tube to the catheter. She looked up now, smiling slightly. "You're the least of my concerns."

* * *

Mrs. Kijek was a widow. Her husband, Lena's father, had been a professor of civil law at the university in Lwów, one of the twenty-five professors the SS death squads had shot in July 1941. Tolya knew that because she brought him clothes that had been her husband's—store-bought, machine-made clothes, finer than anything Tolya had ever owned and only a little too big—and when he tried to protest she told him that it wasn't as though Adrian would mind, and she must have mistaken the blankness in his face for a question because then she told him why.

He didn't want to take those clothes. All he had left of his own was his threadbare uniform trousers, bloodstained and clammy even after washing, but he didn't want to lie in her attic wearing her dead husband's clothes when it had been Ukrainian nationalists supplying Polish names and addresses for the Nazis' kill lists. He didn't tell her that, of course, but he told her he didn't want to take them. And she said that was too bad, but they were his whether he liked it or not because otherwise they were only going to go for bandages.

So now he had smart gray wool trousers and a suit jacket, and a crisp, collared shirt, and buttery-smooth leather shoes.

He could guess some of the rest. She didn't tell him, and he didn't ask, but she must have had medical schooling, which meant she'd come from money, not just married into it, which probably meant this was her house—her ancestral house, not the house of her widowhood.

It was a sprawling old house, all timber-framed white clay—shuttered and sheeted and moth-eaten now, but still grand. There was an old clock down the stairs that chimed the quarter hours like a church bell. There was a bathroom with marble counters and a tub as big as a swimming pool. There was a magnificent old dining room with a paving-stone floor and a vaulted, trussed ceiling and diamond-paned windows and half-paneled brick walls, and there was a study with a wide brick hearth and fireplace running the whole length of one wall. There was a crowned Polish eagle carved into the mantelpiece, its proud wings spread as wide as Tolya was tall.

There was the piano in the drawing room, and sometimes in the long, twilit evenings he could hear Mrs. Kijek playing. She played beautifully. He didn't know any of the pieces except one, Liebesträum no. 3. He knew that was the Hungarian, Liszt, because it had been Aunt Olena's favorite piece and she'd had

Rubinstein's recording for the phonograph, until her husband, Ivan, smashed the record over the tabletop—"fascist foolery," he said. When Aunt Olena said nothing, Ivan broke the phonograph too.

One more reason why Tolya had never called him uncle.

All that week it was just Tolya and Mrs. Kijek and the tabby cat Maja in the house. In the gray half-light before dawn each morning, Mrs. Kijek would stir up the coals in the stove and put the kettle on, and then she would go out to the yard to feed the chickens and get the eggs, coming back in just as the kettle whistled. Then she would come up the stairs with coddled eggs and porridge and rye toast and butter and black-currant jam and tea—real black tea with sugar and cream—and she would sit with Maja on her lap, listening to the news out of Warsaw on the wireless while Tolya ate. There was fighting in Warsaw. The Soviet advance had stalled on the east bank of the Vistula, but the Polish Resistance was fighting.

Twice a day Mrs. Kijek would change the dressings on Tolya's back and shoulder and at the crook of his arm, around the catheter, and once a day she would change the intravenous solution. It didn't occur to Tolya until he'd been almost the whole week in that room, with nothing much to do but think, to wonder where she got the medicine. The butter and sugar and tea and wine could be explained away. He knew there was a black market in Lwów, and he knew Mrs. Kijek had money, and he didn't doubt she had black market contacts. But antibiotics didn't go to civilians, even on the black market—not when the NKVD could be bribed with them—and he'd only ever seen those American morphine syrettes once before.

He didn't ask. He didn't say anything about the syrettes. He was afraid of how much he might give up if he said anything—how much they would try to make him give up, about Anna and Iryna and the Red Cross station in Toporiv and anything else about the UPA that they weren't asking because they didn't think he knew. He was afraid of them knowing that he did.

* * *

Lena and Janek came back that Sunday night. It must have been their routine—maybe not always Lena and Janek, but some two or three of them coming down on Sundays for a hot meal—because he could hear Mrs. Kijek already laying the table when they got there. While Janek was out splitting wood for the stove, Lena came up the attic stairs with a bundle of rifles. She unstrapped one to show him. It was a German Karabiner modified for sniping, with a Zeiss scope, a blued steel barrel, and a smooth, blond oak stock. She gave it to him and let him test the sights.

"Pretty, isn't it?" she said. "Have you ever used one?"

He leaned on his elbows over the cat, who was curled up asleep on the pillow. He shouldered the rifle and sighted the darkening wood through the window.

"Yeah," he said, "once." Comrade Lieutenant Spirin had carried a German rifle, a prize from the Battle of Moscow. He'd let Tolya try it at Voronezh. One of the NKVD men had taken it after Spirin's execution.

Lena knelt to pull up a floorboard. She dropped the rifles into the space between the joists. She brought out a cartridge box from her pocket and held it up so he could see.

"In case you ever need it," she said.

He didn't say anything. Her trust shamed him, the way Mrs. Kijek's silence had shamed him. He was suddenly very conscious of wearing Lena's dead father's shirt and trousers and jacket and shoes. He handed her the German rifle, and she put it down with the others between the joists. She laid the floorboard back down. Then she sat back on her heels and looked at him.

"Are you all right? Do you need anything?"

"No," he said. "I mean yes, I'm all right."

"You must be bored to death up here. I'd be bored to death."

"I'm all right."

"Do you like to read?"

"No," he said. He could read passably in Ukrainian and Russian. He didn't want to tell her that he couldn't read at all in Polish.

"What do you like to do?" she asked. Then she corrected herself a little. "What did you like to do before the war?"

He thought about it. He didn't think about Kuz'myn. Kuz'myn was only hunger and death. He thought about Kyiv in those last two years before the war, when it was just him and Aunt Olena. He thought about Aunt Olena's apartment, the new apartment in Pechersk, with the tall French windows opening onto the balcony, and the cobbled street below lined with flowering horse-chestnut trees, and the boats on the Dnieper, and Bohdan Khmelnytsky, hero of the Cossacks, astride his proud horse under the golden spires of Holy Sophia—which of course was no longer Holy Sophia but only a museum.

"I played football," he said.

"In Tarnopol?"

"No," he said into Maja's fur.

"Where? You sound Galician."

He thought about lying. It would have been easy to lie. But her trust shamed him.

"In Kyiv," he said.

She tilted her head, studying him. "You're Ukrainian."

It was a realization, not a question. He didn't say anything.

"I assumed you were a Polish conscript. They took thousands of us after the invasion. It was that or be shot."

He didn't say anything. What was there to say? He wasn't Polish, and he wasn't Ukrainian. He was a traitor to his father's people on account of his mother, and a traitor to his mother's people on account of his father, and a traitor to both on account of the Reds, and a traitor to the Reds on account of Zampolit Petrov.

Lena got up, treading on the floorboard to make sure it was flush. "Will you go back?"

"What?"

"To Kijów. After the war."

"I don't know," he said, and he realized in that moment that he'd stopped thinking about *after*.

"You've got family there?"

"Not anymore."

She looked up, glancing over his face. "I'm sorry."

"Why? I'm Ukrainian."

She didn't say anything, and he looked away. He hadn't meant to say it. He hadn't really meant it at all, except there was the bitter, shamed part of him that knew how and why Adrian Kijek had died.

He lay looking at the wall, blinking furiously, while her footsteps went away down the stairs. Then he clamped the tube, peeled off the dressing, and took the catheter out. He took Adrian Kijek's jacket and shoes, and he took the German rifle and the box of cartridges. He moved Maja off the bed so he could straighten the sheet. Then he opened the window and went out onto the roof, shutting the window behind him so Maja wouldn't come out.

34

THEY WOULD HUNT HIM.

He knew that. They would hunt him by necessity because he knew too much—because he knew names, real names, and faces, and because he knew about the guns under the attic floorboards. And they would hunt him for vengeance because of Adrian Kijek.

That was all right. He was sorry, though, about the clothes. He didn't want to take them. He was sorry too about Mrs. Kijek's medicine and the German rifle, and most of all about Lena's trust. The medicine and the rifle it might be possible to repay —someday, somehow, *after*, if he lived. But he couldn't really repay her father's clothes, and he would never be able to repay her trust. He couldn't give Lena her father back, and he couldn't go back and change the reason her father had died.

Outside, it was blue twilight, and the nightingales were singing. The hollow *thump* of Janek's hatchet echoed up from the side yard. There was a quarter moon hanging over the wood, a breath of wind coming off the hill. The yard was dark and cool below him. He slipped down the mossed shingles and handed himself carefully into the yard from the low, guttered ledge— left foot first, reaching with his toes, keeping his weight off his right foot.

"I'd have made you a pack if you'd asked," Lena said.

She was sitting on the kitchen step in the half-light, smoking a cigarette, watching him.

He straightened slowly, shifting his weight onto his heels. He steadied himself with one hand on the wall. The rifle was slung across his back, and the cartridges were in his pocket. Her submachine gun was beside her against the wall. Her pistol, Zampolit Petrov's pistol, was holstered at her belt, under her jacket. He could see it when she touched the cigarette to her lips.

"Is this because of *that*?" She jerked her chin toward the attic window.

She could have the pistol out and trained before he got the sling over his head, never mind loading. He didn't move.

"I know what happened to your father," he said.

She was silent for a moment, pulling on her cigarette. "You think I blame you?"

"I think you've got the right."

"That doesn't work, you know—doesn't solve anything. Punishing the many for the sins of the few. That's how you get *this*." She waved her cigarette in a vague circle. "That's how *you* end up strapped to a post in a root cellar."

He didn't say anything. The *thump* of Janek's hatchet was still echoing over the yard, rolling away into the trees up the hill.

"You know, it was a Ukrainian who got Mama out of the city." Lena flicked away the ash from her cigarette with quick fingers. "I wasn't there. I'd been with cousins in England since the war began. They took Papa at the house—the SS—but Mama was on duty in the ward that night. He got her out before they could track her down. He was a nationalist—one of the Nachtigallen, Ukrainian volunteers fighting with the Wehrmacht. The idea was the Germans were going to help them set up an independent Ukrainian state." She let out a low, smoky breath. "We'd been in school together, he and I, before the war. He was a couple years older—brilliant, but his Polish wasn't very good, so they kept holding him back. They'd shut the Ukrainian schools back in the twenties. Made all the Ukrainian kids start coming to Polish schools. Well, technically our schools were supposed to be bilingual, Polish and Ukrainian. That was the way the law was written. But everybody knew that didn't happen."

She took a fierce drag on her cigarette.

"He tried, at first, really tried, but—no Polish friends, and he wasn't getting it at home. He never really stood much chance. We bullied him badly, and he stopped trying. He dropped out. Six years later he was a nationalist gunman." She shrugged. "Maybe they got too radical for him. Maybe collaboration with the Nazis was the last straw. I don't know. I don't know how much he knew of the plan beforehand. I don't know if he saw the list. I guess he must have: He knew they'd be watching for those names at the checkpoints out of the city. He got Mama out through the sewers." She hesitated, trailing smoke softly from her lips. "I like to think they shot him for it. Of all the things they could have done to him—I like to think they shot him. Quick and easy. But they always put the body on display after they shot somebody—as a lesson for the rest of us, you know—and I never saw his, which I guess means I'm fooling myself."

She held her cigarette in two fingers and took another drag, more calmly this time.

"I wonder," she said. "How much of that was his fault, and how much of it was ours? Who are you supposed to blame? Who are you supposed to punish? He was the one trying to atone." She tapped the ash from her cigarette absently. "I don't blame him. I don't blame you. If I had to blame anybody, I suppose I'd blame myself. My sins are the only ones I'm sure about."

He didn't say anything, and she looked up.

"I'm being an idiot," she said. "It makes sense in my head. Here—have a cigarette."

She slipped another cigarette from her pocket and held it out.

He took it. He sat down beside her on the step, and she leaned over to light the cigarette for him.

"Does it hurt?" she asked. "Talking about Kijów?"

He cupped the cigarette in his hands and took a drag. It was a real cigarette, not makhorka rolled loosely in scrap paper. He hadn't had a real cigarette since Tarnopol, when they'd found Ecksteins on the German dead.

He leaned his head back against the door jamb, his throat and chest comfortably warm.

"No," he said. Then, because it felt like a lie, he said cautiously, "I'm not from Kijów—not from birth."

"Where from birth?"

"Kuz'myn." He didn't know how to say it in Polish. "Outside Proskuriv—Płoskirów."

"So I was right about Galicia. Just wrong about which side of the border."

"Yeah." He hesitated. "My mother was Polish. There are many Poles in that part of Galicia. There were."

She looked at her nails. They were chipped and bitten, the skin torn. Her face was blank. Tolya waited, expecting questions— the technical questions, how and why and when.

Instead, she said, "Kuz'myn is the one that hurts, isn't it?"

He looked away. He had the images but not the words. He remembered, in blurred snapshots, the fields stripped and black and dust scoured, and bodies swollen with hunger, and the air yellow and sour with smoke and rot and the stink of death, always the stink of death, and the whole village made, at gunpoint, to stand in a circle and watch while the NKVD knouted young Avgust Vovk against the cross in the churchyard (twenty-five strokes, enough to kill, except Papa had broken on the twelfth), and Mama curled over her knees against the base of the garden wall, on the little plot of collective land they'd been allowed to call their own.

"Yeah," he said. His hands were shaking. He took another drag on the cigarette. He glanced at her. "Like Lwów for you—but you came back."

She was tapping the ash from her cigarette, not looking at him.

"Like an idiot," she said, "to fight a war that was lost five years ago."

She rubbed the cigarette between her fingertips and looked up, smiling a slight, sad smile—Mrs. Kijek's smile, in perfect duplicate.

"We've lost Lwów. We'll lose Warsaw. I don't know who will win, but we've lost."

He didn't say anything. On the radio that morning, they said the Germans had executed forty thousand Polish civilians in the center of Warsaw—forty thousand in just one week, in reprisal for the Resistance uprising. He didn't know what you were supposed to say to that. *It's all right*, Solovey would say because there was nothing else to say, *it's all right*—but you knew he didn't mean it.

Lena let out a soft breath between her teeth.

"One more week. Finish this round of antibiotics. Then I'll get you out of here, all right? I'll take you into the mountains. You can make the coast before the weather turns. Find a ship for Turkey or something."

"I thought you said you needed a sniper."

"It's not your war to lose," she said.

He didn't say anything. What was he supposed to say? They weren't his people. It wasn't his war. It had never really been his war.

Janek came over from the woodshed, carrying an armful of split logs.

"Enough to start with," he said.

He paused in midstep, noticing Tolya.

"What's he doing down here?"

"Fresh air," Lena said blandly, stubbing out her cigarette on the step. "Does him good."

"He shouldn't be down here."

She shrugged.

Janek gestured brusquely with his armful of logs. "Here. I'm going to finish the rest, just to have it done."

"Come in to dinner," Lena said when Janek had clomped off again to the woodshed.

"I'll go up," Tolya said. He'd seen the anger in Janek's face.

"You're down here anyway," Lena said. "I'll put out another plate."

* * *

He'd been downstairs before, twice to have a bath in the swimming-pool tub and once to have his hair cut in the kitchen, but he'd never been down there to eat. He perched on the edge of a chair, looking intently at his hands in his lap—*peasant hands*, Koval would say—to keep from staring at all the crystal and silver. Mrs. Kijek must have noticed his discomfort because after a while she gave him a bowl of boiled potatoes to cut up for a salad while she finished mixing the mayonnaise.

Lena had a newspaper in pieces at the head of the table.

"Moscow's trying to claim it's only their puppet 'People's Army' fighting," she said.

"The ink, dear," Mrs. Kijek said mildly. "That's Great-Grandmother Helena's silk tablecloth."

"It's lasted seven wars."

"I'd like it to last eight."

Janek came in from the yard, shutting the door quickly and locking it. He had his pistol out.

"Lena, get away from the windows."

"What's the matter?"

"Get away from the windows." He came around the table and snapped the heavy draperies shut. "NKVD—up in the wood. They must have left a signalman watching the house."

Without a word, Mrs. Kijek doused the lamp on the table. Lena scraped her chair back, unslinging her submachine gun.

"How many?"

"At least six. Two gun crews—they've got machine guns covering the yard. I saw them setting the mounts."

"Go get Jerzy. We've got time. Go out through the cellar—it's unlocked. I'll cover you to the wood."

"Leave you here?"

"Yes."

"Like hell I'm leaving you here. We'll all make a break."

Lena shook her head. "We've got time, unless you keep arguing about it. They'll negotiate. They'll want us alive."

"They only need one of us. If they storm the house—"

"We'll barricade ourselves in the attic. We could hold them off for a week from that attic."

"Unless they burn you out."

"Look—"

"I'll go," Tolya said.

They all looked at him. He put down his knife and potato.

"I'll go," he said. "I've just got to get to the wood."

"What are you talking about?" Janek snapped. "You don't even know where the camp is."

"I'll take out the guns." He slipped the sling of the German rifle over his head. "I can cover you from the high ground when the nests are clear."

Machine-gun fire tore through the windows, shredding the draperies.

He hit the floor with the rifle beneath him, curling up to shield himself against the needle-sharp flecks of shattered glass and the chewed-up splinters of paneling. Bullets spattered over the walls—one long burst, then silence.

Somebody shouted across the yard.

"Lay down your weapons and come out! You're surrounded!"

Tolya lifted his head. Clay dust hung on the air like smoke, drifting on the breeze through the broken windows. The shadows of the ripped draperies jumped across the walls.

"Cover me," he said to Lena. "I'll go."

"You're not going anywhere," Janek said. He was on his stomach in the kitchen doorway, propped up on his forearms, his pistol in his hands.

"Cover me from the attic." He reached into his pocket for the cartridge box, careful to avoid Janek's eyes. "You can come out by the roof when I've cleared the nests."

"Janek." Lena jerked her chin. "You and Mama in the attic. I'll cover from the cellar until he gets across the yard."

"He's one of them," Janek said.

"Don't be an idiot."

"He's one of them." Janek lifted his pistol. "He's afraid they're going to cut their losses."

"Lower the gun, Janek." That was Mrs. Kijek, speaking quietly from against the wall. "It's not helping."

"Lena," Janek said, appealing.

"He might as well go," Lena said. Her eyes held Tolya's evenly. "He's not much good as a hostage, even if he is theirs. There are three of us and only one of him. I doubt they'll make that trade—or any kind of trade we'd want."

Tolya popped the bolt on the German rifle. Janek was still holding the pistol on him. He pretended not to notice, focusing on the rifle. The action was very much like that of his Mosin. He stripped a five-round clip into the magazine and shoved the bolt in, glad they couldn't see the way his hands were shaking.

"Janek," Lena said.

There was another spray of machine-gun fire through the shattered windows.

"Last chance, *ublyudki*! Lay down your weapons and come out!"

"Janek," Lena said through shut teeth.

Janek shut his eyes briefly. Then he lowered his pistol and shoved it into his holster. He pushed up on his hands.

"All right," he said, "all right, but I'm taking the cellar. Give me your gun."

"I'm the better shot."

"I know. I'm no good for distance, but I can lay down covering fire. Give me your gun."

Lena locked the bolt and shoved the submachine gun to Janek across the paving stones. "Only because *I'm* not going to waste ten minutes arguing about it."

"Later," Janek said. "Go."

35

TOLYA FOLLOWED JANEK IN THE HALF-LIGHT
through the kitchen and down into the cool, damp darkness of
the cellar. He stumbled a little at the smell of raw earth, remembering. Just for a second, panic slid over his throat like cold
fingers, tightening like a fist in the pit of his stomach. He had
the sudden urge to curl up small and invisible there on the steps,
covering his head with his arms.

Something bowled into him from behind, carrying him up off
his feet and flinging him down the steps with a *bang*.

He landed on his hands on bare dirt, his ears ringing, his
breath snatched away. Pinpricks of white light scattered into the
darkness. His head spun. He tasted smoke and blood. He tried
to move. Something big and solid and heavy was pinning him
flat to the floor.

Janek bent over him. "Are you all right?"

"I can't move."

"You've got the door on top of you—luckily. That was a
grenade. Here, give me a second."

Distantly above, there was a spattering of gunfire.

"Listen," Janek said, dragging the door off him and pulling him up by an elbow. "Maybe you're theirs. Maybe you're not. I don't know." He pushed Tolya down at the base of the steps going up to the outside doors. "The thing is, they won't know either—and the difference is that they won't care. Do you understand? They're going to be shooting, not asking questions, whoever goes out these doors. Understand?"

"Yes."

Janek shoved his pistol at him. "Keep that rifle slung. Use this to the wood—it's handier. Mind the crossfire. And mind I've got a gun on your back in case you get any funny ideas."

"Where are the nests?"

"One at the edge of the wood—eleven o'clock, so you'll want to keep on this side of the barn. One at the side yard, toward the road. That's the crossfire you're minding." Janek unlocked the bolt of the submachine gun. "Are you ready?"

"Yes," Tolya said.

"Prove me wrong," Janek said.

He flung open the doors. He sprawled flat on his stomach across the steps, keeping his head low, bracing the barrel of the submachine gun on the top step.

"Now," he said, "go now"—and then he was shouting to Lena and Mrs. Kijek: "*Już! Już!* Now! Now!"

He opened fire in a sweeping arc. Tolya pushed up on his hands. He lunged up the steps. It was twenty meters across the yard to the barn, then ten meters over open ground from the barn to the wood. He ran, veering from side to side. The yard had cleared quickly when Janek opened fire. There was one NKVD soldier dead at the kitchen step, two more between the henhouse and the toolshed. The rest had scattered for cover, diving behind the woodpile and the raised garden beds.

Bullets snapped and sang across the yard. A rifle shot whined past his ear, very close. Submachine-gun fire spattered over the barn doors. He heard the *thud, thud, thud* of the machine guns. The tracers swung toward him in two long, white streams. He ducked, gasping, into the shadow of the barn, under the long northern wall.

A grenade roared somewhere behind him. The shiver of the concussion ran through the soles of his shoes. The barn wall shuddered under his hand. He looked back. Two NKVD submachine gunners stood at the cellar doors, silhouetted against the flame and ash and curling smoke, firing in tandem down the steps.

No—please, God, no.

And then: *Please, let me prove him wrong.*

He bolted for the wood across that last ten meters of open ground. The machine gun on the slope above the barn picked him up again. The muzzle flashed. Bullets cut across his path, kicking up dirt in little plumes. He dove on his face into the cover of the trees. The bullets hissed and snarled after him, thudding into the tree trunks. Bark and leaves and bits of twig showered down on him. He crawled up the slope, belly down, pulling himself along on his elbows, pushing with the sides of his feet, until the gunner gave him up in the darkness of the trees. Then he got up and ran.

Two of them followed him, crashing through the underbrush up the slope behind him. He swung around behind a fat beech tree, braced his shoulder on the trunk, and cupped Janek's pistol in his hands. He shot the first man squarely in the chest, just under the second of the three brass buttons down the placket of his tunic. He wasted two more shots on the other because this one slid behind a tree when the first man fell. The bullets glanced uselessly off the trunk. He didn't have time or ammunition for this game. He stuck the pistol in his waistband, unslung the German rifle, and shot through the fuze cap of the F1 grenade on the dead man's belt. Then he ran again, because the explosion had given away his position.

He cut across the shoulder of the hill, southward, moving quickly and quietly from tree to tree, until he was straightaway up the slope from the barn—two hundred meters, maybe. He could see the first nest below, just to the right of the barn, and the second in the old, flat ricks of unbaled hay past the yard gate, where the road from Zarudce ran to nothing in the tall grass. There were three men to each nest—gunner, loader, spotter. He couldn't see any NKVD still in the yard except for the three dead men, but gunfire echoed distantly across the yard from somewhere inside the house. Muzzle flashes glinted on the windowpanes.

He rested the barrel of the German rifle on a fallen log. He stretched out carefully on his stomach, shouldering the butt. He leaned his cheek on the stock and shut his left eye. The Zeiss scope gave him six-power magnification, and he could see the nest very clearly in the moonlight. The gunner's head was bent to the sights, his shoulders straining against the jerk of the gun. He was shooting at the windows in intermittent bursts.

Tolya sighted—distance two hundred meters, negative-elevation differential of thirty, half wind from five o'clock, off the ridge. He squeezed the trigger. The rifle jumped lightly against his shoulder. The bullet sparked off the wheel of the mount, just clear of the gunner's left hand.

The spotter's head whipped around. Tolya slipped the bolt back and ejected the spent cartridge. He adjusted quickly for wind, fumbling with hasty fingers. The spotter lifted a subma-chine gun and let off a blind, wild spray of bullets into the trees down the slope, fifty meters short.

Tolya bent his cheek and shut his eye. He brought the back of the gunner's head into the crosshairs. This time when the rifle jumped under his hands the gunner lurched and fell forward across the barrel of the machine gun. The loader pushed the gun-ner's body off and dragged the machine gun around, and Tolya shot him in the forehead as he turned.

The spotter stumbled up jerkily and ran for the nest in the hayricks. Tolya followed him through the scope. His hands were steady now, his head cool and clear. He dropped the running man just outside the yard gate. He pulled the bolt, ejected the cartridge, and shoved the bolt back in, lifting his head to gauge the distance to the second gun. Six hundred meters, or very nearly, across the wind—and the thing about shooting at machine guns at six hundred meters, Comrade Lieutenant Spirin would say, was that machine guns could shoot *back* at six hundred meters, with a comparative minimum of effort.

He adjusted the knobs on the scope. The gun crew in the hayricks had seen the spotter fall. Through the scope, Tolya watched them wheel the machine gun around to face the hillside. He could see the pale, moonlit blur of the gunner's face above the barrel of the gun. He pressed his cheek to the stock and squeezed his eye shut, curling his finger over the trigger.

The mouth of a pistol pushed cold and hard against the base of his skull.

He froze. A quick, rough hand pried the rifle from his hands, slinging it away. Fingers tore Janek's pistol from his waistband.

"Tell those idiots we've got him," a voice said in Russian over Tolya's head, "before they shoot us all to shreds."

A booted foot jabbed Tolya's ribs. "Up, you bastard—slowly. I'll blow your brains out if you so much as twitch."

An electric torch flashed in Tolya's eyes. The voice barked a harsh laugh. The pistol slid under Tolya's jaw, forcing his chin up, turning his face directly to the light.

"Tasha, look. It's your boyfriend."

The second soldier had stooped to pick up the German rifle.

Tolya saw her face as she straightened—her eyes mothy-green in the glare of the electric torch, her smooth blond hair slipping its neat bun in the breeze off the ridge—

Koval, alive.

Koval, wearing the uniform of the NKVD.

36

KOVAL LIFTED THE GERMAN RIFLE AND PUT A
bullet between the first soldier's eyes.

His head snapped back. He reeled and flopped over the log at
Tolya's feet. Koval lowered the rifle. She came over and nudged
his body away with the toe of her boot. She knelt, propping the
barrel of the rifle on the log. She pulled the bolt. The spent cartridge spun out. She looked up.

"Do you have another clip?"

He blinked at her.

"Tolya," she prompted, "another clip."

He moved somehow. He crouched beside her. He gave her
the cartridge box from his pocket wordlessly. His hands were
numb. He didn't trust himself to speak. He wasn't sure in that
moment that she was really there. He watched her push the new
clip into the magazine and shove the bolt home with her palm.
She shouldered the butt and sighted, breathing long and slowly
through her nose, biting her lower lip in concentration as she
always did when she was shooting. Her arm just brushed his arm

as she crooked her elbow on the log. The loose strands of blond hair whipped this way and that in the breeze off the ridge.

She was there, beside him, *alive*.

She was wearing the uniform of the NKVD.

Solovey had lied.

These three things spun around in his head, crashing into each other and breaking apart again, while Koval cleared the machine-gun nest. She did it with three quick shots, sliding the barrel of the rifle smoothly along the top of the log. Then she threw back the bolt and sat up, lowering the rifle to her lap.

"You're hurt," she said.

"What?" Like an idiot.

She jerked her chin. He looked down. There was blood on Adrian Kijek's trousers, soaking the cuff where it bunched up at his right ankle. He leaned back, shifting his weight off his toes. Blood squelched under his heel. He pulled up the trouser leg with stumbling fingers. Shrapnel, not a bullet—there was a jagged metal splinter the width of his thumb sticking out below the ankle bone. There was no pain. That was shock. There would be pain later.

The blood cleared his head a little. "Koval."

"Sit down. Let me see it."

"I need the rifle," he said.

She held the rifle for him while he eased himself stiffly down onto his forearms and stomach.

"You move like a grandfather," she said.

He didn't say anything. He still didn't quite trust himself to speak. He shouldered the butt and sighted the attic window. He watched through the scope, finger on the trigger, while they opened the window and came down the mossy shingles—first Lena, then Mrs. Kijek, following the roof down to the low drop by the kitchen step.

Koval took his shoe off and rolled the trouser leg up his calf.

"Listen," she said, "I've got to radio this in, but I can buy you some time. There's a car down the road—pulled off on the shoulder about a kilometer out of Zarudce. The ignition's unlocked. All you've got to do is flip the starter switch."

He was keeping the window in the crosshairs, watching the kitchen door peripherally, while Lena and Mrs. Kijek crossed the yard to the barn. It took him a second to really hear what she was saying.

"Radio this in," he repeated.

"To headquarters." She tore off a strip of trouser leg. "And then I'll have to hunt you."

He lifted his head from the rifle and looked at her over his shoulder. She was holding his ankle under her hands, looking at the wound.

"This might hurt," she said.

He looked away, swallowing. He leaned his cheek back on the stock of the rifle.

"When?"

It was a question that could be taken several different ways, but she knew what he meant.

"I joined up eighteen months ago." She picked out the splinter quickly and calmly, wrapping the gash with the strip of trouser cloth. "Just before we met."

"Kharkiv."

"They recruited me there. They were afraid the UPA might try to infiltrate the Front when we moved into Ukraine. We had assignments—marks. Potential *anti-Soviet elements*." Her fingers paused just for a second, resting lightly on his ankle. "You were mine."

He watched Lena and Mrs. Kijek move along in the shadow of the barn. His throat was tight, so tight. "Why?"

"It was random. They gave me a name."

"I mean I hadn't done anything."

"You were CSIR—*chlen sem'i izmennika rodiny*, the son of traitors. They'd found a file on your parents when Spirin recommended you for the Red Star." She tied off the wrapping and laced his shoe back on. "You *did* make a good candidate: an orphan, a loner, 'resistant to re-education.' By Tarnopol, we knew the UPA had an informant in the Front, and we thought— after Petrov had Spirin shot, and you went off on him like that—"

"You thought it was me."

"We suspected. Petrov was sure. He wanted to *deal with you* then. It took Colonel Sokolov saying no. He'd lost Spirin. He didn't want to lose you. Moot point, as it turns out. If you were the informant, you'd have known better than to shoot Petrov in the street. But you gave us another option."

Shadows shifted in the attic. Any second now, the window would be flung open, or the kitchen door would swing in, and an NKVD gunman would lean out to see what had become of the vanished defenders.

Koval crouched at his elbow. "You were—not *bait*, exactly, because we didn't know they'd come for you. More like a homing signal. We let them take you. At first, the plan was just to follow from a distance, mark the position of the camp, attack that night. Then we found your rat Yakiv's message in the stolen car. He had the watch the next night, and in exchange for amnesty he would make sure there was no alarm. He gave us the coordinates for the camp and for that munitions dump up in the hills."

There was the attic window opening, and the nose of a submachine gun sticking cautiously out. Tolya squeezed his eye shut and shot the gunman through the windowpane.

"Not us," he said.

"What?"

"Not *us*. You're not one of them."

She was silent for a moment. She started to say something. Then she stopped.

"Listen," she said finally, "I've got to go—unless you want to explain this to *them*." She jerked her chin at Lena and Mrs. Kijek, who were crossing the last stretch of open ground between the barn and the wood. "You'll have about an hour. That's how long it will take me to bring up reinforcements from Lwów." She paused on one knee. "I *will* bring them up, Tolya."

"Then why let me go?"

"Self-preservation. I'm afraid of what you'll tell them under interrogation."

"You could just put a bullet in my head."

"They want you alive. They'd want to know *why* I put a bullet in your head."

"They wouldn't have to know it was you. Maybe it was him. Maybe you killed him for it."

"With an eight-millimeter Mauser, the same as killed both gun crews. Questions and more questions."

"What are you afraid I'll tell them under interrogation?"

She shrugged. "I told you to run to Stryy."

"I didn't."

"Doesn't matter. You'll tell them I told you to, and they'll assume I meant it—and then they'll assume I meant *this*."

She leaned in on her knee. She took his chin in her fingers, turning his face up to hers, cupping his cheek in her hand. She bent her head and slid her lips over his—softly, slowly, as though she were being very careful not to break him.

"Mistaken assumptions," she murmured against the corner of his mouth. "That's what I'm afraid of."

Underbrush crackled distantly down the slope—Lena and Mrs. Kijek, coming up through the trees from the yard.

Tolya shut his eyes. She was holding him close, stroking the back of his neck gently with her fingertips, and he was trembling against her, throat aching, breathless, and there were too many things he wanted to say, too many things he *needed* to say and needed to know and needed *her* to know—too many things to fit into words, a year and a half of things that wouldn't fit into words—all stuck in a sore, tight knot at the base of his tongue.

The only thing that came out was her name.

"Nataliya," he said—and she put her hand over his mouth because there wasn't any time.

"I'm not Nataliya." Her fingers traced his lips, his cheekbones, his throat, the line of his jaw. "I'm not Koval, I'm not Tasha, and I'm not from Kyiv. I don't have a sister there either." She ducked her head to kiss him quickly on the cheek. "An hour, Tolya. Then you'd better hope you never see me again."

VI
ALEKSEY

Friday, July 4
1941

37

IF YOU FOLLOW THE TUNNELS OUT OF ŁYCZA-
kowski District, going east and south, after a couple of kilometers
or so you spill out into Pasieka Creek, with nothing but beech
and elm woodland and maybe some cows around you. There are
low hills farther on—nothing much for hunting or fishing because
you're too close to the dairy farms, but from the hilltops you've
got a pretty good view of that whole eastern slice of the city,
from the Wulka Hills in the south to our own Zamarstynów in
the north, and of the main east road to Tarnopol.

We stopped there, just over the ridge—or I collapsed and
everybody else stopped. That was enough, Mrs. Kijek said. She
gave me one of the sulfa tablets from Andriy's packet and two
aspirin from her handbag and sent Mykola with the rifle back up
the slope to watch the creek and the road, and we settled in to
spend the night.

It was still dark when I woke up. Two thirty, maybe three—
the moon had set. It was a cool, clear, starlit night. Mykola was
asleep between two fat, mossy roots, curled up in a tight ball

with his head burrowed between his arms. Mrs. Kijek slept sitting up against an elm trunk, her coat around her shoulders. Andriy was on watch. He was hunched against a tree with his elbows on his knees, the rifle propped up on his shoulder, his chin on his hands. I rolled carefully onto my stomach and crawled over to him.

"Anything?" I asked. The city lay blacked out and silent below us. Light flashed noiselessly on the horizon, north and east—thunderstorm or artillery bombardment, I couldn't tell.

Andriy shook his head without lifting his chin from his hands. "Just routine patrols."

We sat in silence for a while, listening to the nightingales. I could feel the wariness in him. It occurred to me that he probably thought I'd come up to make sure he didn't slip off into the dark.

"Hey," I said. "I'm sorry."

He turned his chin and looked at me inquiringly.

"I should have told you about Strilka. You found out when you were getting the vitamins, didn't you? That I'd killed him—that was why they'd put a price on my head."

He looked away.

"Oh," he said. "Yes."

"It wasn't fair. I should have told you. I'm sorry."

He dug his chin into his hands and studied his boots.

"I don't blame you for leaving," I said. "I was being stupid earlier. I know it wasn't about the money."

"Makes it worse," he said.

"What?"

He rocked on his feet a little. "No questions. Just—whatever he wanted, I did it. Anything for him. Worse than doing it for money."

"He saved your life. You felt you owed him. It's understandable."

"Understandable," he agreed hollowly. "Everything's *understandable*."

I recognized his tone. He didn't want my justifications. Nothing I said was going to make any difference when he was at war with himself.

"I wanted to apologize." Andriy dug at the dirt with the toe of his boot. "Didn't know how. Hung around that apartment block for two days, trying to figure out how. Didn't think you'd want to hear it anyway." He shrugged tightly. "Vitalik said you would—said you'd listen. Said I had to try. I didn't know he'd been watching."

"Did you know he was going to do *that*—double-cross the Nachtigallen?"

Andriy shook his head.

"I don't think anybody ever really knows with Vitalik," he said.

"Who is he?"

"Strilka thought he was NKVD. Vitalik said the NKVD didn't need agents in the UPA as long as we had officers like Strilka. They didn't like each other."

"I guess not," I said.

"I always thought—" he started. Then he darted a glance at me, as though making sure of me. "I don't know. I always thought—I mean, it's probably stupid, but I don't think he's Ukrainian."

"What—Polish?"

Andriy hesitated.

"I think he's Russian. I think he's a White."

"An émigré?" Thousands of anti-Communist Russians, Whites, the last remnants of the old czarist regime, had filtered into Poland in the years after the Russian Revolution.

"His people anyway. I know he comes from money. I mean—he tries to hide it, to fit in, but I can tell, and I think Strilka could too." Andriy shrugged again. "I don't think he cares about us—about Ukraine, I mean. I think he cares about fighting the Reds."

"Is that why he wouldn't come with us?"

Andriy toed the dirt and looked away.

"No," he said. "That was because he killed your father."

* * *

They'd sent him into Brygidki prison two years ago, right after the Red invasion, with orders to assassinate Papa and make it look like a suicide. They'd been afraid Papa still knew too much about the Ukrainian underground, even after five years—too many names, too many damning details. They'd been afraid of what the Reds might be able to jog from his memory. So they'd sent Vitalik to kill him.

Strilka had known. Andriy wasn't sure about that—the order had come straight from Shukhevych—but I was. Strilka wouldn't have told me, of course. He wanted me safely in the fold. He wouldn't tell me the UPA had killed my father. But he could put his pistol in my hand and tell me to kill Vitalik. It was too theatrically perfect for me to believe he hadn't known.

I sent Andriy down to sleep. I got the impression he hadn't done much of that in the past few days, and I wasn't going to get back to sleep anyway. My legs were hurting pretty badly, and I didn't want to have to wake Mrs. Kijek up to ask for more aspirin. At first I distracted myself by picking out the constellations, the way we used to pick them out over the lake in Brzuchowice before the world went to hell. Then I ran out of constellations and started musing over whether I'd have killed Vitalik after all, if I'd known he'd killed Papa.

Then I gave up and cried—for Papa and Mama and Grandfather and Father Yosyp and Mr. Kijek and all the rest of my dead—because *would haves* didn't do any good.

I cried very quietly and was careful not to sniff, but Mykola came up anyway. He slid in silently beside me in the dark, and he sat there without a word until Mrs. Kijek came up to say we'd better move off the ridge before dawn.

VII
TOLYA

Sunday, August 13
1944

38

NOW HE WAS WATCHING THE GRAY, HEATHER-
choked fields speed past under clouded moonlight.

The green radium dials of the clock on the dashboard said
11:22. It wasn't quite an hour since he'd been in the wood with
Koval. Tolya was stretched out on the back seat with his right
foot propped up on the far door. Lena was in the passenger's
seat, her submachine gun on her lap, the German rifle slung over
her shoulder. She looked back over the seat.

"It's not much farther," she said. "Four kilometers. We're
almost there."

She hadn't spoken once of Janek—neither she nor her
mother—but in the moonlight in the wood above the Zarudce
road, when they'd gone to take the car, he'd seen the tears on
her face.

"We'll have to leave the car," Mrs. Kijek said. "There's a
roadblock below Żółkiew."

"Leave it in the Wiśniewskis' barn. We'll go by the river."

Now the car was turning off the paved road and going down a soft mud lane between two low rail fences. They were going slowly and without headlights. Mud and rain spattered lightly on the windshield.

"Let it rain, let it rain," Lena said, bending to look out the window. She squinted through the streaks on the glass.

"Rain won't cover these tracks," Mrs. Kijek said.

"It'll slow them down coming through Kulików."

The lane went down to a little farm that was tucked away from the road in a fold between the low hills. There was a small mud yard and a house and a stock barn, and through the rain-beaded window Tolya could see where there'd been out-buildings and a grain barn, but now they were just bald, burned patches on the wet, gray grass.

Lena got out to open the barn doors. They put the car in the empty barn, and Tolya stood leaning on the peeling outer wall, blinking the rain out of his eyes, while they shut the doors. The barn was half burned, gaping open to the sky. The bare posts and beams stuck up and curved over like broken ribs. The house, too, was burned and skeletal—four charred walls leaning in on the collapsed ruin of the roof.

Lena came over to pull his arm across her shoulders.

"UPA?" Tolya asked.

"Last year. This farm and the Nowaks', across the river."

They went down to the water. The moon was gone behind clouds. The rain fell softly and steadily. A low mist was rising off the water. There was a rowboat stowed under a brush screen in the trees along the bank. They put the boat out into the water, and Mrs. Kijek sat handling the rudder while Lena rowed.

They went along quietly in the mist and darkness. He was sitting in the bottom of the boat, his legs stretched out on the floor under the seat, and he was listening to the nightingales in the trees on the banks and the soft patter of the rain on the water and the plashing of the oars, and he was slipping away and coming back, slipping away and coming back, his head and shoulder tucked into the curving side of the boat, the rain on his face.

You knew, he was saying to Solovey in the darkness, *you knew. You knew she was still alive. You knew she was NKVD.*

I knew, Solovey said.

You found out that first night—when you went down to talk to your commander. That's why you couldn't get her out.

It's one reason.

You said she was dead.

I suggested.

You lied.

I told you what I was ordered to tell you.

When has that ever been good enough for you—orders for the sake of orders? Was it orders *when you took Mrs. Kijek out through the sewers that night?*

A pause.

If I didn't know you had the emotional range of a boiled potato, Solovey said, *I'd think you were angry.*

Shut up and answer me.

I can't do both.

Answer me. Was it orders *to let me live?*

Tolya—

Or were you going to put a bullet in my brain after all? Plug me in the forehead—is that it?

Tolya—

Because that's what you told your commander you were going to do. You told him you were going to kill me as soon as you had me kill Comrade Colonel Volkov. That's the only reason he let you get me out.

I've lost track of which question I'm supposed to be answering.

Orders for the sake of orders. You were supposed to kill me when Volkov was dead.

Extract all useful intelligence and execute you as a collaborator, to be exact.

My point is that you didn't.

Volkov isn't dead.

You weren't going to anyway, or you'd have done it the night they attacked the camp.

Then, like a true philosopher, you've answered your own question. What do you need from me?

I want to know why you lied. Don't try to tell me it was just because of your orders.

It was safer that way.

Safer for who? You?

For her.

Tolya's turn to pause now.

Nataliya, he said.

Yes.

Nataliya is your informant in the Front.

That's not really her name, you understand.

She's been working for you this whole time.

For the UPA, yes.

But then—

Yes.

She knew about Yakiv. She knew about the attack.

She had her orders too.

She could have warned you.

She did what was necessary to maintain her cover.

She could have warned you.

We all make sacrifices.

She could have found a way to warn you.

She probably assumed you'd be halfway over the Carpathians by then, if it makes you feel any better. She'd never have expected you to stay with me.

It doesn't.

Give it some time, Solovey said.

* * *

Now the boat shifted and shuddered beneath him. It was still raining softly, and the boat was knocking gently against a low dock, and somebody was saying, "Careful, careful," and hands, many hands, were prying him up from the floor of the boat.

"I can walk," he said to the world in general.

"Hush." That was Mrs. Kijek.

"I can walk."

They ignored him. They put him on a stretcher and took him up the bank. There was a farmhouse up from the water. There was warm, yellow lamplight winking through the trees. Lena was walking beside him, her hand on his arm, and he knew, though she hadn't said anything, that they were leaving him here.

The farmhouse belonged to a family named Kostyshyn. The daughter of the family had been Mrs. Kijek's aide at the Medical Institute in Lwów. They put him in the kitchen, on the floor by the woodstove, and he saw the girl's face when she was heating the water to sterilize her instruments—"This is Anna," Mrs. Kijek told him, "Anna Kostyshyn"—and he met her eyes over the pot.

She didn't say anything, so he didn't either, but later they were alone in the kitchen, and she was taking off his shoe, cutting it away with a scalpel because his foot had swollen so.

"Not so lucky this time, were you?" she said. "It's going to be a while before you walk again."

And his tongue knotted up because he didn't know whether she knew Solovey was dead.

Then it occurred to him that she could have heard it from Vitalik.

Then it occurred to him that she might think *he* had done it if she'd heard it from Vitalik.

She peeled away the shoe gingerly. Her callused red hands were warm and steady.

"Ruslan and Taras came through about two weeks ago," she said quietly. "They told me what happened—as much as they knew to tell anyway." She held his ankle under her hand and unwound Koval's bandage. Without looking up, she said, "Is he dead?"

She didn't know.

"He's dead," Tolya said.

"I was afraid—" she said, then stopped. She bit her lip. "You saw it?"

"Yes."

"Quick?"

"Yes."

"How?"

"He shot himself. He was wounded. He shot himself so I would leave him—so I would make it away."

She was silent for a moment, wiping the dried blood off his foot. Then she said, "I'm glad you were with him."

She wiped her hands on her apron and reached for her bag.

"There's still shrapnel in here. I'm not going to try to dig it out tonight—not in this light. I'll dope you up so you can sleep."

* * *

Now he was lying in a bed of blankets on the Kostyshyns' kitchen floor, listening to the rustle of the rain on the thatched roof and the snap of the fire in the stove, comfortably warm and still and heavy headed, his eyes nearly shut, his legs stretched out and the ankle numbed and wrapped in new, clean gauze—and Lena was crouching beside him in the half-light, bending very close to his ear, whispering because she thought he was asleep: "I'll be back for you, Comrade, all right?"

And he was going to tell her what he hadn't been able to tell her on the kitchen step: that she was wrong, that it was his war the same as hers—the same as it was Anna's and Koval's, the same as it had been Solovey's, and Comrade Lieutenant Spirin's, and Aunt Olena's, and Father Dmytro's, just the same as it had been his mother's and his father's. Anyway, he had to stay because he had to show Anna where Vitalik's squad had buried Solovey. He'd been thinking it through, and he was pretty sure he could find it if he could find the lake. He remembered the cut and the place in the streambed where the bank ran down.

But she was gone when he opened his eyes, and then he wasn't sure whether she'd really been there at all.

LIST OF MILITARY AND PARAMILITARY FORCES

Gestapo—Geheime Staatspolizei, the Nazi secret police

Luftwaffe—the air force of Nazi Germany

Nachtigallen—Bataillon Ukrainische Gruppe Nachtigall (Ukrainian Battalion, Nightingale Group), a special-forces unit of the German army, comprised of Ukrainian volunteers

NKVD—Narodnyĭ Komissariat Vnutrennikh Del (People's Commissariat for Internal Affairs), the Soviet secret police from 1934 to 1946, eventually succeeded by the KGB

Polish Resistance—collective name for the armed forces of the Polish underground state that fought German and Soviet occupation in Poland

SS—Schutzstaffel (Protection Squadrons), originally Hitler's bodyguard, expanded into an elite Nazi security force responsible for implementing racial policies

UPA—Ukrainska Povstanska Armiia (Ukrainian Insurgent Army), the military arm of the Ukrainian nationalist movement, fighting at various times against the Soviets, the Germans, and the Polish Resistance alike

Wehrmacht—the army of Nazi Germany

LIST OF CHARACTERS

FIRST UKRAINIAN FRONT OF THE SOVIET RED ARMY

NIKOLAI VATUTIN, commander (until his assassination by the UPA in February 1944)

FYODOR VOLKOV, commander of the Front's NKVD rifle division

100th Rifle Division, 106th Rifle Corps, 60th Army

SOKOLOV, commander

SERGEI PETROV, political officer (*zampolit*)

MAKSYM RUDENKO, lieutenant

SPIRIN, lieutenant

NATALIYA KOVAL, junior sergeant, sniper

ANATOLIY "TOLYA" KOROLENKO, sniper

VASYA, YURA, and PETYA, soldiers

UKRAINIAN NATIONALISTS

ALEKSEY KOBRYN, nom de guerre SOLOVEY, elder son of jailed nationalist leader Yevhen Kobryn

MYKOLA KOBRYN, younger son of Yevhen Kobryn

Nachtigallen

ROMAN SHUKHEVYCH, commander

STRILKA, MARKO, ANDRIY, and VITALIK, soldiers

UPA

SOLOVEY, squad leader

VITALIK, squad leader

ANDRIY, TARAS, YAKIV, RUSLAN, and VALENTYN, soldiers

ANNA and IRYNA, Red Cross nurses

POLISH RESISTANCE

RENATA KIJEK, director of pediatrics at the State Medical Institute

ADRIAN KIJEK, Renata's husband, professor of civil law at
Lwów University

LENA KIJEK, daughter of Renata and Adrian, squad leader

JANEK, JERZY, KOSTEK, and RYŚ, soldiers

OTHERS

FATHERS STEPAN and DMYTRO, priests at the village church in
Kuz'myn, Ukraine S.S.R.

FATHERS YOSYP and KLIMENT, priests at the Dormition Church
in Lwów

OLENA, Tolya's aunt

IVAN, Olena's husband

JANINA, nurse at the State Medical Institute

ALTSHULER, pharmacist in Lwów

AUTHOR'S NOTE

In 1943 and 1944, as the Soviet Red Army pushed the German Wehrmacht slowly back westward, historic tensions between Ukrainians and Poles in the disputed regions of Galicia and Volhynia burst into brutal violence. The Organization of Ukrainian Nationalists had cooperated with German leadership until the Germans imprisoned key OUN leaders shortly after the beginning of Operation Barbarossa—the invasion of the Soviet Union—in mid-1941, crushing OUN hopes for an independent Ukraine. Betrayed by their erstwhile allies, an OUN faction led by Stepan Bandera fielded its own paramilitary and partisan army, the Ukrainian Insurgent Army (Ukrainska Povstanska Armiia, UPA), which carried out a systematic cleansing of the Galician and Volhynian Polish population. Tens of thousands of Poles—men, women, and children—died at the hands of the UPA, often horrifically. Regional elements of the Polish Resistance responded in kind by killing thousands of Ukrainians.

For clarity's sake, I've referred to the military arm of the Ukrainian nationalist movement throughout as the UPA—an admittedly oversimplified composite of several different factions within the movement, and also an anachronism in Aleksey's storyline, as the UPA didn't officially exist until 1942. My main characters are all fictional, though some are composites of real people. The places are real, though some of the names have changed: Lwów is now L'viv, Ukraine, and Andriy's Proskuriv is now Khmelnytskyy. Most of the major events mentioned really took place, and I've tried to follow the historical timeline as accurately as possible.

Some particulars: "Dekulakization," the extermination of the land-owning peasant class—in actual practice, anybody who resisted the Soviets' forced collectivization of farms—resulted in deportation or death for untold millions of peasants across the Soviet Union between 1929 and 1932. In Ukraine, the twin processes of dekulakization and collectivization produced a catastrophic famine that killed *roughly* four million people in 1932–33. Some historians place the death toll much higher. Tolya knows it simply as "the famine"; history knows it as the Holodomor, genocide by hunger.

During the purges of the late 1930s, Soviet authorities targeted ethnic Poles living in the Soviet Union as enemies of the state. Owning a rosary could be taken as sufficient evidence of Polishness and was a punishable offense until Stalin relaxed the restrictions on religious practice during the Second World War. Whether the UPA made as direct a connection as I portray— with Solovey and Vitalik immediately identifying Tolya as Polish by the fact that he carries a rosary—is less certain, though not (I would contend) unreasonable. The UPA targeted Catholic priests and places of worship and were known to ferret out victims by forcing suspected Poles to pray in Ukrainian. There was, and is, a large Eastern rite Catholic community in and around Lwów, but as Tolya observes, praying the rosary isn't a traditional element of Eastern rite worship.

The killing of the Polish university professors in Lwów took place over the first week of July 1941, with most of the executions taking place early in the morning of July 4. The extent to which Ukrainian nationalists were responsible for supplying names and addresses to the SS death squads, or even openly collaborating with them, remains a matter for debate—as does the extent of UPA involvement in atrocities against Jews. Most historians agree that the Nachtigall Battalion, the all-Ukrainian special-forces unit that marched into Lwów with the Germans in late June 1941, took part in the pogroms that followed; and many former members of the Nachtigall Battalion went on to join the UPA when it formed in 1942.

Not all Ukrainians agreed with the UPA's campaign of ethnic cleansing, even within the UPA's own ranks. Not all participated. Many actively resisted by sheltering their Polish neighbors, at the risk of their own lives. Historian Timothy Snyder estimates that the UPA killed as many of these "traitor" Ukrainians as it did Poles. Late-war and postwar collaborations between the remnants of the UPA and the Polish Resistance suggest that both groups had begun to regard their common enemy, the Soviet occupation force, as the primary threat. It was too little too late; both groups were effectively defunct by the 1950s.

The Warsaw Uprising, which took place between August and October 1944, was a heroic but doomed attempt by the Polish Resistance to liberate Warsaw with the expectation of receiving Soviet help; at the outset of the uprising, Soviet general Konstantin Rokossovsky's First Belorussian Front was only about ten kilometers away from the city center. Rather than intervene to assist the badly outnumbered Resistance, however, the Red Army units sat out the action on the east bank of the Vistula River. Attempts by the western Allies—mainly Britain—to assist the Resistance through airdrops were actively hindered by the Soviets. British planes were prevented from landing on Soviet airfields, forced instead to make long-distance flights from bases in Italy. In several instances, the Soviets actually fired on British planes that strayed into Soviet airspace. While Soviet leadership argued at the time that Rokossovsky's front was too badly worn down to provide effective support, the general consensus among historians is that Stalin deliberately allowed the uprising to fail.

* * *

There is a dearth of scholarly material in English on the UPA and the Polish-Ukrainian conflict in Galicia and Volhynia. Snyder's is probably the most accessible. *Bloodlands: Europe Between Hitler and Stalin* provides an excellent broad overview of Eastern Europe under Nazi and Soviet occupation, while *The Reconstruction of Nations: Poland, Ukraine, Lithuania, Belarus, 1569–1999* deals particularly with wartime ethnic cleansings in Galicia and Volhynia. Stephen Rapawy's *The Culmination of Conflict: The Ukrainian-Polish Civil War and the Expulsion of Ukrainians After the Second World War* delves into some of the root causes underlying Polish-Ukrainian tensions. Grzegorz Rossoliński-Liebe's *Stepan Bandera: The Life and Afterlife of a Ukrainian Nationalist; Fascism, Genocide, and Cult* is an exhaustive and damning source on the history and ideology of the UPA—from a Polish perspective. Maria Savchyn Pyskir's autobiography *Thousands of Roads: A Memoir of a Young Woman's Life in the Ukrainian Underground During and After World War II* provides an interesting Ukrainian counterpoint.

Material on the Polish Resistance is more readily available. I've worked primarily from David G. Williamson's *The Polish Underground 1939–1947*, an encyclopedic source on major campaigns undertaken by the Resistance throughout Poland.

For general information on the common soldier's day-to-day experience in the Red Army, I've referred to Vasily Grossman (*A Writer at War: A Soviet Journalist with the Red Army, 1941–1945*) and Catherine Merridale (*Ivan's War: Life and Death in the Red Army, 1939–1945*). For the recreation of historical Lwów, I've relied heavily on Tarik Cyril Amar's *The Paradox of Ukrainian Lviv: A Borderland City Between Stalinists, Nazis, and Nationalists.* I've also made extensive use of the outstanding resources at the Center for Urban History of East Central Europe's website (lvivcenter.org) and the Internet Encyclopedia of Ukraine (encyclopediaofukraine.com). Any inaccuracies are my own.